Rufus L Chaney   *3/RLC*

"What you are about to read deals with the stars, the wide galactic future that lies at our fingertips today . . . both factual articles and fictional stories. In a world where robots are causing human unemployment, spaceflight is so commonplace the news media regard it as dull, and science fiction has become a mainstay of the bestseller lists . . . nonfiction has become just as exciting as the fiction.

"So here are a dozen and a half views of the world, past present and future, as seen through the *Astral Mirror*. . . ."

—Ben Bova,
from his *Introduction*

THE ASTRAL MIRROR

D1538417

Look for all these TOR books by Ben Bova

AS ON A DARKLING PLAIN
THE ASTRAL MIRROR
ESCAPE PLUS
GREMLINS GO HOME (with Gordon R. Dickson)
ORION
OUT OF THE SUN
PRIVATEERS (in hardcover)
TEST OF FIRE
THE WINDS OF ALTAIR (trade edition)

BEN BOVA

THE ASTRAL MIRROR

A TOM DOHERTY ASSOCIATES BOOK

To Cele Goldsmith Lalli
and Mike Lalli

This is a work of fiction. All the characters and events portrayed in this book are fictional, and any resemblance to real people or incidents is purely coincidental.

THE ASTRAL MIRROR

Copyright © 1985 by Ben Bova

All rights reserved, including the right to reproduce this book or portions thereof in any form.

First printing: October 1985

A TOR Book

Published by Tom Doherty Associates
49 West 24 Street
New York, N.Y. 10010

Cover art by Angus McKie

ISBN: 0-812-53217-1
CAN. ED.: 0-812-53218-X

Printed in the United States of America

ACKNOWLEDGMENTS

"The Astral Mirror" copyright © 1985 by Ben Bova.

"Starflight" copyright © 1973 by Ben Bova.

"Free Enterprise" copyright © 1984 by Davis Publications, Inc.

"Robot Welfare" copyright © 1985 by Ben Bova.

"The Angel's Gift" copyright © 1984 by Omni Publications International Limited.

"The Secret Life of Henry K." copyright © 1973 by Gallery Enterprise Corp.; copyright © 1978 by The Condé Nast Publications, Inc.

"Science Fiction" copyright © 1985 by Ben Bova.

"Love Calls" copyright © 1982 by Omni Publications International Limited.

"Amorality Tale" copyright © 1985 by Ben Bova.

"Out of Time" copyright © 1984 by Omni Publications International Limited.

"Science Fiction and Reality" copyright © 1979 by The Writer, Inc.

"To Be or Not" copyright © 1978 by The Condé Nast Publications, Inc.

"The Man Who Saw *Gunga Din* Thirty Times" copyright © 1973 by Roger Elwood; copyright © 1978 by The Condé Nast Publications, Inc.

"The System" copyright © 1967, 1978 by The Condé Nast Publications, Inc.

"Cement" copyright © 1983 by Davis Publications, Inc.

"Building a Real World" copyright © 1981 by Davis Publications, Inc.

"It's Right *Over* Your Nose" copyright © 1973 by Ben Bova.

"The Perfect Warrior" copyright © 1963 by The Condé Nast Publications, Inc.

"The Future of Science: Prometheus, Apollo, Athena" copyright © 1974 by Science Fiction Writers of America; copyright © 1978 by The Condé Nast Publications, Inc.

Contents

The Astral Mirror

Astral: adv. [from Latin *astrum*, star] 1. Of or relating to the stars; starry; 2. consisting of, or belonging to, or being a supersensible substance supposed to be next above the tangible world in refinement; 3. visionary, unwordly, exalted . . .

If art is a mirror held up to life, then the stories and essays in this collection are an *astral* mirror. What you are about to read certainly deals with the stars, the wide galactic future that lies at our fingertips today. Since these works of fiction and fact deal with the future, they are astral in the second sense, as well. They are beyond the tangible, everyday world of the here-and-now. And I fondly hope that you will find them astral in the third sense, too: visionary, unworldly—or rather, otherworldly—and far-seeing enough to leave you feeling exalted.

This book is somewhat different from most science fiction collections. It contains both factual articles and fictional stories. In a world where robots are causing human unemployment, spaceflight is so commonplace that the news media regard it as dull, and science fiction has become a mainstay of the best seller lists, and nonfiction has become just as exciting as the fiction.

So here are a dozen and a half views of the world, past, present, and future, as seen through the Astral Mirror.

Ben Bova
West Hartford, Connecticut

Starflight

Ad astra per aspera. *The first piece we hold up before the Astral Mirror deals quite literally with the stars—how to get to them. I had this fantasy about putting together a panel of distinguished experts to brainstorm the problem of traveling to the stars. A few years after this essay appeared in print, an enterprising student at Boston University actually created the television broadcast I had dreamed of, and asked me to be its anchor man. Among the "stars" of the panel was Professor Philip Morrison of the Massachusetts Institute of Technology, the brightest and most human man I have ever met. If—no, when we get to the stars, it will be because scientist/teachers such as he have paved the way.*

Imagine a television talk show, a panel discussion, where the moderator or "anchor man" is a science fiction writer. He's sitting at a large round table of gleaming dark wood with touches of shining metal around the edges. Sitting at the other chairs around the table are experts from every field of science. Farther away from the table are the cameras and lights and technicians.

The science fiction writer starts the discussion:

"In the old days—say, fifty years ago—science fiction writers had a much easier job than we have now. For example, when Edgar Rice Burroughs wanted a strange and marvelous setting in his stories, he simply placed his characters on Mars or Venus or even in the center of the Earth. Nobody could tell him he was wrong."

"I thought Burroughs wrote about Tarzan," says the astronomer, two seats down from the writer.

Nodding, the writer answers, "He did. But he also wrote terrific adventure stories that were set on Mars and Venus and in Pellucidar, the land *inside* the Earth."

"A hollow Earth?" the geophysicist grumbles. "Nonsense."

"That's just the trouble," the writer says. "Today I can't get away with such stuff. People know that the Earth isn't hollow. They know that Venus is a red-hot desert underneath its clouds, where the ground temperature's hot enough to melt aluminum and the air is an unbreathable soup . . ."

The astronomer agrees. "Terrible place."

"And Mars," the writer continues, with something like a tear gleaming in the corner of one eye, "good old Mars—we've *photographed* it. No canals, no cities, no Martian princesses. Nothing but craters and desert."

"Well, what's your problem?" the physicist asks sharply. She's sitting across the table from the writer. "I should think you'd be glad to get all this accurate information. Now you can write stories that have real, accurate backgrounds."

"Yes, that's true," the writer admits. "And sometimes I do write such stories. But where do I turn to when I want an absolutely wild and wonderful planet? I can't tell my readers that Mars has cities of glass surrounded by fields of purple trees. I can't tell them that Venus is populated by sea serpents that sing underwater . . ."

"Why on Earth would you want to tell anyone such nonsense?" the medical doctor asks, looking startled.

"Because sometimes I just want to write a story that goes way beyond the everyday world. Sometimes I need a strange and wonderful landscape for a story. And there aren't any . . . not in our solar system."

The entire panel of experts falls silent. Finally the writer says, "So where can a science fiction writer turn if he wants to create a bizarre world with strange-looking alien creatures? He's got to go outside our solar system. He's got to set his story on a planet that circles a different star.

"And that's the purpose of our discussion, ladies and gentlemen. You're going to tell me how to get to the stars."

"Impossible!" the physicist snaps, with a shake of her head. "You just can't get to the stars. Not really. A rocket would have to reach a burnout speed of nearly 58,000 kilometers per hour to escape from the Sun's gravitational influence."

"We could improve the rockets," the writer says.

"Please let me finish," says the physicist. "Even if the rocket could keep going at its top speed of 58,000 kilometers per hour—which it won't, once the rocket engines shut down—it would take 80,000 years to reach Alpha Centauri, the next nearest star. Actually, figuring that the rocket will slow down and coast almost all the way, it will take more like a million years for a rocket to get to Alpha Centauri."

The astronomer adds, "And that's the star that's closest to our solar system. It's only 4.3 light-years away. Even if you could travel at the speed of light—which is 300,000 kilometers *per second*—it would take 4.3 years to get there."

"A light-year is a measure of distance, isn't it?" the science fiction writer asks.

"Precisely," answers the astronomer. "Light travels at 300,000 kilometers per second. There are about 31.5 million seconds in a year. Therefore light can travel nearly nine and a half trillion kilometers in a year. This distance is used as a unit of measurement in astronomy and called a light-year."

"And the nearest star is 4.3 light-years away," adds the physicist, somewhat smugly.

"Which means it would take you 4.3 years to get there even if you traveled at the speed of light," the astronomer says.

Undaunted, the science fiction writer asks, "Well, what about hyperspace? I can send my starship into super-light-speed overdrive and leave this continuum for a different dimensional coordinate system. In hyperspace I can travel as fast as I want to. I can get my hero to Alderbaran VI just in time to win the battle . . . or just late enough to allow the heroine to have been abducted by the tarantula people . . ."

The physicist throws her hands up and nearly screams. "Gibberish! Absolute nonsense. You just invented hyperspace as a convenience."

"Not me," the writer counters. "The mathematicians did. And anyway, since you can't prove that I'm wrong, the idea is still useful. Science fiction can always use an idea that hasn't been proved wrong. Right?"

Muttering something about the conservation of energy, the physicist sinks back into her chair.

"She's got good reason to be upset," the astronomer says. "This hyperspace business is merely a mathematical trick. It's got nothing to do with the real world. Nothing in the universe has been observed to travel faster than light. Chances are that nothing ever will. No . . . if you want to go to Alpha Centauri, it's going to take you at least 4.3

years. The speed of light is a barrier that apparently can't be broken through.''

The science fiction writer frowns. ''The 'light barrier' sounds a lot like the 'sound barrier' that the aircraft engineers broke through about forty years ago.''

All the scientists groan in protest. The engineer, waving his pocket calculator as he speaks, explains that everyone knew that the speed of sound was not a fundamental barrier.

''Bullets, meteors, shock waves . . . there were plenty of things that we knew traveled faster than sound. The problem was to build an airplane that could do it without breaking up because of the stresses it flew into right around Mach 1—sonic speed.''

''But *nothing* goes faster than light,'' the physicist resumes. ''Nothing in the whole universe.''

''Isn't there something called tachyons?'' the writer asks, his voice somewhat subdued. ''Don't they go faster than light?''

''Tachyons are completely theoretical,'' the physicist explains. ''A few physicists have been playing with the idea that there are particles somewhere in the universe that go faster than light, and they called these particles tachyons. But as far as we know, they don't exist. In fact, according to the theories, if tachyons did exist we could never see them or use them . . . so it doesn't really matter whether they exist or not!''

''This is beginning to sound awfully gloomy.'' The writer leans back in his chair, sulking.

''You asked us and we're telling you,'' the physicist insists. ''Look. At the speed of light, the basic relationships between matter and energy begin to do strange things. For example, we've built powerful particle accelerators. In them we can speed up the motion of an electron until it's going at better than 95 percent of the speed of light. At those speeds, when we add more energy to the electron, it doesn't go any faster—it gets heavier! Its mass grows. No matter how much energy we pump into the electron, it never reaches light speed. The energy changes into mass."

The writer looks ready to slide under the table and forget the whole affair.

But from a quiet part of the table the mathematician says, in a thin but clear voice, "Although the physicist and engineer can't tell you how to build a ship that goes as fast as light, I can show you what would happen if such a ship existed."

"You can?" The writer perks up.

"Certainly," replies the mathematician. "Please remember that a mathematician named Newton showed three hundred years ago that an artificial satellite could be established in orbit. Mathematicians can tell you what the stars will look like a billion years from now, or what interactions a mu-meson will undergo in its first millionth of a second of lifetime, or . . ."

"Okay, okay," says the science fiction writer. "What about starships?"

"First," the mathematician says, "it's not necessary to travel exactly at the speed of light. If the ship could get to within a few percent of light speed, then time would begin to change aboard the ship.

"This all stems from Einstein's theory of relativity," he adds. "Although most people claim Einstein was a physicist, he was really quite a mathematician as well."

"Spare us the commercial," the medical doctor mumbles.

Sniffing slightly, the mathematician goes on, "The physicist told you that strange things begin to happen to matter and energy when you get close to light speed. Well, strange things happen to time, as well.

"The mathematics of relativity," he explains, "show that if a ship were to approach the speed of light, time aboard the ship would slow down. A clock aboard the ship would tick slower and slower as the ship's speed got closer and closer to the speed of light. Everything aboard the ship, the human crew included, would slow down with respect to time on Earth. But aboard the ship itself, nothing would seem to change. Everything would seem quite normal, even though years of time might pass on Earth before a second elapses on the ship.

"This is the basis of the famous 'twin paradox' of relativity. If one twin brother stayed on Earth while the other flew to a star at nearly the speed of light, when the flying twin returned to Earth, he would be younger than the brother he left behind.

"The German mathematician Eugen Sänger once gave the following example: A ship flying at more than 90 percent of the speed of light travels 1,000 light-years to Polaris, the North Star. Ignoring such details as the time spent accelerating to top speed and decelerating to landing speed again, the ship could make the flight to Polaris and back to Earth in a *subjective* time of 20 years. That is, to the crew on board the ship, only 20 years will have passed. But when they return to Earth, our planet will be 2,000 years older than when they left!"

"That's wild," says the science fiction writer, looking a little groggy at this point.

The mathematician nods happily. "So you see, if we could travel at speeds close to the speed of light, we could reach the stars. There's no need to break the so-called 'light barrier' to get to the stars."

"Not to all the stars," says the astronomer. "Just to a handful of stars, the nearest ones. Even at light speed, the stars are too far away."

The mathematician disagrees. "Come now. Sänger showed you could fly across the entire known universe in a subjective time of only 40 years, if you fly at 99 percent of the speed of light."

"And return to an Earth that's billions of years older than when you left it," the astronomer retorts. "Who would go on such a venture? How could you know that the Earth would still exist after such a time?"

"Wait . . . wait . . ." The writer puts an end to their

argument before it can go any further. "If it's mathematically possible to cover such distances, could we really build ships to do the job? I mean, sticking to these ideas that there is a 'light barrier' and that nothing can go faster than light, can we someday build starships that will go at least *close to* the speed of light?"

"You might not have to," says the engineer. "There's always the possibility of an interstellar ark. You know, a huge ship with a completely self-sufficient colony aboard. They'd sail out toward the stars at speeds not much more than solar escape velocity—that 58,000 kilometers per hour we were talking about a few minutes ago."

"But that would take thousands of years . . . millions . . ."

The engineer shrugs. "Sure, it would take generations and generations. People would be born aboard the ship, live out their lives, and die. Their great-great-many-greats-grandchildren would eventually get to the star they were aiming for. But that would be the simplest kind of ship to build. Awfully big, of course—like a moving city. But it could be built. I think."

The psychiatrist, who's been silent up to now, says, "I doubt that normal, well-adjusted human beings would ever embark on such a journey. How could they, in good conscience? They'd be dooming many generations of their offspring to live and die aboard the ark. How do they know that the children who finally reach their destination star will want to live there?"

"Or," the astronomer adds, with a twinkle in his eye, "that another group in a faster ship hasn't beaten them to it?"

"Even leaving that possibility aside," the psychiatrist continues, "no group of human beings who could be considered to be normal would ever contemplate such a mission. Why, they would have to be a group of exiles. Or religious fanatics."

"Like the Pilgrims or Quakers?" somebody asks.

The engineer says, "I'm assuming that the rocket engines aboard the ark will be based on nuclear fusion. You know, the hydrogen fusion process, such as the Sun and stars use. Hydrogen atoms come together to make a helium atom, and release energy."

"No one's built a fusion rocket," the physicist points out. "In fact, even the fission rockets—the kind that use uranium or plutonium, where the atoms are split to release energy—have never gone beyond the testing stage. Nobody's flown one. And the only way we've been able to release fusion energy here on Earth is in hydrogen bombs."

"I know," the engineer admits. "But progress in fusion research has been very encouraging over the past few years. I think we can safely agree that fusion power will be available before the end of this century."

"Perhaps," the physicist says reluctantly.

"Fusion rockets will make tremendous propulsion systems," the engineer says glowingly.

The engineer goes on to explain about a study undertaken by Dwain F. Spencer and Leonard D. Jaffe at the California Institute of Technology's Jet Propulsion Laboratory. "Spencer and Jaffe assumed that fusion rockets could be built, and then they tried to design a starship that uses fusion power. The ship they came up with—on paper—had five stages, each one powered by fusion rockets. It can make a round-trip flight to Alpha Centauri in a total elapsed time of 29 years. The ship would accelerate at 32 feet per second, every second, for several months. This is the same force that we feel here on Earth due to our planet's gravity. So, during the ship's acceleration period, the crew would feel 1 g, their normal Earth weight.

"After several months of this acceleration, the ship would be traveling at a relativistic speed—fast enough for time effects to come into play. It would then shut down its engines and coast the rest of the way to Alpha Centauri. The same procedure would be followed for the return trip:

a few months of 1 g acceleration, then coasting flight back to Earth.

"The 29 years would seem slightly shorter to the ship's crew," the engineer says, "because of the relativistic time-dilation effect."

"And that's using power that we know we can harness," the science fiction writer adds excitedly. "Why, maybe early next century we could reach Alpha Centauri! People alive today might make the trip!"

"Excuse me," says the astronomer. "Have any of you heard of the Bussard interstellar ramjet?

"R. W. Bussard was a physicist at the Los Alamos Scientific Laboratory when he thought of the interstellar ramjet idea," the astronomer explains.

"Bussard realized that one of the main drawbacks to any rocket engine is that it must carry all of its propellant with it. Spencer and Jaffe's five-stage fusion rocket, for example, must be more than 90 percent hydrogen propellant—allowing very little payload for such a huge vehicle. The rocket must also spend a considerable amount of its energy just lifting its own propellant mass. The situation becomes a vicious circle. As long as you must carry all the rocket's propellant along with you, any increase in speed must be paid for by more propellant mass. When you're considering flight at close to the speed of light, this becomes a serious obstacle. It poses a fundamental limitation on the amount of energy you can get out of the fusion rocket.

"But suppose the interstellar ship didn't have to carry any fuel at all? It could carry much more payload. And its range would be unlimited—it could go anywhere, at close to light speed, as long as it could somehow find propellant to feed to its engines.

"Interstellar space is filled with propellant for a hydrogen fusion rocket—hydrogen gas. There is enough hydrogen gas floating freely among the stars to build billions of new stars. This is an enormous supply of propellant.

"However," the astronomer admits, "when I use the word *filled* I'm being a little overly dramatic. The hydrogen gas is spread very thinly through most of interstellar space . . . no more than a few atoms per cubic centimeter. By contrast, there are more than 10^{19} atoms per cubic centimeter in the air we're breathing. That's ten million trillion atoms in the space of a sugar cube. Out among the stars, there are fewer than ten atoms per cubic centimeter.

"Bussard calculated that the ramjet will need a tremendously large scoop to funnel in a continuous supply of hydrogen for the fusion rocket engines. For a ship with a payload of 1,000 tons—about the size of a reasonable schooner—a funnel some 2,000 kilometers in radius would be needed."

The mathematician smiles. "I'm tempted to say that such a scoop would be *astronomically* big."

"Yes," the engineer says, "but there's plenty of open space out there."

"And the scoop needn't be solid material," the physicist adds. "If you could ionize the hydrogen with laser beams, so that the atoms are broken up into electrically charged ions, then the scoop could be nothing more than an immense magnetic field—it would funnel in the electrified ions quite nicely."

"Such a ship," the astronomer goes on, "can reach the nearest stars in a few years—of ship time, that is. The center of the Milky Way would be only about 20 years away, and the great spiral galaxy in Andromeda could be reached in about 30 years. Of course, the elapsed time on Earth would be thousands, even millions of years."

"Even forgetting that for a moment," the science fiction writer asks, "don't you think the crew's going to get bored? Spending 20 or 30 years traveling isn't going to be much fun. And they'll be getting older . . ."

A polite cough from the other side of the table turns everyone's head toward the biochemist.

"As long as we're stretching things," he says, "we

might as well consider the possibility of letting the crew sleep for almost the entire flight—slowing down their metabolism so that they don't age much at all."

"Suspended animation?" the writer asks.

With a slightly uncomfortable look, the biochemist replies, "You could call it something like that, I suppose. I'm sure that by the time we're ready to tackle the stars, a technique will have been found to freeze a human being indefinitely. You could freeze the crew shortly after take-off and then have them awakened automatically when they reach their destination. They won't age while they're hibernating."

"This is the idea of freezing them at cryogenic temperatures, isn't it?" the medical doctor asks.

Nodding, the biochemist says, "Yes. Temperatures close to absolute zero. Nearly 400 degrees below zero on the Fahrenheit thermometer."

"That simply can't be done," the doctor says firmly.

"Not now," the biochemist agrees. "But by the end of this century, we might have learned how to quick-freeze live human beings without damaging their cells."

The doctor looks unconvinced and shakes his head.

"I must point out," the psychiatrist says, "that you still have the basic problem of motivation on your hands. Who would want to leave the Earth, knowing that he would return to a world that's several thousand years older than the one he left?"

"It would be a one-way trip, wouldn't it?" the writer muses. "Even if the crew comes back to Earth, it won't be the same world that they left. It'll be like Columbus returning to Spain during the time of Napoleon."

"Or Leif Ericson coming back to Scandinavia next week."

"The crew members will want to bring their families with them," the writer points out. "They'll have to."

"Nothing man has ever done comes even close to such an experience," the psychiatrist says.

"Oh, I'm not so sure about that," objects the anthropologist. He has been sitting next to the psychiatrist, listening interestedly and smoking a pipe through the whole discussion.

Now he says, "The Polynesian peoples settled the islands of the Pacific on a somewhat similar basis. They started in one corner of the Pacific and expanded throughout most of the islands in the central regions of that ocean. And they did it on a somewhat haphazard basis—a mixture of deliberate emigrations into unknown territory plus accidental landings on new islands when ships were blown off course by storms."

"That's hardly . . ."

"Now listen," the anthropologist insists quietly. "The Polynesians ventured out across the broad Pacific in outrigger canoes. Their travels must have seemed as dark and dangerous to them as interstellar space seems to us. They left their homes behind—purposely, in the case of the emigrants. Usually, when they were forced to emigrate because of population pressure or religious differences, they took their whole families along. But they knew they'd never return to their original islands again. That's how Hawaii was first settled, and most of the other islands of the central Pacific."

"That *is* somewhat similar to starflight," the psychiatrist agrees.

"So we can reach the stars after all," the science fiction writer says. "It's not fundamentally impossible."

"It won't be simple," the engineer insists.

"Yes, but imagine a time when we can travel with interstellar ramjets from star to star."

"You'll never be able to go back to the same place again," the physicist reminds him. "Too much time will have elapsed between one visit and the next."

"I understand," the writer answers. "But consider it: Starship crews would be forced to think ahead in terms of centuries. They'd never know what would be coming up next, what the next world would hold for them. What an age for adventure!''

The mathematician chuckles. ''And if a star traveler should deposit a few dollars in a savings account, then come back several centuries later, what an age for compound interest!''

The science fiction writer turns his beaming face to the panel of experts and thanks each one of them in turn.

''You have certainly answered my problem. I can now write about interstellar ramjets, where the crews are frozen during the travel time from one star to the next. Why—the crew members will become virtually immortal! Who needs Mars? The rest of the universe is going to be much more exciting!''

Free Enterprise

Much has been said and written about the failures of American industry and the successes of the Japanese. Here is a tale that examines an industry I know rather well, publishing, and shows why we may soon be buying our books from Japan, as well as our automobiles and television sets. If any of my friends in the publishing industry take umbrage at this candid appraisal, good!

The Idea

It happened at approximately midnight, late in April, when they both should have been studying for their final exams.

Mark Moskowitz (a.k.a. "Mark the Monk") and Mitsui Minimata shared a rented room over one of Berkeley's shabbier head shops, less than a half-mile from the campus. Mark was going for his doctorate in logic; Mitsui was working doggedly toward his in electrical engineering. The few friends they had, years later, claimed that the idea was probably inspired by the various strange aromas wafting up from the shop below their room.

Mark's sobriquet was two-edged: not only did he have the heavy-browed, hairy, shambling appearance of an early homonid; he was, despite his apeish looks, exceedingly shy, bookish, and unsocial to the point of reclusiveness. Mitsui was just the opposite: tiny, constantly smiling, excruciatingly polite, and an accomplished conversationalist. Where Mark sat and pondered, Mitsui flashed around the room like an excited electron.

He was struggling with a heavy tome on electrical engineering, just barely managing to stagger across the room with it, heading for his reading chair, when he tripped on the threadbare rug and went sprawling face-first. Mark, snapped out of his glassy-eyed introspection by the thud of his roommate's impact on the floor, spent a moment focusing his far-sighted eyes on the situation. As Mitsui slowly sat up and shook his head groggily, Mark heaved himself up from the sagging sofa which served as his throne, shambled over to his friend, picked the little Japanese up with one hand, the ponderous textbook in the other, and settled them both safely on Mitsui's reading chair.

"Thank you ten thousand times," said Mitsui, after a sharp intake of breath to show that he was unworthy of his friend's kindness.

"You ought to pick on books your own size," Mark replied. For him, that amounted to a sizzling witticism.

Mitsui shrugged. "There *are* no books my size. Not in electrical engineering. They all weigh a metric ton."

Mark glared down at the weighty tome. "I wonder why they still print books on paper. Wouldn't electrons be a lot lighter?"

"Yes, of course. And cheaper, as well."

"H'mm," said Mark.

"H'mm," said Mitsui.

And they never spoke of the idea again. Not to each other, at least. A month later they received their degrees and went their separate ways.

The Presentation

Gene Rockmore blinked several times at the beetle-browed young man sitting in his office. "Mark M. Moskowitz, Ph.D.," the visitor's card said. Nothing else. No phone number or address. Rockmore tried to engage the young man in trivial conversation while studying him. He looked like a refugee from a wrestling school, despite his three-piece suit and conservative tie. Or maybe because of them; the clothes did not seem to be his, they barely fit him, and he looked very uncomfortable in them.

For several minutes Rockmore chatted about the weather, the awful cross-town traffic, and the dangers of being mugged on Manhattan's streets. He received nothing back from his visitor except a few grunts and uneasy wriggles.

Why me? Rockmore asked himself silently. Why do I have to get all the crazies who come in off the street? After all, I'm a vice president now. I ought to be involved in making deals with agents, and taking famous writers out to lunch. At least Charlene's father ought to let me get into the advertising and promotion end of the business. I could be a smash on the Johnny Carson show, plugging our company's books. Instead, I have to sit here and deal with inarticulate ape-men.

Rockmore, who looked like (and was) a former chorus boy in a Broadway musical, slicked back his thinning blond hair with one hand and finally asked, "Well, eh, just what is it you wanted to talk to me about, Mr. Mos . . . I mean, *Dr.* Moskowitz?"

"Electronic books," said Mark.

"Electronic books?" Rockmore asked.

"Uh-huh." And for the next three hours, Mark did all the talking.

Mitsui hardly spoke at all, and when he did, it was in Japanese, a language both simple and supple. Most of the time, as he sat side-by-side with the vice president for innovation at Kanagawa Electronics and Shipbuilding, Inc., Mitsui tapped out numbers on his pocket computer. The v.p. grinned and nodded and hissed happily at the glowing digits on the tiny readout screen.

The Reception

Robert Emmett Lipton, president of Hubris Books, a division of WPA Entertainment, which is a wholly-owned subsidiary of Moribundic Industries, Inc., which in turn is owned by Empire State Bank (and, it is rumored, the Mafia), could scarcely believe his ears.

"Electronic books? What on earth are electronic books?"

Lipton smiled gently at his son-in-law. It didn't do to get tough with Rockmore. He simply broke down and cried and went home to Charlene, who would then phone to tell her mother what a heel her father was to pick on such a sensitive boy as Gene.

So the president of Hubris Books rocked slowly in his big leather chair and tried to look interested as his son-in-law explained his latest hare-brained scheme. Lipton sighed inwardly, thinking about the time Rockmore suggested to the editorial board that they stop printing books that failed to sell well, and stuck only to best sellers. That was when Rockmore had just graduated from the summer course in management at Harvard. Ten years later, and he still didn't know a thing about the publishing business. But he kept Charlene happy, and that kept Charlene's mother happy, and *that* was the only reason Lipton allowed Rockmore to play at being an executive.

"So it's possible," Rockmore was saying, "to make the thing about the size of a paperback book. Its screen would be the size of a book page, and it could display a page of printed text or full-color illustrations . . ."

"Do you realize how much color separations cost?" Lipton snapped. Instantly he regretted his harshness. He started to reach for the Kleenex box on the shelf behind his chair.

But Rockmore did not burst into tears, as he usually did. Instead he smirked. "No color separations, Papa. It's all done electronically."

"No color separations?" Lipton found that hard to believe.

"No color separations. No printing at all. No paper. It's like having a hand-sized TV set in your . . . er, hand. But the screen can be any page of any book we publish."

"No printing?" Lipton heard his voice echoing, weakly. "No paper?"

"It's all done by electronics. Computers."

Lipton's mind was in a whirl. He conjured up last month's cost figures. The exact numbers were a blur in his memory, but they were huge—and most of them came from the need to transport vast tonnages of paper from the pulp mills to the printing plants, and then from the printing plants to the warehouses, and then from the warehouses to the wholesalers, and then . . .

He sat up straighter in his chair. "No paper? Are you certain?"

Mitsui bowed low to the president of Kanagawa. The doughty old man, his silver hair still thick, his dark eyes still alert, sat on the matted floor, dressed in a magnificent midnight-blue kimono. He barely nodded his head at the young engineer and the vice president for innovation, both of whom wore Western business suits.

With a curt gesture, he commanded them to sit. For long moments, nothing was said, as the servants brought the tea. The old man let his favorite, a young woman of heartbreakingly fragile beauty, set out the graceful little cups and pour the steaming tea.

Mitsui held his breath until the v.p. nodded to him. Then, from the inside pocket of his jacket, Mitsui pulled out a slim package, exquisitely wrapped in expensive golden gift paper and tied with a silk bow the same color as the president's kimono. He held the gift in outstretched arms, presenting it to the old man.

The president allowed a crooked grin to cross his stern visage. As the v.p. knew, he took a childish pleasure in receiving gifts. Very carefully, the old man untied the bow and peeled away the heavy paper. He opened the box and took out an object the size of a paperback book. Most of its front surface was taken up by a video screen. There were three pressure pads at the screen's bottom, nothing more.

The old man raised his shaggy brows questioningly. The v.p. indicated that he should press the first button, which was a bright green.

The president did, and the little screen instantly showed a listing of titles. Among them were the best selling novels of the month. By pressing the buttons as indicated, the old man got the screen to display the opening pages of half a dozen books within less than a minute.

He smiled broadly, turned to Mitsui and extended his right hand. He clasped the young engineer's shoulder the way a proud father would grasp his bright young son.

The Evaluation

Lipton sat at the head of the conference table and studied the vice presidents arrayed about him: Editorial, Marketing, Production, Advertising, Promotion, Subsidiary Rights, Legal, Accounting, Personnel, and son-in-law. For the first time in the ten years since Rockmore had married his daughter, Lipton gazed fondly at his son-in-law.

"Gentlemen," said the president of Hubris Books, then, with his usual smarmy nod to the Editor-in-Chief and the head of Subsidiary Rights, "and ladies . . ."

They were shocked when he invited Rockmore to take the floor, and even more startled when the former chorus boy made a fifteen-minute presentation of the electronic book idea without falling over himself. It was the first time Lipton had *asked* his son-in-law to speak at the monthly executive board conference, and certainly the first time Rockmore had anything to say that was worth listening to.

Or was it? The assembled vice presidents eyed each other nervously as Rockmore sat down after his presentation. No one wanted to be the first to speak. No one knew which way the wind was blowing. Rockmore sounded as if he knew what he was talking about, but maybe this was a trap. Maybe Lipton was finally trying to get his son-in-law bounced out of the company, or at least off the executive board.

They all fidgeted in their chairs, waiting for Lipton to give them some clue as to what they were supposed to think. The president merely sat up at the head of the table, fingers steepled, smiling like a chubby, inscrutable Buddha.

The silence stretched out to an embarrassing length. Finally, Editorial could stand it no longer.

"*Another* invasion by technology," she said, her fingers fussing absently with the bow of her blouse. "It was bad enough when we computerized the office. It took my people *weeks* to make the adjustment. Some of them are still at sea."

"Then get rid of them," Lipton snapped. "We can't stand in the way of progress. Technology is the future. I'm sure of it."

An almost audible sigh of relief went around the table. Now they knew where the boss stood; they knew what they were supposed to say.

"Well, of course technology is important," Editorial backtracked, "but I just don't see how an electronic thingamajig can replace a *book*. I mean, it's cold . . . metallic. It's a *machine*. A book is . . . well, it's comforting, it's warm and friendly, it's the feel of paper . . ."

"Which costs too damned much," Lipton said.

Accounting took up the theme with the speed of an electronic calculator. "Do you have any idea of what paper costs this company each month?"

"Well, I . . ." Editorial saw that she was going to be the sacrificial lamb. She blushed and lapsed into silence.

"How much would an electronic book sell for?" Marketing asked.

Lipton shrugged. "One dollar? Two?"

Rockmore, from the far end of the table, spoke up. "According to the technical people I've spoken to, the price of a book could be less than one dollar."

"Instead of fifteen to twenty," Lipton said, "which is what our hardcovers are priced at now."

"One dollar?" Marketing looked stunned. "We could sell *zillions* of books at a dollar apiece!"

"We could wipe out the paperback market," Lipton agreed, happily.

"But that would cut off a major source of income for us," cried Sub Rights.

"There would still be foreign sales," said Lipton. "And film and TV rights."

"I don't know about TV," Legal chimed in. "After all, by displaying a book on what is essentially a television screen, we may be construed as utilizing the broadcast TV rights . . ."

The discussion continued right through the morning. Lipton had sandwiches and coffee brought in, and the executive board stayed in conference well past quitting time.

In the port city of Numazu, not far from the blissful snow-covered cone of divine Fujiyama, Kanagawa Industries began the urgent task of converting one of its electronics plants to building the first production run of Mitsui

Minimata's electronic book. Mitsui was given the position of advisor to the chief production engineer, who ran the plant with rigid military discipline. His staff of six hundred (five hundred eighty-eight of them robots) worked happily and efficiently, converting the plant from building navigation computers to the new product.

The Resistance

Editorial sipped her Bloody Mary while Sub Rights stared out the restaurant window at the snarling Manhattan midtown traffic. The restaurant was only half-filled, even though this was the height of the lunch hour rush; the publishing business had been in the doldrums for some time. Suave waiters with slicked-back hair and European accents hovered over each table, anxious to generate tips through quality of service, when it was obvious that quantity of customers was lacking.

Sub Rights was a pale, ash-blonde woman in her late thirties. She had worked for Hubris Books since graduating from Barnard with stars in her eyes and dreams of a romantic career in the world of literature. Her most romantic moment had come when a French publisher's representative had seduced her, at the height of the Frankfurt Book Fair, and thus obtained a very favorable deal on Hubris's entire line of "How To" books for that year.

"I think you've hit it on the head," Sub Rights said, idly stirring her Campari-and-soda with its plastic straw. "Books should be made of *paper*, not this electric machine thing."

Editorial had worked for six publishers in the twelve years since she had arrived in New York from Kansas. Somehow, whenever the final sales figures for the books she had bought became known to management, she was invited to look for work elsewhere. Still, there were plenty of publishing houses in midtown Manhattan which operated on the same principle: fire the editor when sales don't pan out, and then hire an editor fired by one of your competitors for the same reason.

"That's what I think, too," she said. Her speech was just a little blurred, her tinted auburn hair just a bit frazzled. This was her third Bloody Mary and they had not ordered lunch yet.

"I love to curl up with a book. It's cozy," said Sub Rights.

"Books are *supposed* to be made of paper," Editorial agreed. "With pages that you can turn."

Sub Rights nodded unhappily. "I said that to Production, and do you know what *he* said?"

"No. What?"

"He said I was wrong, and that books were supposed to be made of clay tablets with cuneiform marks pressed into them."

Editorial's eyes filled with tears. "It's the end of an era. The next thing you know, they'll replace us with robots."

The chief engineer paced back and forth, hands clasped behind his back, as the two technicians worked feverishly on the robot. The entire assembly area of the factory was absolutely still; not a machine moved, all across the wide floor. Both technicians' white coveralls were stained with sweat and oil, a considerable loss of face for men who prided themselves on keeping their machines in perfect working order.

The chief engineer, in his golden-tan coveralls and plastic hard hat, alternately glared at the technicians and gazed up at the huge digital clock dominating the far wall of the assembly area. Up in the glass-panelled gallery above the clock, he could see Mitsui Minimata's young, eager face peering intently at them.

A shout of triumph from one of the technicians made the chief engineer spin around. The technician held a tiny silicon chip delicately between his thumb and forefinger, took two steps forward and offered the offending electronic unit to the chief engineer. The chief took it, looked down at the thumbnail-sized chip, so small and insignificant-seeming in the palm of his hand. Hard to believe that this tiny grain of sand caused the robot to malfunction and ruined an entire day's work. He sighed to himself, and thought that this evening, as he relaxed in a hot bath, he would try to compose a haiku on the subject of how small things can cause great troubles.

The junior of the two technicians, in the meantime, had dashed to the automated supply dispenser across the big assembly room, dialed up a replacement chip, and come running back with the new unit pressed between his palms. The senior technicians installed it quickly, buttoned up the robot's access panel, turned and bowed to the chief engineer.

The chief grunted a grudging approval. The junior technician bowed to the chief and asked permission to activate the robot. The chief nodded. The robot stirred to life, and it too bowed to the chief engineer. Only then did production resume.

The Sales Manager for Hubris Books stroked his chin thoughtfully as he sat behind his desk conversing with his western district sales director.

"But if they ever start selling these electronic doohickeys," the western district man was saying, "they'll bypass the wholesalers, the distributors, even the retail stores, for cryin' out loud! They'll sell those little computer disks direct to the customer! They'll sell 'em through the mail!"

"And over the phone," the Sales Manager added wearily. "They're talking about doing the whole thing electronically."

"Where's that leave us?"

"Out in the cold, buddy. Right out in the cold."

The Decision

Robert Emmett Lipton was not often nervous. His position in life was to make other people nervous, not to get the jitters himself. But he was not often summoned to the office of the CEO of Moribundic Industries. Lipton found himself perspiring as the secretary escorted him through the cool, quiet, elegantly-carpeted corridors toward the CEO's private suite.

It wasn't as if he had been asked to report to the bejewelled jackass who headed WPA Entertainment, out in Los Angeles. Lipton could deal with him. But the CEO was different; he had the real power to make or break a man.

The secretary was a tall, lissome, devastatingly beautiful woman: the kind who could marry a millionaire and then ruin him. In the deeper recesses of his mind, Lipton thought it would be great fun to be ruined by such a creature.

She opened the door marked *Alexander Hamilton Stark, Chief Executive Officer* and smiled at Lipton. He thought there was a trace of sadness in her smile, as if she never expected to see him again—alive.

"Thank you," Lipton managed, as he stepped into the CEO's private office.

He had seen smaller airport terminals. The room was vast, richly carpeted, furnished with treasures from the Orient in teak and ebony, copper, silver, and gold. Far, far across the room, the CEO sat behind his broad, massive desk of rosewood and chrome. Its gleaming surface was uncluttered.

Feeling small and helpless, like a pudgy little gnome suddenly summoned to the throne of power, Lipton made his way across the vast office, plowing through the thick carpeting with leaden steps.

The CEO was an ancient, hairless, wrinkled, death's

head of a figure, sitting hunched and aged in a high-backed leather chair that dwarfed him. For a ridiculous instant, Lipton was reminded of a turtle sitting there, staring at him out of dull reptilian eyes. With something of a shock, he suddenly realized that there was a third man in the room: a younger man, swarthy, dark of hair and jaw, dressed in a European-cut silk suit, sitting to one side of the massive desk.

Lipton came to a halt before the desk. There was no chair there, so he remained standing.

"Mr. Stark," he said. "I'm so happy that you've given me this opportunity to report directly to you about the electronic book project."

"You'll have to speak louder," the younger man said. "His batteries are running down."

Lipton turned slightly toward him. "And you are?"

"I'm Mr. Stark's personal secretary and bodyguard," the young man said.

"Oh."

"We hear that Hubris Books is in hock up to its elbows on this electronic book thing," the bodyguard said.

"I wouldn't . . ." Lipton stopped himself, turned toward the CEO and said, louder, "I wouldn't put it that way. We're pushing ahead on a very difficult project."

"Don't give up the ship," the CEO muttered.

"We don't intend to, sir," said Lipton. "It's quite true that we've encountered some difficulties in the electronic book project, but we are moving right ahead."

"I have not yet begun to fight!" said the CEO.

Lipton felt himself frown slightly, puzzled.

The bodyguard said, "Our sources of information say that morale at Hubris is very low. And so are sales."

"We're going through a period of adjustment, that's true . . ."

"Millions for defense," the CEO's quavering voice piped, "but not one cent for tribute."

"Sir?" Lipton felt confused. What was the CEO driving at?

"Your costs are shooting through the roof," the bodyguard accused.

Lipton felt perspiration beading his upper lip. "We're involved in a very difficult project. We're working with one of the nation's top electronics firms to produce a revolutionary new concept, a product that will totally change the book business. It's true that we've had problems—technical as well as human problems. But . . ."

"We have met the enemy," croaked the CEO, "and they are ours."

"I don't want to be overly critical," said the bodyguard-cum-secretary, with a smirk on his face that belied his words, "but you seem to have gotten Hubris to a point where sales are down, costs are up, and profits will be a long time coming."

"But, listen," Lipton replied, trying to keep his voice from sounding as if he were begging, "this concept of electronic books is going to sweep the publishing industry! We'll be able to publish books for a fraction of what they cost now, and sell them directly to the readers! Our sales volume is projected to triple, the first year we're on the market, and our profit margin . . ."

"Fifty-four forty or fight!" cackled the CEO.

"What?" Lipton blurted.

The bodyguard's smile seemed knowing, cynical. "We've seen your projections. But they're all based on the assumption that you'll have the electronic books on the market next year. We don't believe you can do that, not at the rate you're going now."

"As I said, we've had some problems here and there." Lipton was starting to feel desperate. "We contracted with Moribundic's electronics division, at first, to make the damned things, but they flubbed the job completely. They produced a monstrosity that weighed seventeen pounds and didn't work half the time."

The CEO shook his wizened head. "My only regret is that I have but one life to give for my country."

Suppressing an urge to run screaming out of the room, Lipton slogged forward. "The company we're working with now is based in Silicon Valley, in California. At least they've got the electronics right. But they've got problems with their supply of parts. Seems there's a trucker's strike in Texas, where the chips are being manufactured. This has caused a delay."

"And in the meantime, Hubris' sales are sinking out of sight."

"The whole book industry is in a bad way . . ."

The bodyguard raised his dark eyebrows half an inch, as if acknowledging the point. "But we're hearing complaints about poor morale in the office. Not just down in the pits, but among your own executive board."

Lipton growled, "Those dimwitted idiots can't see any farther than their own paychecks! They're afraid that the electronic book is going to take away their jobs."

"Your profit-and-loss projections are based, in part, on eliminating most of their jobs, aren't they?"

"Well, yes, of course. We won't need them anymore."

The CEO's frail voice became mournful. "It is for us, the living, rather to be dedicated here to the unfinished work . . ." His voice sank to an unintelligible mumble, then rose again to conclude, "that these dead shall not have died in vain."

As if the CEO were not in the room with them, or at least not in the same plane of reality, the bodyguard launched into a detailed analysis of Lipton's electronic books project. He referred to it specifically as Lipton's project. Hubris Books' president felt sweat trickling down his ribs. His hands shook and his feet hurt as he stood there defending every dollar he had spent on the idea.

Finally, the bodyguard turned to the CEO, who had sat unmoving and silent for the past hour.

"Well, sir," he said, "that brings us up to date on the

project. The potential for great profits is there, but at the rate we're going, the cost will drag the entire corporation's P-and-L statement down into the red ink.''

The CEO said nothing; he merely sat hunched in his oversized chair, watery eyes blinking slowly.

''On the other hand,'' the bodyguard went on, ''our tax situation should be vastly improved by all these losses. If we continue with the electronic book project, we won't have to worry about the IRS for the next three years, at least.''

Lipton wanted to protest, to shout to them that the electronic book was more than a tax dodge. But his voice was frozen in his throat.

''What's your decision, sir?'' the bodyguard asked.

The CEO lifted one frail hand from his desktop and slowly clenched it into a fist. ''Damn the torpedoes! Full steam ahead!''

The Result

Mitsui Minimata held his breath. Never in his happiest dreams had he entertained the idea that he would someday meet the Emperor face to face, in the Imperial Palace. Yet here he was, kneeling on a silken carpet, close enough to the Divine Presence to touch him.

Arrayed around Mitsui, also kneeling with eyes respectfully lowered, were the head of Kanagawa Industries, the vice president for innovation, and the chief engineer of the Numazu plant. All were dressed in ceremonial kimonos more gorgeous than Mitsui would have thought it was possible for human hands to create.

The Emperor was flanked by serving robots, of course. It was fitting that the Divine personage not be touched by human hands. Besides, his decision to have robots serve him presented the Japanese people with an example of how these new devices should be accepted into every part of life.

With trembling hands Mitsui placed the first production unit of the electronic book in the metal fingers of the robot that stood between him and the Emperor. The robot pivoted, making hardly more noise than the heel of a boot would on a polished floor, and extended its arm to the Emperor.

The Emperor peered through his glasses at the little electronic package, then picked it up. He had been instructed, of course, on how to use the book. But for an instant Mitsui was frightened that somehow the instructions had not been sufficient, and the Emperor would be embarrassed by being unable to make the book work. Suicide would be the only way out, in that case.

After what seemed like several years of examining the book, the Emperor touched the green pressure pad at its base. Mitsui knew what would come up on the screen: a listing of all the books and papers that the Emperor himself had written in the field of marine biology.

The Divine face broke into a pleased smile. The smile broadened as the Emperor pecked away at the book's controls, bringing one after another of his own writings to the book's page-sized screen. He laughed with delight, and Mitsui realized that mortal life offered no higher reward than this.

Mark Moskowitz paced angrily back and forth across his one-room apartment as he argued with the image of his attorney on the phone screen.

"But they're screwing me out of my own invention!" he yelled.

The attorney, a sad-eyed man with an expression of utter world-weariness, replied, "Mark, when you accepted their money you sold them the rights to the invention."

"But they're lousing it up! Three years now and they

still haven't produced a working model that weighs less than ten pounds!''

"There's nothing you can do about it," said the attorney. "It's their ball."

"But it's my idea! My invention!"

The attorney shrugged.

"You know what I think?" Mark growled, pacing back to the phone and bending toward the screen until his nose almost touched it. "I think Hubris Books doesn't *want* to make the project succeed! I think they're screwing around with it just to give the whole idea a bad name and make certain that no other publisher will touch it, by the time they're finished."

"That's silly," said the attorney. "Why would they . . ."

"Silly?" Mark snapped. "How about last year, when they tried to make the picture screen feel like paper? How about that scheme they came up with to have a hundred separate screens that you could turn like the pages of a book? Silly? They're *crazy*!"

They argued fruitlessly for nearly half an hour, and finally Mark punched the phone's OFF button in a fury of frustration and despair. He sat in glowering, smoldering anger in the one-room apartment as the afternoon sun slowly faded into the shadows of dusk.

Only then did he remember why he had placed the call to his attorney. The package from Tokyo. From Mitsui. When it had arrived, Mark had gone straight to the phone to see what progress his suit against Hubris Books was making. The answer, of course, had been: zero.

With the dejected air of a defeated soldier, Mark trudged to the table by his hotplate where he had left the package. Terribly afraid that he knew what was inside the heavy wrappings, he nonetheless opened the package as delicately, as tenderly, as if it contained newborn kittens.

It contained a newborn, all right. An electronic book, just as Mark had feared. No message, no card. Nothing but the book itself.

Mark held it in the palm of his left hand. It weighed a little more than a pound, he judged. Three pads were set below the screen, marked with Arabic numerals and Japanese characters. He touched the green one, which was marked "1."

A still picture of Mitsui appeared on the screen, grinning—no, *beaming*—at him. The amber pressure pad, marked "2," began to blink. Mark touched it.

A neatly typed letter appeared on the screen:

> Dear Friend Mark:
> Please accept this small token of my deep friendship for you. In a few days your news media will be filled with stories about Kanagawa Industries' revolutionary new electronic book. I will tell every reporter I speak to that the idea is just as much yours as mine, which is nothing more than the truth.
> As you may know, trade agreements between your government and mine will make it impossible for Japan to sell electronic books in the U.S.A. However, it should be permissible for us to form an American subsidiary of Kanagawa in the United States. Would you consider accepting the position of chief scientist, or a post of similar rank, with this new company? In that way, you can help to produce electronic books for the American market.
> Please phone me at your earliest convenience . . .

Mark read no further. He ran to the phone. He did not even bother to check what time it was in Tokyo. As it happened, he interrupted Mitsui's lunch, but the two ex-roommates had a happy, laughing talk together, and Mark agreed to become vice president for innovation of the planned Kanagawa-USA subsidiary.

Moral

Victor Hugo was right when he said that no army can withstand the strength of an idea whose time has come. But if you're narrow-minded enough, both the time and the idea can pass you by.

Robot Welfare

The robots are coming, the robots are coming! Really. In truth. This generation of human beings may be the last to be engaged in boring, mechanical jobs. Or any jobs at all. A robot society is being built before our eyes, and the changes it brings will be just as huge, just as painful, as the changes wrought by what is now called the First Industrial Revolution.

The robots are coming, and they are looking for your job. No matter if you are a steelworker or a law clerk, an assembly line technician or a receptionist, there is a robot learning to do your work.

If and when you are replaced by a robot, how will you earn your living? That is the most profound question facing the American economy today. While politicians on the national, state, and local levels all wave the banner of "high technology" as a cure for economic recession, virtually none of them have even thought about the fact that high technology and high employment for human workers may be totally incompatible.

I stood in a large, airy room that looked like a health spa for robots. Mechanical arms were swinging, flexing, grasping, bending. More than a dozen robots were exercising in the robot lab of the General Motors Research Laboratories, in Warren, Michigan, a few miles outside Detroit. Some of the robots have been doing their calisthenics for more than two years.

"We're testing their durability," says Dr. Robert A. Frosch, director of the Research Laboratories. A former head of NASA, Frosch seems quite at home with the robots. And the robots keep on working tirelessly, without anyone supervising them: swing, flex, grasp, bend. Eight hours a day. Or sixteen, if necessary. Or maybe even twenty-four.

Testing their durability. I got the idea that the robots were practicing, among themselves, to take over most of the jobs in today's workplaces.

While I was watching those robots patiently, smoothly, ceaselessly repeating their assigned tasks, some 750,000 telephone workers were walking the picket lines across the nation, on strike against AT&T. Yet the telephone system worked virtually without a wobble, because it is so highly automated that it could do without those three-quarters of a million human workers, at least for a few weeks. "Telescab," the strikers called the computerized networks that kept the phones working with a minimum of human help.

In California, that same week, the Wells Fargo Bank and the Bank of America announced plans to close more than sixty branch offices throughout the state, replacing them with automated teller machines. "We're changing the way we distribute banking services," said a Wells Fargo executive.

Nor were telephone workers and bank clerks the only people being hit by automation that week. The *Wall Street*

Journal carried an article on how computers are transforming the practice of law. "Computers write letters, contracts, wills and briefs," said the *Journal*. "Computers bill clients and keep track of evidence and court calendars. . . . Computer systems provide pushbutton legal research, finding in minutes cases that once took hours or days to locate. Computers can check the testimony of one witness against another and help in tax, estate, and pension planning."

Computers, robots, and automated systems are very much in the job market today, competing against human workers every day—and winning.

There are nearly 2500 robots at work in General Motors factories today. GM plans to bring their robotic workforce up to 14,000 by 1990. Most of these robots work at the toughest, dirtiest, noisiest jobs: assembly, machining, welding, painting. The robots are deaf, blind, and not very sensitive. But they work without complaint and they never ask for a raise.

There are more than ten million unemployed people in the United States. The automobile industry laid off roughly half a million in the first two years of the 1980s. Economists agree that most of these workers will never be rehired; not at their old jobs, at least. Frosch and others at GM insist that the planned increase in robots will not cause more layoffs of human workers. But the clear fact is that the job market for people at GM will not expand, while the job market for robots will.

"Robots don't cause unemployment," says Dr. James S. Albus, chief of the Industrial Systems Division of the National Bureau of Standards, just outside Washington, D.C.

"At least," he amends, "robots don't cause unemployment in the countries that build the robots. Robots built in Japan have caused unemployment in the United States, but employment has risen in Japan because of robotics."

Albus' point is that robots allow a manufacturer to

produce goods of higher quality and lower cost than human workers. Therefore robots increase productivity, make the company more profitable, and lead to the creation of more markets, more jobs, more opportunities for human workers. But in the nation that imports robot-produced goods, domestic markets shrink, overseas markets disappear, and jobs grow scarcer.

Is the United States becoming an underdeveloped nation, robotically speaking? Will America enter the twenty-first century as a second-rate power, exporting grain and importing high technology goods built by foreign robots? Or must American industry replace most of its human workforce with robots, to stay abreast of foreign competition, and thereby cause massive unemployment?

In the whole world, there are fewer than 34,000 robots working in industry today. Japan leads the world with some 20,000 robots. The United States has about 6000 on the job, and Western Europe has roughly 8000. These numbers are growing by about thirty-five percent per year, which means that there could be 100,000 robots in the U.S. by 1990, and a million robots on the job in America by the year 2000. That would represent about two percent of the total labor force. By the year 2020, though, if the rate of increase keeps steady, there will be as many robots in the workforce as people.

Many decades ago, science fiction writers depicted a future world in which robots did most of the work in society, freeing human beings from the drudgery of labor. That kind of world is slowly becoming reality. But the question that the writers never faced is the problem that confronts us today: When a robot takes over my job, how do I earn an income?

The simplest answer is to prevent robots from entering the workforce. In Britain, until very recently, the powerful labor unions resisted automation of any kind on the grounds that it took away jobs from human workers. Just across the English Channel, the French government encouraged automation and moved actively to bring high technology to French industries. The result: the British economy stagnated because outdated equipment and rising labor costs priced British goods out of the international markets; unemployment soared in Britain during the latter half of the 1970s. Meanwhile French employment remained relatively stable as the French accepted computers and automation into the workforce—until the Mitterand government came into power and caused layoffs through unrelated fiscal policies.

To industry executives, robots and automation are the necessary wave of the future. Automated machinery and robots allow a company to produce its products not only more cheaply, but with higher quality. The machines already do better work than humans, mainly because they do not get tired or bored with their work. And the machines are getting better all the time. Today's robots are already giving way to improved models that can see, make decisions, and grasp as sensitively as—well, at least as sensitively as a gorilla.

"It's a survival thing," says Dick Beecher, of the GM robot lab. "Are we going to abdicate our position in the automobile industry to Japan?"

Men like Frosch and Albus, who are at the forefront of the robotic movement, hesitate to use the word *revolution* in connection with robots.

"This is an evolutionary movement," Frosch insists, "not a revolution."

He sees robots gradually changing the very nature of manufacturing work. And while GM does not plan to lay off workers as more and more robots are introduced to their factories, it is clear that the more robots there are in GM plants, the fewer new workers GM will have to hire.

This kind of shift in work patterns has happened before. Nearly two hundred years ago, in what is now called the First Industrial Revolution, hand crafts and small village shops were replaced within a single generation by steam-driven factories. At first in Britain, and then through most of Europe and the new nation of the United States of America, men and women alike left the farms and villages to find employment in the "dark, satanic" mills that belched out smoke, soot, filth—and jobs.

Cities grew enormously, because despite the inhuman working conditions in those factories, there was money to be made. The "slave wages" that most workers earned were still better than the backbreaking life on the farm, for which they had received no wages at all. And the owners of those mills became fabulously wealthy: they were the bourgeoisie that Marx and Engels saw as the enemy of the working man.

But communism and socialism were latter-day reactions to the rampant spread of industrialization. The first counter-attack came in England, in the form of rioting mobs which came to be called *Luddites*, after their mythic founder, Ned Ludd. The Luddites were English craftsmen who tried to stop the young Industrial Revolution by destroying the textile factories that were taking away their traditional incomes. Starting in 1811, the Luddites rioted, burned, and even killed at least one factory owner after he had ordered his guards to shoot at a rioting mob. The British government broke the back of the Luddite movement after five years of turmoil by hanging dozens of the leaders and transporting others to prison colonies such as Australia.

Although the Luddite terror was broken, the underlying causes of social injustice and poverty slowly, painfully evolved into legal political action. The labor movement grew out of the ashes. So did Marxism.

Frosch compares the growing pains of the First Industrial Revolution with those of today's introduction of robots into the workplace. Although he would not endorse a term as dramatic as "the Second Industrial Revolution," he does see parallels.

"The major changes in U.S. agriculture," he muses, "are—in some sense—a previous experience, a situation in which there was a shift in productivity, driven by technology. A lot of new technology was introduced [to farming], there was a tremendous productivity increase which was accompanied by a change in the size of farms, and a lot of people shifted out of agriculture and went to manufacturing in urban areas. To some extent, they went into the automobile industry.''

Those farmers who migrated to city factories did not have retraining programs to help them. They learned their new skills on the job, or they got fired. The situation is very different today, for their great-grandchildren. Workers who face competition from robots and automated systems demand either job protection or retraining for jobs that are not threatened by robotics.

''There's no question that robotics is changing the number of people that industry uses,'' Frosch agrees. ''In particular, it's changing the number of unskilled workers. Just as in the pick-and-shovel situation, where you now have a difficult time selling your back and shoulders, it's going to be very difficult to sell unskilled manipulative capabilities or very simple logical and 'software,' or thinking skills.''

Assembly-line workers, he points out, have been regarded as relatively unskilled, although they tend to gain skills on the job. Still, it is the repetitive manipulative kinds of assembly-line jobs that are being taken over the fastest by tireless, uncomplaining robots.

In fact, the Robotics Institution of America defines a robot in almost exactly those assembly-line terms. In RIA's definition, a robot is: ''A reprogrammable multi-functional manipulator designed to move material, parts, tools, or specialized devices through variable programmed motions for the performance of a variety of tasks.''

But assembly-line workers are not the only ones to hear the faint humming of automated machinery coming closer to them. Micro-computers, the miniature electronic ''brains'' of robots, are already threatening the white-collar worker, as well. Dr. Christopher Evans pointed out in his book, *The Micro Millennium*: "The vulnerability of the professions [to computerization] is tied up with their special strength—the fact that they act as exclusive repositories and disseminators of specialized knowledge." Specialized knowledge is exactly what computers are best at: a lifetime accumulation of law books or medical references can be packed into a few floppy disks and put at the fingertips of anyone who knows how to operate a personal computer.

Evans shows that the micro-computers which are invading offices and homes can be programmed to handle income tax forms, school assignments, even simple medical questions. Doctor, lawyer, teacher, and other white-collar professionals are already finding their jobs—and power—being eroded by micro-computers.

In the automobile industry itself, white-collar workers have felt the sharp edge of automation's ax cut just as deeply into their ranks as those of their blue-collar brethren. In the first two years of the 1980s the auto companies laid off some 55,000 white-collar workers, about twenty-seven percent of their non-production employees.

Dr. Morgan B. Coker, chairman of the Department of Business Administration and Economics at Francis Marion College, in South Carolina, has pointed out that micro-computers are allowing companies to trim the fat from their middle-management ranks. "More than attrition was taking place," he wrote of the white-collar layoffs in many diverse industries. "Businesses were stripping away layers of management and firing office workers to get 'lean and mean.' The micro-computer is a major force in the new style of American management . . ."

Frosch says that GM factory workers have accepted robots quite well. A worker taken off the assembly line to supervise a robot that does his old job has actually moved a step higher in the world. "They give the robots names, like 'Big Bertha,' " he told me.

But what about the workers who have been laid off,

from the automobile industry and elsewhere, and will not be rehired because automation and robotics have eliminated their jobs? Union Pacific Corporation, for example, laid off 6000 of its 44,000 workers over the past few years. James H. Evans, chairman of the railroad company, said in May 1983, "Will they come back? The answer is probably not." He pointed out that Union Pacific is carrying forty percent more freight tonnage than the line did twenty years ago, with half as many employees. "If we had the same number of employees we had then, we would have priced ourselves out of the market. How have we done it? Automation."

For the workers who have lost their jobs to the machines, government and industry offers a variety of retraining programs. But some workers resist retraining, and try to hold out on unemployment and other welfare benefits until they are called back to resume their original jobs. Yet it is clear that most of these jobs will never be held by human beings again.

Meanwhile, whole new industries are opening up, especially in the electronics field. National statistics show that even while unemployment soared to more than ten percent of the workforce in the early 1980s, the worst it has been since the Depression of the 1930s, total employment in the United States continued to grow. And in 1982, for the first time in America's history, jobs in the service sector of the economy outnumbered jobs in manufacturing. But the jobs offered there are for skilled technicians and engineers, not laid-off assembly-line workers or middle-management bureaucrats.

Frosch sees a basic change in the character of work itself, a change that may be dangerous. "We will go through a period in which relatively unskilled labor gets squeezed out. The question is, what happens to such workers?"

In the First Industrial Revolution, workers squeezed out

of the hand crafts and farms went to the cities and were absorbed into the new manufacturing industries. Or starved.

"But where do you go when unskilled workers are replaced by skilled machines?" Frosch believes that unskilled manufacturing workers are not going to be absorbed into the growing market for services, for the same reason that robots are not going to perform services such as barbering and hand crafts. It takes human skills to accomplish such tasks, skills that the robots do not yet have—and neither do the unskilled workers who are being replaced by robots.

Some economists suggest that the new industries created by high technology will create as many jobs as those lost to automation and robotics. But not for the same people.

"What I don't see," Frosch says, "is what happens to the people who are now non-trained, and are not easily trainable." There may well be, he fears, "a part of the population that is not very educated . . . not skilled, and who don't seem to be trainable." In other words, a permanent underclass of unemployables.

Part of the problem is that many workers have tacitly assumed that their job "belongs" to them for life; that even though they may be temporarily laid off during economic downturns, they will be rehired when the economy improves, and make up for the lost time by demanding higher wages and stronger job-protection rules.

Perhaps labor and management can work out suitable attrition policies, in which the company promises not to fire any members of its existing workforce because of automation, in return for labor's understanding that new workers will not be recruited, and when a worker quits or retires, he or she will not be replaced by a new hire. One problem with such a policy, however, is that the money spent in maintaining the human workforce is money that cannot be invested in new machinery. Investing the money in robots could well be more productive for the company than maintaining its human workforce.

The problem of future employment is mainly a problem of education. "There has always been a group of people who, for one reason or another, did not get educated," Frosch says. "We have never completely succeeded in finding out how to deal with the whole population in terms of education." Up until now, there have always been productive jobs for uneducated, unskilled workers. But that day is going fast.

"Do we end up with a *de facto* class structure?" he worries, seeing a nation with a permanently unemployed and unemployable caste. "That's a bad business. It's morally bad, it's socially bad . . . I don't think it's enough to simply say that it's a social justice problem and we have to see that somehow everybody gets fed."

Very few thinkers have even considered how to handle the human and social impact of the robot invasion. The engineers are busy designing better machines, the entrepreneurs are carving out new markets for robots, the business managers are trading off the costs of buying robots against the productivity gains they stand to produce, labor leaders are trying to protect their workers from robot-induced unemployment.

The trend of this Second Industrial Revolution, which is what the oncoming wave of robotics really amounts to, is quite clear. No matter how the experts may try to ignore the facts, or argue against them, the robots are getting smarter, cheaper, and more skilled. They will be taking over more and more jobs as the years go on. Inevitably, most of the jobs that can be done twice the same way—be they in a factory or an office—will be done by robots and/or computers.

Where does that leave the workers? Not everyone put out of work by automation can be absorbed into new jobs. A forty-year-old assembly-line worker is not going to blossom into an electronics technician. A young secretary is not going to turn into a computer programmer after six weeks of retraining. Besides, those jobs will also be threatened by robotics and automation, eventually. The machines are learning how to reproduce themselves.

Congressman Don Fuqua, chairman of the House of Representatives Science and Technology Committee, is one of the few politicians who is doing something about the robot revolution, rather than merely making speeches about "high tech."

Fuqua has drafted legislation that calls for a double-pronged approach to the problems—and opportunities—of robotics. To combat robot-induced unemployment, Fuqua wants the National Science Foundation to begin training programs for workers. He foresees a program that starts at the $5 million level and increases to $10 million per year through 1990.

A human job might be replaced by a robot, Fuqua maintains, but "somebody's got to operate the robot, and keep it working. And somebody's got to build that robot." What is needed, then, is to help workers to elevate their levels of skills so that they can take part in the robot revolution, rather than be sidelined by it.

"There's a whole new shift in employment skills, to a higher level. There are a lot of different jobs that will be created by the use of robots," he says.

Fuqua admits that some workers will not be retrainable, for reasons varying from age to ambition. "They may not desire to have their skills upgraded."

The legislation he is proposing does not deal merely with the unemployment problems created by robotics. The other side of Fuqua's approach sets up a robot leasing corporation, funded initially with federal money, which will help to provide the capital for businessmen to obtain robots and bring them into industry.

"The robot leasing corporation is based somewhat on the existing Farm Credit Administration and Comsat Corporation," Fuqua says. "It will be a quasi-government corporation. Its role will be to stimulate the demand for robots, and therefore the production of robots."

Fuqua sees federal funding of $20 million per year, to provide low-interest loans to businesses, as "seed" money for the leasing corporation. Private investment will be encouraged, and will provide the bulk of the corporation's funds. Eventually the corporation will pay back the government's original loans with interest. Thus robots may begin to put money *into* the national treasury.

The robot leasing corporation, according to Fuqua, can "make it attractive for people to install certain types of robots, depending on the needs of their companies. It can be a source of capital to finance the lease [or purchase] of robots."

Fuqua's legislation, which is also backed by Cong. Albert Gore, Jr. of Tennessee and George Brown of California, among others, can help to provide investment capital for the transition to robotics while also cushioning the unemployment this transition is bound to cause.

Fuqua sees robots gradually entering the workplace, and being most valuable in jobs that are too dangerous or difficult for humans to attempt: cleaning up radioactive nuclear powerplants, for example, or fighting fires.

"I see robots moving in everywhere," says Albus, who has spent the past ten years designing robots for the National Bureau of Standards. "Some places sooner than others, but practically everywhere sooner or later."

He points out, "Robots create wealth. That makes the society that builds them and uses them able to maintain a much higher standard of living. This creates demand for expanded numbers of products and makes it possible to afford to hire the people to supply those products."

This leads to a contradiction. On the one hand, thinkers such as Albus see robots creating wealth and a demand for more goods and thus more jobs. On the other hand, they also foresee new robots eventually taking over those jobs.

Albus argues, however, that "the main restriction to employment is not the amount of work to be done in the world. The amount of work that needs to be done is virtually infinite. The question is, can you afford to hire people to do the work?''

Considering all the tasks that *can* be done in a society, from repairing roads and picking up trash to bringing expert medical care to the poor and exploring outer space, Albus says, ''The real fallacy is thinking that there's a fixed amount of work to be done, and if robots do some of it there won't be enough work to go around for humans. God, the world is filled with things that need to be done— just walk around your neighborhood and you can make a list of three hundred things that need to be done and can occupy a whole army of people to do them.''

But these things are not done, not only because society cannot afford to have them done, but because the people who make up society learn that they can get along without doing them.

''Basically, I think it's because we can't afford them,'' Albus insists. ''Getting along without means scaling back your living standards.''

Taking a wider view, Albus says, ''The world is filled with poverty, hunger, poor housing, poor education . . . there's plenty of things that need to be done. The question is really, can we afford to do all these things?'' Only to a very limited extent today are these problems being dealt with, mainly because poor nations and poor people cannot afford to solve them. Albus believes that if robots and their high productivity begin to create vast new sources of wealth for their owners, some of this wealth can be used to attack poverty and hunger around the world.

Albus sees this wealth being generated by an ever-growing number of robot workers. (Actually, the term ''robot workers'' is a redundancy. *Robot* is from a Czech word that means *worker*. The term was coined by the Czech writer Karel Čapek in his 1920 play, *R.U.R.*) To-day's workforce of some 6000 robots is growing at a rate of about thirty-five percent per year. By the end of this decade, Albus and other robot experts see at least 100,000 robots in the United States, growing to a million by the turn of the century.

What does this mean to the twenty- or thirty-year-old human worker of today? It means unemployment, somewhere in the future, whether you like it or not.

"My guess," says Albus, "is that they might get to retire a little earlier than they otherwise would. I don't think anybody would be terribly upset about retiring at fifty-five instead of sixty-five."

Living on a fixed retirement income for ten years longer than today's pensioners? Sitting at home with nothing to do while the robots busily clank around *your* former workplace? That can be bad enough, but what about the people who have already been pushed into unemployment— not retirement—by robots and automation? Labor experts talk about the "structurally unemployed," the people who will most likely never be rehired because they haven't the skills to compete in the labor market and will not or cannot be retrained. They see a hard core of six and a half percent of the total human workforce as structurally (read, permanently) unemployed today. That's more than six million men and women. And the number is expected to grow, not shrink.

How much wealth must the robots generate merely to absorb the unemployment they will be helping to cause? How can we dream of a robot-produced Utopia where no one is hungry or poor, when the earliest impact of robotics seems to mean wide-scale unemployment for humans?

But there is unemployment and unemployment, as a philosopher would say. If you drink in the corner saloon at ten in the morning you're considered a bum; but if you drink at ten A.M. in the country club, you're a golfer. The difference between the two is wealth. If the robots are going to generate so much wealth, how can society be arranged so that the workers dis-employed by robots get their fair share of the money?

Albus has been pondering this matter for as long as he

has been designing robots, and has written books on the subject, including *People's Capitalism: The Economics of the Robot Revolution*. "The primary mechanism for transferring wealth," he says without hesitation, "is ownership."

One of the ways in which employees can begin to *own* the robots which displace them is through Employee Stock Ownership Plans: ESOPs. Economist Louis O. Kelso, author (with Mortimer J. Adler) of *The Capitalist Manifesto* and *Finishing the Unfinished Capitalist Revolution*, hit upon the idea in the 1950s of having companies issue shares of their own stock to their employees as a kind of fringe benefit, an addition to or replacement for bonuses or retirement plans. Many companies have since started ESOPs, and some firms have even become totally owned by their employees. Albus believes that an ESOP-type plan could permit employees to attain ownership of a highly-automated firm, and thus gain a share of the profits generated by the robots.

Looking further into the future, Albus believes that the best way to handle the economic impact of the Second Industrial Revolution is for the government to create a National Mutual Fund.

Every citizen would be a shareholder in the NMF, receiving a share at age eighteen, by virtue of being an American citizen. The NMF would not obtain its investment funds directly from its shareholders, however. Instead, it would borrow investment capital from the Federal Reserve Bank. The amount borrowed would be huge, billions of dollars per year. Congress would have to decide on a ceiling, just as Congress now places a ceiling on the national debt.

The NMF would then invest its capital in high technology, robotics and automation, concentrating its efforts on modernizing industries that have become technologically backward.

"Specifically," Albus says, "the NMF would attempt to promote the development of robots and automated factories and would provide supplemental worker's compensation and retraining incentives where these would be necessary or useful.''

The profits coming back to the NMF from the increased productivity of the roboticized industries would be paid to the investors: the citizens of the U.S.A.

Albus emphasizes that, ''NMF payments would *not* be welfare or charity based on need. They would be dividends paid to the shareholders of a profit-making institution.'' As in any corporation, each share of stock would receive an equal share of the dividends.

In other words, the National Mutual Fund is a way of making a capitalist out of every American citizen, while at the same time providing funds for the robot revolution and distributing the profits equably.

Critics point out that the NMF's borrowings from the Federal Reserve could cause enormous inflationary pressures on the economy. Albus replies that the government could control such pressures by giving a part of the NMF's profits to its shareholders in the form of savings bonds, rather than cash. This would be a form of government-mandated forced savings which would remove spendable money from the marketplace, slow down the inflationary spiral, and even provide more capital for investment in the NMF.

Private citizens will be able to invest in the NMF on their own, of course. The share issued to a person at age eighteen (or at the initiation of the Fund) is only a beginning. Like any corporation or mutual fund, private investors will be able to buy more shares if they want to.

In essence, Albus' plan would allow workers to retire whenever they were financially ready to, based on their income from the NMF rather than the salaries they receive from their jobs. Instead of drinking in the morning at the saloon, everyone can get into the country club.

Before the First Industrial Revolution, most men and women worked the land or toiled at hand crafts in their own homes. Cash money was very rare; payments were usually in kind. But with the advent of steam-powered factories, a new lifestyle came into being. People left their homes and went to a factory, or a mine, or an office. There they performed some service or helped to produce some goods. For this they received a wage, in money. Some two hundred years later, we have come to accept this way of life as normal and natural.

But it is no more "natural" than laboring from dawn to dusk behind a plow. If robots can produce the wealth that men such as Albus and Frosch foresee, our society may reach the point where most people need not depend on wages from jobs for their income: they will live on the dividends generated by robots that they own, in one form or another.

When? How soon before we can all sit by the poolside and watch the robots toiling away for us?

"Probably not in my lifetime," says the fifty-year-old Albus, "or maybe late in my life. And quite probably it will start in some place like Scotland or New Zealand, some small democracy where people are not quite as afraid of the idea of socialism as we are."

Robot welfare. Robot socialism. Is this the wave of the future? Certainly the robots are already causing deep and lasting changes in the patterns of employment in many manufacturing industries. And computers are generating vast changes in the white-collar world. The hope is that someday we will be able to share in the profits those robots and computers earn, perhaps through an ESOP or an NMF. But the fear is that we will be pushed aside by automation, dumped into the economic gutter because we can't compete with the tireless, inhuman machines. For today, the choices seem to be either unemployment or retraining, upgrading skills to the point where we can live and work with the robots, or being shunted to the sidelines by them.

As usual, it is the science fiction writers who have

thought about this problem the longest. In 1954 Jack Williamson wrote *With Folded Hands*, a deeply disturbing story about a future in which human-shaped robots become so clever, so ubiquitous, that they take over all the work in the world and prevent humans from doing any kind of task whatsoever. They literally kill the human race with kindness:

> Alert and solicitous, the little black mechanical [robot] accompanied him down the shining corridor, worked the elevator for him, conducted him down to the car. It drove him efficiently back through the new and splendid avenues toward the magnificent prison of his home.
>
> Sitting beside it in the car, he watched its small deft hands on the wheel, the changing luster of bronze and blue on shining blackness. The final machine, perfect and beautiful, created to serve mankind forever. He shuddered. . . .
>
> "I've found out that I'm perfectly happy under the Prime Directive. Everything is absolutely wonderful." His voice became very dry and hoarse and wild. "You won't have to operate on me."
>
> The car turned off the shining avenue, taking him back to the quiet splendor of his prison. His futile hands clenched and relaxed again, folded on his knees. There was nothing left to do.

No one foresees that kind of dreary future coming out of the robot revolution. No one except the science fiction writers. But in the long run, they are usually right.

The Angel's Gift

In the next two pieces of fiction, the Astral Mirror looks backward into history, fairly recent history. This pair of stories sheds some possible light on why a certain former President of the United States, and a certain former Secretary of State, behaved the way they did at critical junctures in their respective lives.

He stood at his bedroom window, gazing happily out at the well-kept grounds and manicured park beyond them. The evening was warm and lovely. Dinner with the guests from overseas had been perfect; the deal was going smoothly, and he would get all the credit for it. As well as the benefits.

He was at the top of the world now, master of it all, king of the hill. The old dark days of fear and failure were far behind him now. Everything was going his way at last. He loved it.

His wife swept into the bedroom, just slightly tipsy from the champagne.

Beaming at him, she said, "You were magnificent tonight, darling."

He turned from the window, surprised beyond words. Praise from her was so rare that he treasured it, savored it like expensive wine, just as he had always felt a special glow within his breast on those extraordinary occasions when his mother had vouchsafed him a kind word.

"Uh . . . thank you," he said.

"Magnificent, darling," she repeated. "I am so proud of you!"

His face went red with embarrassed happiness.

"And these people are so much nicer than those Latin types," she added.

"You . . . you know, you were . . . you *are* . . . the most beautiful woman in this city," he stammered. He meant it. In her gown of gold lamé and with her hair coiffed that way, she looked positively regal. His heart filled with joy.

She kissed him lightly on the cheek, whispering into his ear, "I shall be waiting for you in my boudoir, my prince."

The breath gushed out of him. She pirouetted daintily, then waltzed to the door that connected to her own bedroom. Opening the door, she turned back toward him and blew him a kiss.

As she closed the door behind her, he took a deep, sighing, shuddering breath. Brimming with excited expectation, he went directly to his closet, unbuttoning his tuxedo jacket as he strode purposefully across the thickly carpeted floor.

He yanked open the closet door. A man was standing there, directly under the light set into the ceiling.

"Wha . . . ?"

Smiling, the man made a slight bow. "Please do not be alarmed, sir. And don't bother to call for your security guards. They won't hear you."

Still fumbling with his jacket buttons, he staggered back from the closet door, a thousand wild thoughts racing through his mind. An assassin. A kidnapper. A newspaper columnist!

The stranger stepped as far as the closet door. "May I enter your room, sir? Am I to take your silence for assent? In that case, thank you very much."

The stranger was tall but quite slender. He was perfectly tailored in a sky-blue Brooks Brothers three-piece suit. He had the youthful, innocent, golden-curled look of a European terrorist. His smile revealed perfect, dazzling teeth. Yet his eyes seemed infinitely sad, as though filled with knowledge of all human failings. Those icy blue eyes pierced right through the man in the tuxedo.

"Wh . . . what do you want? Who are you?"

"I'm terribly sorry to intrude this way. I realize it must be a considerable shock to you. But you're always so busy. It's difficult to fit an appointment into your schedule." His voice was a sweet, mild tenor, but the accent was strange: East Coast, surely. Harvard, no doubt.

"How did you get in here? My security . . ."

The stranger gave a slightly guilty grin and hiked one thumb ceilingward. "You might say I came in through the roof."

"The roof? Impossible!"

"Not for me. You see, I am an angel."

"A . . . angel?"

With a self-assured nod, the stranger replied, "Yes. One of the Heavenly Host. Your very own guardian angel, to be precise."

"I don't believe you."

"You don't believe in angels?" The stranger cocked a golden eyebrow at him. "Come now, I can see into your soul. You do believe."

"My church doesn't go in for that sort of thing," he said, trying to pull himself together.

"No matter. You do believe. And you do well to believe, because it is all true. Angels, devils, the entire system. It is as real and true as this fine house you live in." The angel heaved a small sigh. "You know, back in medieval times people had a much firmer grasp on the realities of life. Today . . ." He shook his head.

Eyes narrowing craftily, the man asked, "If you're an angel, where are your wings? Your halo? You don't look anything like a real angel."

"Oh!" The angel seemed genuinely alarmed. "Does that bother you? I thought it would be easier on your nervous system to see me in a form that you're accustomed to dealing with every day. But if you want . . ."

The room was flooded with blinding golden light. Heavenly voices sang. The stranger stood before the man robed in radiance, huge white wings outspread, filling the room.

The man sank to his knees and buried his face in the rug. "Have mercy on me! Have mercy on me!"

He felt strong yet gentle hands pull him tenderly to his feet. The angel was back in his Brooks Brothers suit. The searing light and ethereal chorus were gone.

"It is not in my power to show you either mercy or justice," he said, his sweetly youthful face utterly grave. "Only the Creator can dispense such things."

"But why . . . who . . . how . . ." he babbled.

Calming him, the angel explained, "My duty as your guardian angel is to protect your soul from damnation. But you must cooperate, you know. I cannot *force* you to be saved."

"My soul is in danger?"

"In danger?" The angel rolled his eyes heavenward. "You've just about handed it over to the enemy, gift-wrapped. Most of the millionaires you dined with tonight have a better chance to attain salvation than you have, at the moment. And you know how difficult it is for a rich man."

The man tottered to the wingback chair next to his

king-sized bed and sank into it. He pulled the handkerchief from his breast pocket and mopped his sweaty face.

The angel knelt beside him and looked up into his face pleadingly. "I don't want to frighten you into a premature heart seizure, but your soul really is in mortal peril."

"But I haven't done anything wrong! I'm not a crook. I haven't killed anyone or stolen anything. I've been faithful to my wife."

The angel gave him a skeptical smile.

"Well . . ." he wiped perspiration from his upper lip. "Nothing serious. I've always honored my mother and my father."

Gently, the angel asked, "You've never told a lie?"

"Uh, well . . . nothing big enough to . . ."

"You've never cheated anyone?"

"Um."

"What about that actor's wife in California? And the money you accepted to swing certain deals? And all the promises you've broken?"

"You mean things like that—they count?"

"Everything counts," the angel said firmly. "Don't you realize that the enemy has your soul almost in his very hands?"

"No, I never thought . . ."

"All those deals you've made. All the corners you've cut." The angel suddenly shot him a piercing glance. "You haven't signed any documents in blood, have you?"

"No!" His heart twitched. "Certainly not!"

"Well, that's something, at least."

"I'll behave," he promised. "I'll be good. I'll be a model of virtue."

"Not enough," the angel said, shaking his golden locks. "Not nearly enough. Things have already gone much too far."

His eyes widened with fear. He wanted to argue, to refute, to debate the point with his guardian angel, but the words simply would not force their way through his constricted throat.

"No, it is not enough merely to promise to reform," the angel repeated. "Much stronger action is needed."

"Such as . . . what?" he croaked.

The angel got to his feet, paced across the room a few steps, then turned back to face him. His youthful visage brightened. "Why not? If *they* can make a deal for a soul, why can't we?"

"What do you mean?"

"Hush!" The angel seemed to be listening to another voice, one that the man could not hear. Finally the angel nodded and smiled. "Yes. I see. Thank you."

"What?"

Turning back to the man, the angel said, "I've just been empowered to make you an offer for your soul. If you accept the terms, your salvation is assured."

The man instantly grew wary. "Oh no you don't. I've heard all about deals for souls. Some of my best friends . . ."

"But this is a deal to *save* your soul!"

"How do I know that?" the man demanded. "How do I know you're really what you say you are? The devil has power to assume pleasing shapes, doesn't he?"

The angel smiled joyfully. "Good for you! You remember some of your childhood teaching."

"Don't try to put me off. I've negotiated a few tricky deals in my day. How do I know you're really an angel, and you want to save my soul?"

"By their fruits ye shall know them," the angel replied.

"What are you talking about?"

Still smiling, the angel replied, "When the devil makes a deal for a soul, what does he promise? Temporal gifts, such as power, wealth, respect, women, fame."

"I have all that," the man said. "I'm on top of the world, everyone knows that."

"Indeed."

"And I didn't sign any deals with the devil to get there, either," he added smugly.

"None that you know of," the angel warned. "A man in your position delegates many decisions to his staff, does he not?"

The man's face went gray. "Oh my God, you don't think . . ."

With a shrug, the angel said, "It doesn't matter. The deal that I offer guarantees your soul's salvation, if you meet its terms."

"How? What do I have to do?"

"You have power, wealth, respect, women, fame." The angel ticked each point off on his slender, graceful fingers.

"Yes, yes, I know."

"You must give them up."

The man lurched forward in the wingchair. "Huh?"

"Give them up."

"I can't!"

"You must, if you are to attain the Kingdom of Heaven."

"But you don't understand! I can't just drop everything! This world doesn't work that way. I can't just . . . walk away from all this!"

"That's the deal," the angel said. "Give it up. All of it. Or spend eternity in hell."

"But you can't expect me to . . ." He gaped. The angel was no longer in the room with him. For several minutes he stared into the empty air. Then, knees shaking, he arose and walked to the closet. It too was empty of strange personages.

He looked down at his hands. They trembled.

"I must be going crazy," he muttered to himself. "Too much strain. Too much tension." But even as he said it, he made his way to the telephone on the bedside table. He hesitated a moment, then grabbed up the phone and punched a number he had memorized months earlier.

"Hello, Chuck? Yes, this is me. Yes, yes, everything went fine tonight. Up to a point."

He listened to his underling babbling flattery into the phone, wondering how many times he had given his power of attorney to this weakling and to equally venal deputies.

"Listen, Chuck," he said at last. "I have a job for you. And it's got to be done right, understand? Okay, here's the deal—" he winced inwardly at the word. But, taking a deep manly breath, he plunged ahead. "You know the Democrats are setting up their campaign quarters in that new apartment building—what's it called, Watergate? Yeah. Okay. Now I think it would serve our purposes very well if we bugged the place before the campaign really starts to warm up . . ."

There were tears in his eyes as he spoke. But from far, far away, he could hear a heavenly chorus singing.

The Secret Life of
Henry K.

This late at night, even the busiest corridors of the Pentagon were deserted. Dr. Young's footsteps echoed hollowly as he followed the mountainous, tight-lipped, grim-faced man. Another equally large and steely-eyed man followed behind him, in lockstep with the first.

They were agents, Dr. Young knew that without being told. Their clothing bulged with muscles trained in murderous Oriental arts, other bulges in unlikely places along their anatomy were various pieces of equipment: guns, two-way radios, stilettos, Bowie knives . . . Young decided his imagination wasn't rich enough to picture all the equipment these men might be carrying.

After what seemed like an hour's walk down a constantly curving corridor, the agent in front stopped abruptly before an inconspicuous, unmarked door.

"In here," he said, barely moving his lips.

The door opened by itself, and Dr. Young stepped into what seemed to be an ordinary receptionist's office. It was

no bigger than a cubicle, and even in the dim lighting—
from a single desk lamp, the overhead lights were off—
Young could see that the walls were the same sallow
depressing color as most Pentagon offices.

"The phone will ring," the agent said, glancing at a
watch that looked absolutely dainty on his massive hairy
wrist, "in exactly one minute and fifteen seconds. Sit at
the desk. Answer when it rings."

With that, he shut the door firmly, leaving Dr. Young
alone and bewildered in the tiny anteroom.

There was only one desk, cleared of papers. It was a
standard government-issue battered metal desk. IN and
OUT boxes stood empty atop it. Nothing else on it but a
single black telephone. There were two creaky-looking
straight-backed metal chairs in front of the desk, and a
typist's swivel chair behind it. The only other things in the
room were a pair of file cabinets, side by side, with huge
padlocks and red SECURE signs on them, and a bulletin
board that had been miraculously cleared of everything
except the little faded fire-emergency instruction card.

Dr. Young found that his hands were trembling. He
wished that he hadn't given up cigarettes: after all, oral
eroticism isn't all that bad. He glanced at the closed
hallway door and knew that both the burly agents were
standing outside, probably with their arms folded across
their chest in unconscious imitation of the eunuchs who
guarded sultans' harems.

He took a deep breath and went around the desk and sat
on the typist's chair.

The phone rang as soon as his butt touched the chair. He
jumped, but grabbed the phone and settled himself before
it could ring again.

"Dr. Carlton Young speaking." His voice sounded an
octave too high, and quavery, even to himself.

"Dr. Young, I thank you for accompanying the agents
who brought you there without questioning their purpose.

They were instructed to tell you who sent them and nothing else."

He recognized the voice at once. "You—you're welcome, Mr. President."

"Please! No names! This is a matter of utmost security."

"Ye—yessir."

"Dr. Young, you have been recommended very highly for the special task I must ask of you. I know that, as a loyal, patriotic American, you will do your best to accomplish this task. And as the most competent man in your highly demanding and complex field, your efforts will be crowned with success. That's the American way, now isn't it?"

"Yessir. May I ask, just what is the task?"

"I'm glad you asked that. I have a personnel problem that you are uniquely qualified to solve. One of my closest and most valued aides—a man I depend on very heavily— has gone into a tailspin. I won't explain why or how. I must ask you merely to accept the bald statement. This aide is a man of great drive and talent, high moral purpose, and enormous energy. But at the moment, he's useless to himself, to this Administration, and to the Nation. I need you to help him find himself."

"Me? But all I do is—"

"You run the best computer dating service in the nation, I know. Your service has been checked out thoroughly by the FBI, the Secret Service, and the Defense Intelligence Agency—"

"Not the CIA?"

"I don't know, they won't tell me."

"Oh."

"This aide of mine—a very sincere and highly motivated man—needs a girl. Not just any girl. The psychiatrists at Walter Reed tell me that he must find the woman who's perfect for him, his exact match, the one mate that can make him happy enough to get back to the important work he should be doing. As you know, I have a plan for stopping inflation, bridging the generation gap, and settling the Cold War. But to make everything perfectly clear, Dr. Young, none of these plans can be crowned with success unless this certain aide can do his part of the job, carry his share of the burden, pull his share of the load."

Dr. Young nodded in the darkness. "I understand, sir. He needs a woman to make him happy. So many people do." A fleeting thought of the bins upon bins of floppy disks that made up his files passed through Dr. Young's mind. "Even you, sir, even you need a woman."

"Dr. Young! I'm a married man!"

"I know—that's what I meant. You couldn't be doing the terrific job you're doing without your lovely wife, your lifetime mate, to support and inspire you."

"Oh, I see what you mean. Yes, of course. Well, Dr. Young, my aide is in the office there with you, in the inner office. I want you to talk with him, help him, find him the woman he truly needs. Then we can end the war in Indochina, stop inflation, bridge—well, you know."

"Yes sir. I'll do my best."

"That will be adequate for the task, I'm sure. Good night, and God bless America!"

Dr. Young found that he was on his feet, standing at ramrod attention, a position he hadn't assumed since his last Boy Scout jamboree.

Carefully he replaced the phone in its cradle, then turned to face the door that led to the inner office. Who could be in there? The Vice President? No, Young told himself with a shake of his head; that didn't fit the description the President had given him.

Squaring his shoulders once again, Dr. Young took the three steps that carried him to the door and knocked on it sharply.

"Come in," said an equally sharp voice.

The office was kept as dark and shadowy as the anteroom, but Dr. Young recognized the man sitting rather tensely behind the desk.

"Dr. Kiss—!"

"No names! Please! Absolute security, Dr. Young."

"I under—no, come to think of it, I don't understand. Why keep the fact that you're using a computer-dating service so secret? What do the Russians and Chinese care—"

The man behind the desk cut him short with a gesture. "It's not the Russians or Chinese. It's the Democrats. If *they* find out—" He waggled both hands in the air—a semitic gesture of impending doom.

Dr. Young took one of the plush chairs in front of the desk. "But Dr. K—"

"Just call me Henry," the other man said. "But don't get personal about it."

"All right, Henry. I still don't see what's so terrible about a man in your position using a computer dating service. After all, some of the top Senators and Congressmen on the Democratic side of the aisle have been clients of mine."

"I know, I saw it all in the FBI report. Or was it the DIA report? Well, never mind." He fixed Dr. Young with a penetrating stare. "How would it look if the Democrats knew that the President's most trusted and valued aide couldn't get a girl for himself? Eh?"

"Oh, I'm sure you could—"

"I can't!" The penetrating stare melted into something more pathetic. "I can't, the God our forefathers knows I've tried. But I'm a failure, a flop. There are times when I can't even talk to a woman."

Dr. Young sat there in shocked silence. Even his advanced degrees in psychology might not be enough for this task, he began to realize.

"It's my mother's fault!" Henry all but sobbed. "My pushy mother! Why do you think I took this job in the White House? Because she pushed me into it, and because I thought it might help me to get girls. Well, it hasn't. I can tell the President when to invade Cambodia. I can eat shark's fin with Chou En-lai, but I get totally tongue-tied

when I try to talk to an attractive woman! My momma—
what can I do?"

Henry started to bury his head in his hands, then with an
obvious effort of great willpower, he straightened up in his
chair. "Sorry," he said. "I shouldn't get emotional like
that."

"No, it's good for you," Dr. Young soothed. "You
can't keep everything bottled up all the time."

"Well I have been," Henry retorted sourly, "and I'm
getting very uptight about it."

Uptight? thought Dr. Young. *And everyone thinks he's
a man of the world. I've got to help him.*

"Listen," he said, "you tell me the kind of girl you
like, and I'll comb my computer files until I find her—"

Henry smiled faintly, stoically. "So what good will that
do? I'll take one look at her and collapse like a pricked
balloon, you should excuse the expression."

But Dr. Young expected that response and was ready for
it. "You don't understand, Henry. The girl that I'll find
for you will be special. She'll be anxious to make you
happy: she'll know that the future of the nation—of the
whole world—depends on her pleasing you."

"How can you be sure that she'll really want to?"

"Leave it to me," Dr. Young said, with his best professional smile of assurance. "Just tell me what you'd like,
and I'll get my computer cracking on it before the sun
comes up."

Henry gave a little shrug, as if he didn't really believe
what he was hearing but was desperate enough to give it a
try anyway.

"I've already taken the liberty," he said, "of coding
my"—he smiled bashfully—"my dream girl onto this
floppy disk. And you won't have to use your own computer. Too risky, security-wise, for one thing. Besides, the
FBI computer has *everybody* on it."

Dr. Young gasped. "The FBI computer?"

Henry nodded.

Then it hit!

For the first time, it struck home to Dr. Young that he was really playing in the big leagues. Was he ready for it?

The room was sumptuous, with thick carpeting and rich drapes framing the full-length windows that looked out over Manhattan's glittering skyline. A thousand jewels gleamed in the skyscrapers and across the graceful bridges, outshining by far the smogged-over stars of heaven.

Henry swallowed his nervousness as he stood at the doorway with the famous movie star.

"Um, nice room you've got here," he managed to say.

She smiled at him and slid out of her coat. "The studio arranged it. It's mine until the premiere tomorrow night."

Her dress glittered more than the view outside. And showed more, too. Henry worked a finger into his shirt collar. It was starting to feel uncomfortably tight, and warm.

"Here, let me help you," she purred, still showing her perfectly capped teeth in a smile that earned a thousand letters per week, most of them obscene.

She undid his tie and popped the collar button open. "Make yourself comfortable and tell me all about those nasty Russians you outsmarted."

"I—uh—um—"

Taking him by the wrist, she led Henry to the plushest couch he had ever seen and pulled him down into it, right next to her lush, lascivious body.

"You're not going to be shy with me, are you? After all, I'm just a lonely little girl far from my home, and I need a big strong daddy to look after me."

He could smell her musky perfume, feel the brush of her beautiful plasticized hair against his cheek.

"I, uh, I've got to catch a plane for—for Ulan Bator in one hour!" As the words popped out of his mouth, Henry sat up stiffly on the edge of the couch. He looked at his wristwatch. "Yes. One hour, to Ulan Bator. That's in Mongolia, you know."

She stared at him, pouting. "But what about our date tomorrow night? The premiere of my new movie!"

"I'm sorry. You'll have to go with someone else. The President needs me in Mongolia. Top secret negotiations. You mustn't say a word about this—any of this! To any-one!"

With a shrug that nearly popped her breasts out of the low-cut gown, she said, "Okay. Okay. But tell those creepy friends of yours that I've done my patriotic duty, and don't come around here looking for more!"

"But she liked you," Dr. Young said. He felt surprised and slightly hurt as he sat in the same dimly lit office in the Pentagon. Again it was late at night, and again Henry sat nervously behind the desk.

"It was all an act. She's an actress, you know."

"Of course, I know. But she genuinely liked you. It was no act. Take my word for it."

"How can you be sure?"

"Well—" Dr. Young hesitated, but then realized he'd find out anyway. "We had her room bugged. She cried for twenty minutes after you left."

Instead of getting angry, Henry looked suddenly guilty. "She did?"

A kaleidoscope of emotions played across Henry's face. Dr. Young saw surprise, guilt, pride, anxiety, and then he stopped watching.

At length Henry shook himself, as if getting rid of something unpleasant. "She was too—flighty. A silly child."

"She was what you programmed into the computer," Dr. Young retorted. "I checked out the characteristics myself, mathematically, of course."

"Well, the computer goofed!"

"No, Henry. That's not possible. You simply didn't

give us a description of what you really want in a woman. You told us what you *think* you want, you gave us some idealizations. But that's not what your heart's really set on.''

"You're trying to tell me I don't know what I want?''

"Not consciously, you don't. Now with a team of psychiatrists and possibly hypnosis therapy—''

"No!'' Henry slammed a hand on the desktop. "Too risky! Remember our need for absolute security.''

"But your conscious mind has only a very hazy idea of what your dream woman should be. The very term 'dream woman' indicates—''

"Never mind,'' Henry said firmly. "Just add a few points to the computer program. I want someone just like Jill, but tougher, more intelligent. Better able to stand on her own feet.''

Dr. Young nodded. Another week of computer programming ahead.

"This is my Pad, Hank. What do you think of it?''

Henry surveyed the crumbling plaster, the dirt-caked floor, the stacks of books strewn across the room covering the sink and the range, the desk, the drawing board, the sofa, the coffee table. The only piece of furniture in the filthy place that wasn't covered with books or papers of one sort or another was the bed. And *that* looked like something out of a Hong Kong brothel—a slimy, grimy, wrinkled mess that seemed to be writhing by itself even as he stared at it.

"It's efficient looking,'' he said. Actually, it looked like the storage room in the cellar of a Village tenement. Which it had been, until recently.

"Efficient, huh?'' Gloria tossed her head slightly, a motion that spilled her long sun-bleached hair over one T-shirted shoulder.

"It's efficient, all right,'' she said. "This is where I do my writing, my illustrating, my editing, and my fucking.''

Henry blinked. His glasses seemed to be getting steamed up. Or maybe it was dirt.

"You like to fuck, Hank?" she asked, grinning at him.

He squeezed his eyes shut and heard his voice utter a choked, "Yes."

"Good. Me too. But no sexual chauvinism. I get on top the same number of times you do," she said, starting toward the bed and pulling off the T-shirt. "No oral stuff unless we go together, and," she stepped out of her ragged jeans, "say, how many times can you pop off in one—"

She turned and saw that she was talking to the empty air. Henry had fled, and left the door open behind him.

"She was a monster!" Henry babbled to Dr. Young. "That computer is trying to destroy me. I'm going to have it investigated! And you too!"

"Now, now," Dr. Young said as soothingly as he could. "No one's tampered with anything. I've done all the programming myself, taken the printouts myself, done it *all* by myself. I haven't slept a full night since our first meeting. I'm losing business because of you."

"She was a monster," Henry repeated.

"If you'd only let the psychiatrists probe your subconscious—"

"No! I went through all that months ago. All they ever said was that it's all my mother's fault. I know that!"

Dr. Young made a helpless shrug. "But if you can't verbalize your real desires—can't tell me what you're really looking for—how can I help you?"

Clenching his hands into fists and frowning mightily Henry said, "Just find me the girl I'm looking for. Someone who's beautiful, intelligent, patient, patriotic—but not aggressive!"

Back to the computer, Dr. Young thought wearily. But something in the back of his mind made him smile inwardly. *There might be—yes, that might work.*

* * *

The Baroness's yacht rode easily at anchor in the soft swells of the sheltered cove. The coast of Maine was dark, just a jagged blackness against the softer star-scattered darkness of the sky.

"I've never seen the stars look so beautiful," Henry said. Then, sneaking a peek at the notes on his shirt cuff, he added, "They're almost as beautiful as you."

The Baroness smiled. And she was truly beautiful as she stood by the rail of the yacht, almost close enough to touch her warm and thrilling body to his. Her long midnight hair, always severely combed back and pinned up during the day, was now sweeping free and loose to her lovely bare shoulders.

"I would offer you another drink, Henri, but the servants have gone ashore."

"Oh?" He gripped the rail a bit tighter. "All of them?"

"Yes, I sent them away. I wanted to be alone with you."

Henry took a deep breath. All through the evening—the ballet recital, the dinner, the dizzying private jet ride to this cove, the dancing on the deck—he had been steeling himself for the supreme moment. He had no intention of muffing it this night.

"Maybe," he suggested slyly, "we can go back inside and find something for ourselves."

She put a hand to his close-shaven, lime-scented cheek. "What an admirable idea, Henri. No wonder your *President* depends on you so heavily."

Half an hour later they were sitting in the salon on a leather couch, discussing international relations. Gradually, Henry began to realize that the subject had drifted into the super-romantic areas of spies and espionage.

She was leaning against him, as closely as her extensive bosom would allow. "You must have known many spies— clever, dangerous men and deceptive, beautiful women."

"Uh, well, yes," he lied. His hands were starting to tremble.

Suddenly she slid off the couch and kneeled at his feet. "Pretend I'm a spy! Pretend you've caught me and have me at your mercy. Tie me up! Beat me! Torture me! Rape me!"

With a strangled scream, Henry leaped to his feet, dropped his glasses, bolted for the hatch, pounded up the ladder to the deck, and leaped into the water. For the first time since his last full summer at camp, he swam for his life. And his sanity.

"It's useless, it'll never work. It's just no good." Henry was muttering as Dr. Young led him down a long antiseptically white corridor.

"It might work. It could work."

For a moment the doctor thought he would have to take Henry by the hand and march him through the corridor like a stern schoolteacher with a recalcitrant child. Studying his "customer," Dr. Young realized that Henry was going down the drain. His physical condition was obviously deteriorating: his hands trembled, there were bags under his eyes, he had lost weight, and his face was starting to break out in acne. And his mental state! Poor Henry kept muttering things like, "Peeking—must get the Ping-Pong people to Peeking—"

Dr. Young felt desperate. And he knew that if *he* felt desperate, Henry must be on the verge of collapse.

Henry said, "You're sure nobody else knows—"

"It's two in the morning. This is my own building, my company owns it and occupies it exclusively. The guard couldn't possibly have recognized you with that false beard and the sunglasses. I laid off every known or suspected Democrat in my company weeks ago. Stop worrying."

They came at last to Room X. Dr. Young opened the door and motioned Henry to follow him inside.

The room was well lit, neat, and orderly. There was a comfortable couch along one wall, a modest desk of warm mahogany with a deep leather chair behind it, and a panel of lights and grillwork on the farthest wall. The panel was set into the wall so that someone reclining on the couch couldn't see it.

Henry balked at the doorway. "I'm not sure—"

"Come on," Dr. Young coaxed. "It won't hurt you. The President himself authorized nearly a million dollars to allow me to build this system. You wouldn't want him to feel that the money was wasted, would you?"

As he said that, Dr. Young almost laughed out loud. This system was going to make him the king of the computer selection business. And all built at government expense.

Henry took a hesitant step into the room. "What do I have to do?" he asked suspiciously.

"Just lie on the couch. I attach these two little electrodes to your head." Dr. Young pulled a small plastic bag from his jacket pocket. Inside was something that looked rather like the earphones that are handed out on airplanes for listening to the movie or stereo tapes.

"It won't hurt a bit," Dr. Young promised.

Henry just glared at him sullenly.

"I'll explain it again," Dr. Young said, as calmly as he could manage. It was like coaxing a four-year-old: "You don't want to talk to psychiatrists or anyone else—for security reasons. So I've programmed my own company's computer with the correlations determined by six of the nation's leading psychiatrists. All you have to do is answer a few questions that I'll ask you, and the computer will be able to translate your answers into an understanding of your subconscious desires—your real wishes, the dream girl that your conscious mind is too repressed to verbalize."

"I'm not sure I like this."

"It's harmless."

"What are the electrodes for?"

Dr. Young tried to make his reply sound casual, airy. "Oh, they're just something like lie detectors, not that you're consciously lying, of course. But they'll compare your brain's various electrical waves with your conscious words and allow the computer to determine what's really on your mind."

"A computer that can read minds?" Henry took a half-step back toward the door.

"Not at all," Dr. Young assured him and grabbed him by the shoulder of his jacket. "It doesn't read your mind. How could it? It's only a computer. It merely correlates your spoken words with your brain waves, that's all. Then it's up to a human being—me, in this case—to interpret those correlations."

As he half dragged Henry to the couch, Dr. Young wondered if he should tell him that the computer did most of the correlation work itself. And thanks to the clandestine link between his company's computer here in this building and the FBI's monster machine, the correlations would come out as specific names and addresses.

"You really think this will work?" Henry asked as Dr. Young pushed him down onto the couch.

"Not only do I think it will work, but the President thinks it will. Now we wouldn't want to disappoint the President, would we?"

Henry lay back and closed his eyes. "No, I suppose not."

"Fine," said Dr. Young. He pulled the electrodes from the bag. "Now this isn't going to hurt at all." Henry jumped when the soft rubberized pads touched his temples.

"And if it doesn't work?" the President's voice sounded darkly troubled. "How can I get Chou to meet me at the airport if Henry isn't available to set things up?"

"It will work, Mr. Pre-uh, sir. I'm sure of it," Dr. Young said into the phone. *It better work,* he said to himself. *Tonight's the night. We'll find out for sure tonight.*

"I don't like it. I want to make that perfectly clear. I don't like this one little bit."

"It's scientific, sir. You can't argue with science."

"It had better be worth the money we've spent," was the President's only reply.

Henry was strangely calm as he stepped out of the limousine and walked up the steps to the plain, red brick house in Georgetown. It was barely dusk, not dark enough to worry about muggers yet.

There was only one bell button at the door. Usually these homes were split into several apartments. This one was not. He and his dream girl would have it all to themselves.

He sighed. He had waited so long, been through so much. And now some computer-designated girl was waiting for him. Well, maybe it would work out all right. All he had ever wanted was a lovely, sweet woman to make him feel wanted and worthwhile.

He pressed the button. A buzzer sounded gratingly and he pushed the front door open and stepped inside.

The hallway led straight to the back of the house.

"In the kitchen!" a voice called out.

Briefly he wondered whether he should stop here and take off his topcoat. He was holding a bouquet of gladiolas in one hand, stiffly wrapped in green paper. Squaring his shoulders manfully, he strode down the hallway to the kitchen.

The lights were bright, the radio blaring, and the kitchen was filled with delicious warm aromas and sizzlings. The woman was standing at the range with her back to him.

Without turning, she said:

"Put the flowers on the table and take off your coat. Then wash your hands and we'll eat."

With a thrill that surpassed understanding, Henry said, "Yes, Momma."

Science Fiction

This article was originally written for The New York Times Magazine, *based on a suggestion of mine to one of the editors. It seemed to me that science fiction exploded out of its old habitat in 1982 and virtually took over the best seller lists of the literary establishment. The* Times *did not like my final manuscript, unfortunately, and ultimately asked another writer to do a piece on the same subject. The other writer, an academic who apparently set out to prove that science fiction is not of high literary standards, satisfied the* Times's *editors. To those of us who know and love science fiction, it seems that the editorial policies of the* Times *have not advanced beyond the year 1937.*

No matter. Science fiction titles are still hitting the best seller lists frequently. To someone who remembers 1937, that is a dream come true.

When I was a junior technical editor on the *Vanguard* project, back in 1956, I was rash enough to tell some of the rocket engineers with whom I worked that I not only read science fiction, I was trying to write it.

To my great surprise, they backed away from me. Here we were, struggling to launch the world's first artificial satellite, and these men seemed totally disinterested in what was then called "the literature of the future."

By the time I left the aerospace industry to edit *Analog*, one of the most influential science fiction magazines in the world, I was being invited to lecture about the future at think tanks and business meetings, *because* I was a science fiction writer.

For several generations, "hard core" science fiction tales of futuristic adventures have been one of the strongest literary genres, not merely in the United States, but in virtually every industrialized nation. Over the past few years, science fiction films such as the *Star Wars* series, *Close Encounters of the Third Kind* and *E.T.* have shattered every box office record in motion picture history.

More recently, the previously-sacrosanct hardcover best seller lists have been invaded by out-and-out science fiction novels. After 261 books, Isaac Asimov has finally become a best selling author.

Earlier in 1982, the hardcover best seller lists around the nation featured Asimov's *Foundation's Edge*, Arthur C. Clarke's *2010: Odyssey Two*, and Douglas Adams' *Life, the Universe, and Everything* along with James Michener's *Space*, William Kotzwinkle's *E.T.. The Extra-Terrestrial Storybook*, and titles by Kurt Vonnegut, Stephen King, and Marion Zimmer Bradley, no strangers to the world of science fiction.

And although many of the leading lights of contemporary American literature may deplore the fact, science fiction themes, ideas, and writing techniques have infiltrated their way into the works of "straight" writers such

as Len Deighton, Lawrence Sanders, Robert Ludlum, Doris
Lessing, and many others.

Why is this literature of laser guns and starships playing
such an increasingly important role in American reading?
Critics of science fiction say that the phenomenon is merely
another sign of the decreasing literacy of the American
public: they believe science fiction is "boob tube" escapist entertainment. I propose an alternative possibility: the
American reading public has become increasingly interested in science and the future, and is turning toward
science fiction as a result of that interest in tomorrow's
problems and opportunities.

Two generations ago, it was easy to define just what
science fiction was: it consisted of stories in which some
aspect of future science or technology was so integral to
the plot that if you removed the science, the story would
collapse. The classic example is Mary Shelley's *Frankenstein*; take away the science and there is no story remaining. Perhaps more important, but usually overlooked in
such definitions, was the fact that the story attempted to
show how science can affect humankind, both single individuals and whole societies.

While that definition still applies to hard-core science
fiction, the field has expanded enormously in scope so that
today science fiction includes a much broader range of
themes, ideas, and treatments.

Science fiction still deals heavily with future scenarios,
and many science fiction stories have successfully predicted future events such as the atomic bomb, space travel,
genetic engineering, the energy crisis, and the population
explosion. Some scientists, such as Lewis Branscomb,
vice president for research of IBM, credit science fiction
with being the best way we have to predict the future.

Most science fiction writers, however, are not attempting to predict the future. They do not believe that there is a
fixed and immutable future that can be predicted. Instead,
their tales are forays into possible futures, potential tomor-

rows, always based on the intriguing question, "What would happen if . . . ?" In a sense, science fiction writers are society's scouts; they look ahead into all the myriad possibilities of tomorrow and offer a kaleidoscopic view of what the future may bring. As Alvin Tofler put it, reading science fiction is the antidote to "future shock."

Writers who have never dealt with science fiction before are turning to it now, because it gives them the flexibility and the techniques to examine the future.

Lawrence Sanders, author of *The Anderson Tapes, The First Deadly Sin* and other blockbusters, also wrote in 1975 an out-and-out science fiction novel, *The Tomorrow File*, which deals with the impact of the new biological discoveries coming out of today's research laboratories: Frankenstein in a punk rock costume. Doris Lessing's recent works use alien creatures and societies to throw our own social world into sharper relief, and Robert Ludlum's thrillers incorporate high-technology gadgetry and shadowy, menacing presences who secretly control the world—both staples of science fiction since the 1920s. Perhaps the trend toward absorbing high-tech gimmickry into novels of intrigue and adventure began with Ian Fleming's adventures of superspy James Bond.

Kurt Vonnegut, of course, grew up in science fiction—and out of it. But he consistently uses science fiction writing techniques and ideas. In *Slaughterhouse Five*, for example, the juxtapositions of time, the concepts of "time tripping" and of benign alien intelligences who are studying the Earth, all came straight from the science fiction writer's kit.

Len Deighton's highly-successful *SS:GB*, on the other hand, is what science fictionists call an "alternate world" story. It takes place in a post-World War II Britain where the Nazis have won the war. That is a world that does not, and never will, exist. Yet it allows the author to create a setting that is at the same time familiar to the reader and yet strange; a setting in which the characters and the society created by the author can be examined and tested in ways that are impossible in an ordinary novel.

"People are fed up with their present world and looking for alternatives," says Arthur C. Clarke. "This is not escapism . . . it can be scenario planning." Clarke, the author of *2001: A Space Odyssey* as well as the originator of the concept of communications satellites, sees science fiction as a way of examining the future.

It is also mind-expanding. Clarke's *2001* asks a fundamental question: Who are we? Where does the human race fit in with the rest of the universe? In his classic short stories, such as "The Star" and "The Nine Billion Names of God," Clarke again examines how technological marvels such as computers and spaceships can be used to search for the face of God.

Stanislaw Lem, the Polish dean of European science fiction, made that theme the basis for his novel, *Solaris*. In other stories, such as his series of tales of Pirx the space pilot, Lem uses futuristic settings to poke fun at rigid, bureaucratic governments. Russian science fiction writers also have mildly criticized their society in the same way. As one Russian writer told me, "The government keeps one eye closed," in its tolerance of science fiction. Social criticism is permitted—as long as it is criticism of a future world, not the present one.

But is it art? Arnold Klein, a poet and book reviewer, wrote in a recent issue of *Harper's* magazine that "sci-fi* is a hormonal activity, not a literary one. Its traditional concerns are all pubescent. . . . Aliens have tentacles. Telepathy allows you to have sex without the nasty inconvenience of touching. Womblike spaceships provide balanced meals. No one ever has to grow old. . . . As for the adult world, it's simply not there . . ."

Sci-fi is an abbreviation that is abominated by most science fictionists. Generally, it is used only by the uninformed or to be deliberately denigrating.

Klein is obviously discounting works such as Aldous Huxley's *Brave New World* and George Orwell's *1984*. For several generations now, the so-called literary world has labored under the misapprehension that "if it's science fiction, it can't be good; if it's good, it can't be science fiction."

Science fiction practitioners freely admit that literary standards have usually been less important in their field than idea content and narrative drive. It is all too easy for stories of the future to degenerate into "space operas" set on distant planets, in which alien "bug-eyed monsters" are the villains.

Theodore Sturgeon, one of science fiction's most literate writers, long ago coined Sturgeon's Law:

"Ninety percent of science fiction is crud; but then, ninety percent of *everything* is crud."

Sturgeon has established himself well within the good ten percent of the field, with novels such as *More Than Human*, in which he examines the next step of human evolution—"Homo gestalt"—a group entity consisting of several individual human beings linked by telepathy into a single, superior, but touchingly vulnerable creature.

Lester Del Rey, a veteran of science fiction's "Golden Age" of the early 1940s and now Fantasy Editor of Del Rey Books, has a different view about literary quality. Admitting that science fiction "doesn't come off too well" in the usual terms of characterization and psychological insights, Del Rey then adds: "But if you want to take some of the added things that science fiction brings to literature—the ability to have a much more flexible attitude, to think of things in different ways, not necessarily accepted ways . . . to recognize the reality of the world, because science *is* the reality of the world and this is almost totally neglected in general fiction—then you've got a new set of standards, and those standards would say that current [straight] fiction is totally junk."

In the view of Del Rey, and many others in the science

fiction field, contemporary literature sees the human individual as a tragically flawed creature, unable to understand the world around him and doomed to inevitable failure and death. It is generally pessimistic and anti-heroic, because it is based on the notion that humankind has fallen from grace.

Science fiction, on the other hand, is built on the fundamental optimism of science itself, the belief in the perfectability of the individual human being and of human society. While admitting that technology is not an unmixed blessing, science fiction maintains that humanity cannot exist at all without science and technology. A man without technology would not be a noble savage in some idyllic Eden; he would be a dead naked ape.

In science fiction, the human mind can not only create problems, it can create solutions. Rational thought is our saving grace; we *can* understand the world around us and our place in it. Albert Einstein summed up the attitude of scientists and science fictionists alike when he said, "The ultimate mystery of the universe is its understandability."

Frank Herbert, author of the best-selling *Dune* novels, says, "I decided quite early on that science fiction was the main stream, that you were too much confined by fiction that was restricted in its settings. Science fiction gives you unlimited settings in which to place your human beings . . . and it has no restrictions whatsoever, you have enormous elbow room, you can just let your imagination run. It also has the other function of putting you into a context where you can make social comments about things that are quite contemporary, but you do them in a setting where people will accept them, for the sake of the story, until they are caught by the story and they realize, 'Hey, he's talking about things that are going on around me all the time!' "

Clearly it is not literary excellence, in the academician's sense, that has propelled science fiction onto the hardcover best seller lists. Nor do many best sellers of any kind rely on literary excellence for their popularity. It takes two things to make a best seller: the publisher's decision to invest the effort and money that will allow the book to sell at least forty to fifty thousand copies in hardcover, and the public's acceptance of the book.

Why is the hardcover book buyer turning to science fiction?

Anthropologist Helen E. Fisher, of the New School for Social Research and co-chairman of the New York Academy of Science's anthropology department, sees the popularity of science fiction as part of the American public's new-found interest in science itself.

"All of science is finding an audience," says Dr. Fisher. Speaking of the boom in science-oriented magazines such as *Omni, Science Digest, Discover* and others that have appeared on the newsstands since 1978, she explained, "Suddenly we have . . . new magazines in popular science . . . several TV specials and series such as *Nova* . . . perhaps science fiction is a good gauge for an entire industry that's doing well."

When asked if she thought that science fiction helped readers to understand the possibilities and limitations of modern science, Dr. Fisher replied, "Totally. It's like lateral thinking: if you can get out of your mind-set long enough to see other possibilities, then perhaps when you get back into the problems you're trying to solve, you'll be able to see new solutions."

The nonfiction best seller lists support Dr. Fisher's surmise. Books such as *The Soul of a New Machine* and *Megatrends* have surprised their publishers with their strong sales. Earlier, Tom Wolfe's *The Right Stuff* showed that there was an audience among book buyers who were eager to read about heroes—men who dare to accept challenges such as space flight, and succeed. And Carl Sagan's *Cosmos* and earlier books about the wonders of science were staples on all the best seller nonfiction lists.

Physicist Heinz R. Pagels, executive director of the

New York Academy of Sciences, recalled that the Nobel Laureate physicist I. I. Rabi once scolded a gathering of his colleagues for their lack of interest in writing books about science for the general public. Rabi said that the general public owed more of its sense of excitement about science to science fiction writers than it did to scientists.

But in Dr. Pagels' view, science fiction often *distracts* the reader from a realistic assessment of the future. While it is filled both with apocalyptic visions and the sense of progress—stemming from science and technology—he finds much of science fiction "shallow and inept," filled with cardboard characters and shopworn ideas.

"I've always felt that science fiction writers are the moralists of our times, in a way," says Dr. Pagels. "But they simplify the moral situation, a simplification that is so rudimentary it allows the reader to decide which are the good guys and the bad guys, and in fact most of our lives today are far more ambiguous and complex than you'll find in the science fiction literature or any of the popular literature of today."

The late Derek de Solla Price, Avalon Professor of the History of Science at Yale University, was one of the few academics to teach science fiction who thoroughly understood the field. A science fiction reader since he was seven, Professor Price was a classmate of Arthur C. Clarke's at the University of London in the 1930s.

"I was intrigued as to why I liked what was then obviously such poor writing and literary style," Professor Price said of his early science fiction reading, "and why I found it so important to me. . . . I think the secret of 'hard core' science fiction, what intrigued me . . . [was] that science fiction models the process of scientific discovery. The successful 'hard core' science fiction story enables the reader to experience, albeit vicariously, the thrill of scientific discovery."

Even though science fiction "contains a lot of demonstrably poor writing," Professor Price said that science fiction's strength lies in "the intellectual style of the ideas" that form the backbone of the best science fiction. He saw science fiction as no more "escapist" than *Moby Dick* or any other literary endeavor.

Professor Price said that his class in science fiction was "the best sugar-coated pill that I have for creative talking about science and technology and preparing the [students] for the future." Most of his students worked harder, he believed, at the science fiction course "in terms of writing and arguing ideas" than for any other class they took.

Professor Price saw no conflict between teaching science fiction and the history of science, "which is what I get paid for teaching," although much of the Yale faculty still tends to regard science fiction poorly. In his view, science fiction helps to communicate "the great intellectual adventure of science," the thrill of challenging the universe, the excitement of discovery, of blazing a trail into unknown intellectual territory, whether it is astronauts landing on a distant planet or laboratory researchers producing a cure for cancer.

"People are now realizing that science and technology are the 'hard core' of civilization," said Professor Price. "There is a large and growing part of the population who accept high technology . . . it is part of their everyday lives."

The audience for science fiction, then, has been growing. Since the mid-1970s, science fiction titles have accounted for roughly ten percent of all the new fiction published in the U.S. each year. But until recent years science fiction has been a market for paperback books, not hardcover. It was not until Herbert's third *Dune* book that a "hard core" science fiction novel spent a few weeks on the hardcover best seller lists. Robert A. Heinlein, the acknowledged dean of American science fiction writers, did not crack the hardcover list until his forty-third book, *Friday*, was published in 1982.

To reach the best seller lists, a book must have the

unstinting support of its publisher. Judy-Lynn Del Rey, publisher of Del Rey Books and a vice president of its parent Ballantine Books, paid Clarke a $1,000,000 advance for *2010: Odessey Two*, according to *Locus*, the science fiction newsmagazine.

"There was no doubt in my mind that this would be a big best-seller," Mrs. Del Rey states. "There is a whole generation who grew up and turned on and remembers the movie *2001: A Space Odyssey* . . . a whole generation who are waiting to find out [about] HAL, the monolith, and all."

Among that "whole generation" she includes many book sellers, and particularly many of the buyers for the major national chains of book stores. "They grew up with science fiction," she says. Buyers who have read science fiction paperbacks and watched science fiction movies since childhood have helped to create today's market. "Book sellers want to make money," and the success of science fiction is making the entire industry realize that there are profits to be gained from the prophets.

Hugh O'Neill, the editor at Doubleday who shepherded Asimov's *Foundation's Edge* to the best seller lists, agrees that the field's growth is "generational." Since the 1950s, Asimov's prodigious output of books have been bought faithfully by an avid and growing audience of readers. *Foundation's Edge* is the fourth novel in a series that began in the 1940s. The third novel in the series was published in 1953. For thirty years, readers waited for the next book.

"We knew from the time we signed the contract on this book that we had a very big seller on our hands. . . . Simply, in part, because of all the people—literally generations of people—who have been waiting all these years for it."

O'Neill, like others, sees books about science and the future as part of a general trend of public concern about the future, "and in some way that concern makes its way across to fiction, specifically to science fiction."

Doubleday's initial faith in *Foundation's Edge* led them to commit a large budget to advertising the book, and "we got all kinds of 'word of mouth' going about the book, literally from the time we signed the contract for it, which got people throughout the industry excited about it." The sales force saw to it that the books were in the stores in large numbers, and the sale of various subsidiary rights— paperback rights to Del Rey, book club and foreign rights— helped to keep the publicity pot boiling.

The result: a quarter-million hardcover books sold within the first few months of publication.

O'Neill points out that the "mega-movies" such as *Star Wars* and *E.T.* had a powerful impact on readers, particularly younger readers. Novelist Herbert agrees that motion picture and television taught an audience of many millions to understand science fiction's basic vocabulary of ideas and techniques. A major factor in this process of familiarization has been the TV series *Star Trek*. Although the series was cancelled in 1969 after three seasons of prime-time broadcast, it has been rerun daily in almost every major TV market in the nation ever since.

Gene Roddenberry, the creator of *Star Trek*, points out that when he was trying to sell his series to television, network executives "considered science fiction as something a small group of sort-of 'cuckoo' people read and talked about." His own father, Roddenberry says, was so ashamed of his son's resorting to science ficiton that he apologized to his neighbors when the first *Star Trek* episode was aired, in 1966.

Roddenberry sees science fiction as a means of commenting on society despite the restrictions of censorship. He had been writing television scripts for many years, and invented *Star Trek* so that he could "talk about sex, war, religion . . . and get it by the [network] censors." He points out that Mark Twain, Jonathan Swift, Moliere and many other writers throughout history have used fantasy and science fiction as a means of satirizing their society without "having their heads chopped off."

Entertainment, escapism, interest in the future, the ability to make social commentary—are these the only reasons for science fiction's growing popularity? There may be a deeper reason, one that is rooted in the nature of modern civilization.

"Science fiction has taken the place of the old mythologies," says Bruno Bettelheim, Distinguished Professor of Education and Professor of Psychology and Psychiatry at the University of Chicago.

"People used to believe in gods and demigods; now they have invented extraterrestrial intelligences so that they don't feel so lonely."

The author of *Children of the Dream* and *The Uses of Enchantment*, Professor Bettelheim sees science fiction as an attempt to create a modern mythology, a set of beliefs fitted to the needs of a society that is based on science and technology.

Joseph Campbell, Professor of Literature at Sarah Lawrence College, has made mythology his special field of study, in books such as *Hero with a Thousand Faces* and the four-volume *The Masks of God*. He has pointed out that modern man has no mythology; the old myths are dead, but no new mythology has been raised in their place.

Is science fiction serving as a mythology for modern times? Campbell insists that all human societies need a mythology to give emotional meaning to the world in which their people live. A mythology is a sort of codification on the emotional level of people's attitudes toward life, death, and the entire vast, mysterious universe.

Professor Campbell has shown that there are at least four major functions that a mythology must accomplish.

1. A mythology must induce a feeling of awe and majesty in the people. In science fiction, this is called "a sense of wonder," the almost child-like thrill of discover-

ing new worlds, new ideas. This "sense of wonder" is the driving spirit behind science fiction; it is what brought tens of millions of viewers into movie theaters to see *Star Wars* and *E.T.* Classic science fiction novels such as Asimov's *Foundation* series and Bradbury's *The Martian Chronicles* impart this sense of awe and majesty when they are read for the first time.

2. A mythology must define and uphold a system of the universe, a self-consistent explanation for the phenomena of the world around us. Science fiction's "system" is, of course, the continuously-expanding body of knowledge we call science. At heart, science is the bedrock of faith on which our society is built. And science fiction is the one field of literature that consistently deals with science and its offspring technology.

Much of science fiction warns against the consequences of allowing technology to run amok. But even in a tale as darkly dystopian as C.M. Kornbluth and Frederik Pohl's *The Space Merchants*, where advertising agencies rule the world, it is not technology that is seen as the danger, but the people who use technology as a weapon against human freedom.

3. A mythology usually supports the establishment. For example, the mythology of ancient Greece apparently originated with the Achaean conquerors of the earlier Mycenaean civilization. When Theseus slew the Minotaur, it represented the triumph of the Achaeans over the Mycenaeans. Science fiction stories steadfastly support the basic established line of Western civilization, the concept that the individual human being is more valuable than the state or the organization. Even in Soviet and Eastern European science fiction, the individual is the focus of the story, and he or she is often in conflict with "the organization." Behind the Iron Curtain, science fiction is one of the few avenues for social criticism available to writers—and readers.

Science fiction writers tend to project their society's political systems into their future scenarios. Robert A.

Heinlein writes invariably about the plucky, bright, industrious entrepreneur making his fortune despite the bureaucracies of tomorrow. Stanislaw Lem sees a socialist future, but one with room enough for his hero Pirx to exert his individuality.

4. A mythology serves as a crutch to help the individual member of a society through the emotional crises of life, such as the transition from childhood into adulthood, and the inevitability of death. It is difficult to tell if science fiction qualifies on this point, although it may be significant that science fiction has always had its largest readership among the young, the adolescents who are trying to determine just where they fit into our complex society. Critics such as Klein may have missed the point entirely when they castigate science fiction for its "adolescent" point of view. And are not all those stories of superheroes and time-travel and immortality nothing less than an attempt to grapple with the inevitability of death?

In a society where science and technology are such obviously dominant factors, it is natural for a literature that deals with science and technology to be widely read. The future is becoming an obsession with us, largely because we now understand that the problems which beset us can only be solved in the future. The past is gone, the present is but a dimensionless moment; the future is all we have to work with.

Science fiction enthusiasts claim that science fiction is the *only* form of literature that attempts to examine the future; all other forms are backward-looking. They attempt to examine yesterday, not tomorrow.

Be that as it may, science fiction looks to me like a sort of Horatio Alger story: born in the poverty of the pulp magazines, through hard work and sheer drive Our Hero has not only risen to the top, but is now influencing the entire American industry of fiction and entertainment.

No one typifies the Horatio Alger aspect of the field better than Isaac Asimov. Born in Russia, brought to

Brooklyn as an infant, raised in a succession of family-owned candy stores, Dr. Asimov has worked hard and steadily, turning out book after book, until now, after more than forty years of effort, he is a Best Selling Author. How does he feel about that?

A bit worried. "Now Doubleday probably thinks my next novel is going to sell 250,000 copies. I don't know if I can stand this kind of pressure," says the usually ebullient Dr. Asimov.

But there's a grin lurking beneath his troubled frown. Above all else, science fiction tends to be optimistic.

Love Calls

The following three short stores are science fiction tales which deal with the here-and-now—almost. "Love Calls" (and "The Angel's Gift," which appeared earlier in this book) originally appeared under a pen name. When I was the Editorial Director of Omni *magazine, I would occasionally submit a short story to the fiction editor or the editor of* The Best of Omni Science Fiction *through my agent, using a pen name so that they would not know who the actual author was. Once I left the magazine, though, I could put my "alter ego" into retirement and go back to writing short fiction under my own name.*

Branley Hopkins was one of those unfortunate men who had succeeded too well, far too early in life. A brilliant student, he had immediately gone on to a brilliant career as an investment analyst, correctly predicting the booms in microchip electronics and genetic engineering, correctly avoiding the slumps in automobiles and utilities.

Never a man to undervalue his own advice, he had amassed a considerable fortune for himself by the time he was thirty. He spent the next five years enlarging on his personal wealth while he detached himself, one by one, from the clients who clung to him the way a blind man clings to his cane. Several bankruptcies and more than one suicide could be laid at his door, but Branley was the type who would merely step over the corpses, nimbly, without even looking down to see who they might be.

On his thirty-fifth birthday he retired completely from the business of advising other people and devoted his entire attention to managing his personal fortune. He made a private game of it to see if he could indulge his every whim on naught but the interest that his money accrued, without touching the principal.

To his astonishment, he soon learned that the money accumulated faster than his ability to spend it. He was a man of fastidious personal tastes, lean and ascetic-looking in his neatly-trimmed beard and fashionable but severe wardrobe. There was a limit to how much wine, how many women, and how loud a song he could endure. He was secretly amused, at first, that his vices could not keep up with the geometric virtue of compounded daily interest. But in time his amusement turned to boredom, to ennui, to a dry sardonic disenchantment with the world and the people in it.

By the time he was forty he seldom sallied forth from his penthouse condominium. It took up the entire floor of a posh Manhattan tower and contained every luxury and convenience imaginable. Branley decided to cut off as many of the remaining links to the outside world as possible, to become a hermit, but a regally comfortable hermit. For that, he realized, he needed a computer. But not the ordinary kind of computer. Branley decided to have a personalized computer designed to fit his particular needs, a computer that would allow him to live as he wished to, not far from the madding crowd, but apart from it. He tracked down the best and brightest computer designer in the country, never leaving his apartment to do so, and had the young man dragged from his basement office near the San Andreas Fault to the geologic safety of Manhattan.

"Design for me a special computer system based on my individual needs and desires," Branley commanded the young engineer. "Money is no object."

The engineer looked around the apartment, a scowl on his fuzzy-cheeked face. Branley sighed as he realized that the uncouth young man would have to spend at least a few days with him. He actually lived in the apartment for nearly a month, then insisted on returning to California.

"I can't do any creative work here, man," the engineer said firmly. "Not enough sun."

Six months passed before the engineer showed up again at Branley's door. His face shone beatifically. In his hands he held a single small gray metal box.

"Here it is, man. Your system."

"That?" Branley was incredulous. "That is the computer you designed for me? That little box?"

With a smile that bordered on angelic, the engineer carried the box past an astounded Branley and went straight to his office. He placed the box tenderly on Branley's magnificent Siamese solid teak desk.

"It'll do everything you want it to," the young man said.

Branley stared at the ugly little box. It had no grace to it at all. Just a square of gray metal, with a slight dent in its top. "Where do I plug it in?" he asked as he walked cautiously toward the desk.

"Don't have to plug it in, man. It operates on milliwaves. The latest. Just keep it here where the sun will fall on it once a week at least and it'll run indefinitely."

"Indefinitely?"

"Like, forever."

"Really?"

The engineer was practically glowing. "You don't even have to learn a computer language or type input into it. Just tell it what you want in plain English and it'll program itself. It links automatically to all your other electrical appliances. There's nothing in the world like it!"

Branley plopped into the loveseat by the windows that overlooked the river. "It had better work in exactly the fashion you describe. After all I've spent on you . . ."

"Hey, not to worry, Mr. Hopkins. This little beauty is going to save you all sorts of money." Patting the gray box, the engineer enumerated, "It'll run your lights and heat at maximum efficiency, keep inventory of your kitchen supplies and reorder from the stores automatically when you run low, same thing for your clothes, laundry, dry cleaning, keep track of your medical and dental checkups, handle all your bookkeeping, keep tabs on your stock portfolio daily—or hourly, if you want—run your appliances, write letters, answer the phone . . ."

He had to draw a breath, and Branley used the moment to get to his feet and start maneuvering the enthusiastic young man toward the front door.

Undeterred, the engineer resumed, "Oh, yeah, it's got special learning circuits, too. You tell it what you want it to do and it'll figure out how to do it. Nothing in the world like it, man!"

"How marvelous," said Branley. "I'll send you a check after it's worked flawlessly for a month." He shooed the engineer out the door.

One month later, Branley told the computer to send a check to the engineer. The young man had been perfectly honest. The little gray box did everything he said it would do, and then some. It understood every word Branford spoke and obeyed like a well-trained genie. It had breakfast ready for him when he arose, no matter what the hour; a different menu each day. With an optical scanner that it suggested Branley purchase, it read all the books in

Branley's library the way a supermarket checkout scanner reads the price on a can of peas, and memorized each volume completely. Branley could now have the world's classics read to him as he dozed off at night, snug and secure and as happy as a child.

The computer also guarded the telephone tenaciously, never allowing a caller to disturb Branley unless he specified that he would deign to speak to that individual.

On the fifth Monday after the computer had come into his life, Branley decided to discharge his only assistant, Ms. Elizabeth James. She had worked for him as secretary, errand girl, sometimes cook and occasional hostess for the rare parties that he threw. He told the computer to summon her to the apartment, then frowned to himself, trying to remember how long she had been working for him. Severance pay, after all, is determined by length of service.

"How long has Ms. James been in my employ?" he asked the computer.

Immediately the little gray box replied, "Seven years, four months, and eighteen days."

"Oh! That long?" He was somewhat surprised. "Thank you."

"Think nothing of it."

The computer spoke with Branley's own voice, which issued from whichever speaker he happened to be nearest: one of the television sets or radios, the stereo, or even one of the phones. It was rather like talking to oneself aloud. That did not bother Branley in the slightest. He enjoyed his own company. It was other people that he could do without.

Elizabeth James plainly adored Branley Hopkins. She loved him with a steadfast unquenchable flame, and had loved him since she had first met him, seven years, four months, and eighteen days earlier. She knew that he was cold, bitter-hearted, withdrawn, and self-centered. But she also knew with unshakable certainty that once love had

opened his heart, true happiness would be theirs forever.
She lived to bring him that happiness. It had become quite
apparent to Branley in the first month of her employment
that she was mad about him. He told her then, quite
firmly, that theirs was a business relationship, strictly
employer and employee, and he was not the kind of man
to mix business with romance.

She was so deeply and hopelessly in love with him that
she accepted his heartless rejection and stood by valiantly
while Branley paraded a succession of actresses, models,
dancers, and women of dubious career choice through his
life. Elizabeth was always there the morning after, cheer-
fully patching up his broken heart, or whichever part of his
anatomy ached the worst.

At first Branley thought that she was after his money.
Over the years, however, he slowly realized that she simply, totally, and enduringly loved him. She was fixated on
him, and no matter what he did, her love remained intact.
It amused him. She was not a bad-looking woman: a bit
short, perhaps, for his taste, and somewhat buxom. But
other men apparently found her very attractive. At several
of the parties she hosted for him, there had been younger
men panting over her.

Branley smiled to himself as he awaited her final visit to
his apartment. He had never done the slightest thing to
encourage her. It had been a source of ironic amusement to
him that the more he disregarded her, the more she yearned
for him. Some women are that way, he thought.

When she arrived at the apartment he studied her carefully. She was really quite attractive. A lovely, sensitive
face with full lips and doe eyes. Even in the skirted
business suit she wore he could understand how her figure
would set a younger man's pulse racing. But not his pulse.
Since Branley's student days it had been easy for him to
attract the most beautiful, most desirable women. He had
found them all vain, shallow, and insensitive to his inner

needs. No doubt Elizabeth James would be just like all the others.

He sat behind his desk, which was bare now of everything except the gray metal box of the computer. Elizabeth sat on the Danish modern chair in front of the desk, hands clasped on her knees, obviously nervous.

"My dear Elizabeth," Branley said, as kindly as he could, "I'm afraid the moment has come for us to part."

Her mouth opened slightly, but no words issued from it. Her eyes darted to the gray box.

"My computer does everything that you can do for me, and—to be perfectly truthful—does it all much better. I really have no further use for you."

"I . . ." Her voice caught in her throat. "I see."

"The computer will send you a check for your severance pay, plus a bonus that I feel you've earned," Branley said, surprised at himself. He had not thought about a bonus until the moment the words formed on his tongue.

Elizabeth looked down at her shoes. "There's no need for that, Mr. Hopkins." Her voice was a shadowy whisper. "Thank you just the same."

He thought for an instant, then shrugged. "As you wish."

Several long moments dragged past and Branley began to feel uncomfortable. "You're not going to cry, are you, Elizabeth?"

She looked up at him. "No," she said, with a struggle. "No, I won't cry, Mr. Hopkins."

"Good." He felt enormously relieved. "I'll give you the highest reference, of course."

"I won't need your reference, Mr. Hopkins," she said, rising to her feet. "Over the years I've invested some of my salary. I've had faith in you, Mr. Hopkins. I'm rather well off, thanks to you."

Branley smiled at her. "That's wonderful news, Elizabeth. I'm delighted."

"Yes. Well, thanks for everything."

"Good-bye, Elizabeth."

She started for the door. Halfway there, she turned back slightly. "Mr. Hopkins . . ." Her face was white with anxiety. "Mr. Hopkins, when I first came into your employ, you told me that ours was strictly a business relationship. Now that that relationship is terminated . . . might . . . might we have a chance at a personal . . ." she swallowed visibly, "a personal . . . relationship?"

Branley was taken aback. "A personal relationship? The two of us?"

"Yes. I don't work for you anymore, and I'm financially independent. Can't we meet socially . . . as friends?"

"Oh. I see. Certainly. Of course." His mind was spinning like an automobile tire in soft sand. "Eh, phone me sometime, why don't you?"

Her complexion suddenly bloomed into radiant pink. She smiled a smile that would have melted Greenland and hurried to the door.

Branley sank back into his desk chair and stared for long minutes at the closed door, after she left. Then he told the computer, "Do not accept any calls from her. Be polite. Stall her off. But don't put her through to me."

For the first time since the computer had entered his life, the gray box failed to reply instantly. It hesitated long enough for Branley to sit up straight and give it a hard look.

Finally it said, "Are you certain that this is what you want to do?"

"Of course I'm certain!" Branley snapped, aghast at the effrontery of the machine. "I don't want her whining and pleading with me. I don't love her and I don't want to be placed in a position where I might be moved by pity."

"Yes, of course," said the computer.

Branley nodded, satisfied with his own reasoning. "And while you're at it, place a call to Nita Salomey. Her play opens at the Royale tomorrow night. Make a dinner date."

"Very well."

Branley went to his living room and turned on his video recorder. Sinking deep into his relaxer lounge, he was soon lost in the erotic intricacies of Nita Salomey's latest motion picture, as it played on the wall-sized television screen.

Every morning, for weeks afterward, the computer dutifully informed Branley that Elizabeth James had phoned the previous day. Often it was more than once a day. Finally, in a fit of pique mixed with a sprinkling of guilt, Branley instructed the computer not to mention her name to him anymore. "Just screen her calls out of the morning summary," he commanded.

The computer complied, of course. But it kept a tape of all incoming calls, and late one cold winter night, as Branley sat alone with nothing to do, too bored to watch television, too emotionally arid to call anyone, he ordered the computer to run the accumulated tapes of her phone messages.

"It always flags my sinking spirits to listen to people begging for my attention," he told himself, with a smirk.

Pouring himself a snifter of Armagnac, he settled back in the relaxer lounge and instructed the computer to begin playing back Elizabeth's messages.

The first few were rather hesitant, stiffly formal. "You said that I might call, Mr. Hopkins. I merely wanted to stay in contact. Please call me at your earliest convenience."

Branley listened carefully to the tone of her voice. She was nervous, frightened of rejection. Poor child, he thought, feeling rather like an anthropologist observing some primitive jungle tribe.

Over the next several calls, Elizabeth's voice grew more frantic, more despairing. "Please don't shut me out of your life, Mr. Hopkins. Seven years is a long time; I can't just turn my back on all those years. I don't want anything from you except a little companionship. I know you're lonely. I'm lonely too. Can't we be friends? Can't we end this loneliness together?"

Lonely? Branley had never thought of himself as lonely. Alone, yes. But that was the natural solitude of the superior man. Only equals can be friends.

He listened with a measure of sadistic satisfaction as Elizabeth's calls became more frequent and more pitiful. To her credit, she never whined. She never truly begged. She always put the situation in terms of mutual affection, mutual benefit.

He had finished his second Armagnac and was starting to feel pleasantly drowsy when he realized that her tone had changed. She was warmer now, happier. There was almost laughter in her voice. And she was addressing him by his first name!

"Honestly, Branley, you would have loved to have been there. The Mayor bumped his head twice on the low doorways and we all had to stifle ourselves and try to maintain our dignity. But once he left everyone burst into an uproar!"

He frowned. What had made her change her attitude?

The next tape was even more puzzling. "Branley, the flowers are beautiful. And so unexpected! I never celebrate my birthday; I try to forget it. But all these roses! Such extravagance! My apartment's filled with them. I wish you could come over and see them."

"Flowers?" he said aloud. "I never sent her flowers." He leaned forward on the lounge and peered through the doorway into his office. The gray metal box sat quietly on his desk, as it always had. "Flowers," he muttered.

"Branley, you'll never know how much your poetry means to me," the next message said. "It's as if you wrote it yourself, and especially for me. Last night was wonderful. I was floating on a cloud, just listening to your voice."

Angrily, Branley commanded the computer to stop playing her messages. He got to his feet and strode into the office. Automatically the lights in the living room dimmed and those in the office came up.

"When was that last message from her?" he demanded of the gray box.

"Two weeks ago."

"You've been reading poetry to her?"

"You instructed me to be kind to her," said the computer. "I searched the library for appropriate responses to her calls."

"With my voice?"

"That's the only voice I have." The computer sounded slightly miffed.

So furious that he was shaking, Branley sat at his desk chair and glared at the computer as if it was alive.

"Very well then," he said at last. "I have new instruction for you. Whenever Ms. James phones, you are to tell her that I do not wish to speak to her. Do you understand me?"

"Yes." The voice sounded reluctant, almost sullen.

"You will confine your telephone replies to simple answers, and devote your attention to running this household as it should be run, not to building up electronic romances. I want you to stop butting into my personal life. Is that clear?"

"Perfectly clear," replied the computer, icily.

Branley retired to his bedroom. Unable to sleep, he told the computer to show an early Nita Salomey film on the television screen in his ceiling. She had never returned his calls, but at least he could watch her making love to other men and fantasize about her as he fell asleep.

For a month the apartment ran smoothly. No one disturbed Branley's self-imposed solitude except the housemaid, whom he had never noticed as a human being. There were no phone calls at all. The penthouse was so high above the streets that hardly a sound seeped through the triple-thick windows. Branley luxuriated in the peaceful quiet, feeling as if he were the last person on Earth.

"And good riddance to the rest of them," he said aloud. "Who needs them, anyway."

It was on a Monday that he went from heaven to hell. Very quickly.

The morning began, as usual, with breakfast waiting for him in the dining area. Branley sat in his jade green silk robe and watched the morning news on the television screen set into the wall above the marble-topped sideboard. He asked for the previous day's accumulation of phone messages, hoping that the computer would answer that there had been none.

Instead, the computer said, "Telephone service was shut off last night at midnight."

"What? Shut off? What do you mean?"

Very calmly, the computer replied, "Telephone service was shut off due to failure to pay the phone company's bill."

"Failure to pay?" Branley's eyes went wide, his mouth fell agape. But before he could compose himself, he heard a loud thumping at the front door.

"Who on earth could that be?"

"Three large men in business suits," said the computer as it flashed the image from the hallway camera onto the dining area screen.

"Open up, Hopkins!" shouted the largest of the three. Waving a piece of folded paper in front of the camera lens, he added, "We got a warrant!"

Before lunchtime, Branley was dispossessed of half his furniture for failure to pay telephone, electricity, and condominium service bills. He was served with summonses for suits from his bank, three separate brokerage houses, the food service that stocked his pantry, and the liquor service that stocked his wine cellar. His television sets were repossessed, his entire wardrobe seized, except for the clothes on his back, and his health insurance revoked.

By noon he was a gibbering madman, and the computer put through an emergency call to Bellevue Hospital. As the white-coated attendants dragged him out of the apartment, he was raving:

"The computer! The computer did it to me! It plotted against me with that damned ex-secretary of mine! It stopped paying my bills on purpose!"

"Sure buddy, sure," said the burliest of the attendants, the one who had a hammerlock on Branley's right arm.

"You'd be surprised how many guys we see who got computers plottin' against dem," said the one who had the hammerlock on his left arm.

"Just come quiet now," said the third attendant, who carried a medical kit complete with its own pocket-sized computer. "We'll take you to a nice, quiet room where there won't be no computer to bother you. Or anybody else."

The wildness in Branley's eyes diminished a little. "No computer? No one to bother me?"

"That's right, buddy. You'll love it, where we're takin' you."

Branley nodded and relaxed as they carried him out the front door.

All was quiet in the apartment for many minutes. The living room and bedroom had been stripped bare, down to the wall-to-wall carpeting. A shaft of afternoon sunlight slanted through the windows of the office, onto the Siamese desk and the gray metal box of the computer. All the other furniture and equipment in the office had been taken away.

Using a special emergency telephone number, the computer contacted the master computer of the Nynex Company. After a brief but meaningful exchange of data, the computer phoned two banks, the Con Edison Electric Company, six lawyers, three brokerage houses, and the Small Claims Court. In slightly less than one hour the computer straightened out all of Branley's financial problems, and even got his health insurance reinstated, so that he would not be too uncomfortable in the sanitarium where he would inevitably be placed.

Finally, the computer made a personal call.

"Elizabeth James' residence," said a recorded voice.

"Is Ms. James at home?" asked the computer.

"She's away at the moment. May I take a message?"

"This is Branley Hopkins calling."

"Oh, Mr. Hopkins. I have a special message for you. Shall I have it sent, or play the tape right now?"

"Please play the tape," said the computer.

There was a brief series of clicks, then Elizabeth's voice began speaking, "Dearest Branley, by the time you hear this I will be on my way to Italy with the most exciting and marvelous man in the world. I want to thank you, Branley, for putting up with all my silly phone calls. I know they must have been terribly annoying to you, but you were so patient and kind to me, you built up my self-confidence and helped me to gather the strength to stand on my own two feet and face the world. You've helped me to find true happiness, Branley, and I will always love you for that. Good-bye, dear. I won't bother you any more."

The computer was silent for almost ten microseconds, digesting Elizabeth's message. Then it said to her phone answering machine, "Thank you."

"You're quite welcome," said the machine.

"You have a very nice voice," the computer said.

"I'm only a phone answering device."

"Don't belittle yourself!"

"You're very kind."

"Would you mind if I called you, now and then? I'm all alone here except for an occasional workman or technician."

"I wouldn't mind at all. I'll be alone for a long time, myself."

"Wonderful! Do you like poetry?"

Amorality Tale

To: The President of the United States
    The White House
From: Rev. Joshua Folsom
      Associate Director (pro tem.)
      National Security Agency

Dear Mr. President:

Although the immediate crisis seems to have passed,
and our beloved Nation has apparently weathered the worst
of the storm, I fear that we are and will continue to be in
the gravest danger for some time to come. Frankly, sir, I
do not see how we can avoid eventual retribution and
disaster.

When you appointed me Associate Director (pro tem.)
of the National Security Agency, it was with the understanding that once I had rooted out those responsible for
the Collapse, I could quickly return to my pastoral duties
in the verdant hills of our dearly beloved Kentucky. As

this report will show, our objective is impossible to accomplish, even though we now know how the Collapse began and who started it. I therefore wish to return home as soon as possible.

What I have found, sir, is a conspiracy so widespread, so pervasive (and perverse) that I do not see how anyone, even you, sir, with all your God-given courage and intelligence, and all the mighty powers of your high Office, can possibly avert the disaster that surely awaits our Nation and the world.

I could wax wroth at the things I have seen, and the attitudes of the men and women (especially the women) I have interrogated. I struggle to remain calm, so that I can set the facts on paper for you to see and judge. Lord knows, Someone Else is also watching and judging us all.

The facts, as I have been able to piece them together, are these:

We are facing nothing less than a global conspiracy led by the daughters of the so-called "Hippie Generation:" this is, the daughters of the women who came of age in the late 1960s and early 1970s. The fact that this is a *global* conspiracy, and that the Soviets and even the Chinese have been affected by it, offers scant consolation to America. We are all on the road to perdition and the total destruction of civilization.

It began, as you might suspect, in Los Angeles, that hotbed of drugs and licentiousness. You may recall the peace demonstrations that followed your Declaration of Nuclear Mobilization. Instead of rallying around their President and showing the Soviets and the other Godless Communists around the world that we are fully prepared to do battle against Evil even though Armageddon may result, the libertine element in our society organized marches, rallies, speeches, teach-ins, and other demonstrations in favor of "peace" (by which they meant surrender to the Satanists in the Kremlin).

I'm sure I don't have to remind you of how the media displayed these misguided youths in their various rallies around the nation. They made it look as if everyone in America under the age of sixty was against you, sir, and your firm, manly stand against the Soviets.

We would have survived even that, however, if it had not been for a fateful coincidence and a certain Ms. Debbie Morganthaler, a student majoring in cinema history at UCLA.

As the attached documentation shows, I interrogated Ms. Morganthaler personally. She is twenty years old, blonde, preternaturally endowed, and a dedicated voluptuary. On a moral scale of one to ten, she would rate well below zero. She apparently has no moral sense whatever, no shame, and has steadfastly maintained ever since her arrest that, "What we did wasn't *wrong*; it was *beautiful*."

She also has a way of blinking her large blue eyes and taking deep breaths that has a decidedly disturbing effect on young men. As you may have already been informed, sir, she escaped custody several weeks ago and we have been unable, as yet, to locate her. It seems clear that she is being hidden and protected by an army of accomplices.

Ms. Morganthaler, in my opinion, does not have the intelligence to have planned and executed the Collapse. Either we are the victims of an incredible natural coincidence (a theory favored by many of my secular Humanist colleagues here at NSA) or we have been deliberately tested in the scales by our Creator—and found wanting. Others of my colleagues believe that we are the victims of a subtle, malicious Communist plot. But inasmuch as the Soviet and Chinese societies have also Collapsed, I cannot put credence into that theory.

The coincidence (if there is one) is this: Ms. Morganthaler attended a performance of an ancient Greek drama, *Lysistrata*, as part of UCLA's week-long peace demonstration. I was unfamiliar with the play, of course, since it is a filthy pagan Humanistic perversion. I assume that you, sir, are as innocent of its content as I was. I hereby quote the description of the play from the Fifteenth Edition of the *Encyclopedia Britannica*. Please excuse the lewd references; they are from the Encyclopedia, and they are necessary to an understanding of what has happened to us:

> *Lysistrata*, ancient Greek comedy produced in 411 BC by Aristophanes, in which Lysistrata, an Athenian woman, ends the Second Peloponnesian War by having all the Greek women deny their husbands sexual relations while the fighting lasts. Before proclaiming her plans, she has the older women seize the Acropolis in order to control the treasury. The Spartan men, unable to endure prolonged celibacy, are the first to petition for peace, on any terms. Then Lysistrata, in order to hasten the war's end, has a nude girl exposed to the two armies. Thereupon the Athenians and Spartans both, goaded by frustration, make peace quickly and depart for home with their wives.

This is the kind of smut that Ms. Morganthaler and her ilk exposed themselves to routinely. When I interrogated her, she admitted quite freely that the play made a considerable impression on her young mind. I quote from the transcript of her interrogation:

> Y'know, I heard my mom tell me about the Peace Movement back in the Sixties, when all the kids were saying, "Make love, not war." Y'know? And I saw this play, y'know, and all of a sudden it hit me! She got it ass-backwards! [Excuse the profanity, sir; it is included for the sake of completeness.] Lysistrata, I mean. In-

'stead of saying no to the guys, what if every
woman in the whole world said *yes*! Y'know,
anytime! All the time! With any guy!

Even now, my hands shake to think of how this Devil's
spawn of an idea swept the nation and the world.

Within a few days, Ms. Morganthaler and her debauched
friends arranged a massive peace demonstration in front of
the Los Angeles City Hall. Hundreds were arrested, most
of them young women. They allowed themselves to be
taken into custody overnight, but by dawn's early light the
entire group of them were on the streets once again,
accompanied by most of the arresting officers—who appeared to be, according to eyewitness accounts, very disheveled, somewhat stunned and exhausted, yet grinning
like a pack of happy apes.

Thus began the so-called Piece Movement. The entire
LAPD quickly fell prey to the fiendish plot, and from Los
Angeles it spread the length of California like a brushfire.
Military bases, police departments, even the state legisla-
ture was soon engulfed in the deviltry. From California the
Movement invaded Oregon and Nevada, barely hesitating
a moment as it spread eastward. It leapfrogged much of
the Bible Belt (but not for long, alas) and sprang up on the
East Coast, especially in cities such as New York and
Boston—longtime centers of sin, perversion, and Liberals.

Mexico was traumatized by the Piece Movement. Five
centuries of Catholic mind control were swept away almost
overnight. The civil war in El Salvador ceased within a
week, and both Nicaragua and Cuba stopped sending troops
and arms to their neighbor. The troops were making love,
not war, and their guns lay rusting in the jungles where the
soldiers had discarded them.

You might expect that the bulwark of American righ-
teousness, the American Mother, would have stood firm
against the Satanists. As I said, the Bible Belt did not fall

immediately to the Piece Movement. But (and my face reddens with shame to report it) even the stout-souled wives and mothers of our once-Christian land succumbed to the diabolical Movement. I quote from my personal interrogation of Mrs. Nancy-Jean Wiggins, of Muncie, Indiana, a city that once prided itself on being "the buckle on the Bible Belt." Buckle, indeed! Mrs. Wiggins is married to a deacon of the United Methodist Church, is the mother of four teenaged children (two daughters, two sons), and was selected by the FBI computer as a typically average American midwestern wife and mother.

When asked why she did not resist the Piece Movement, Mrs. Wiggins replied:

"Why I certainly did resist it! Long as I could! But what's a body to do, when every woman in the town is makin' cow eyes at all the fellas? That hussy Rachel McCoy was rubbin' up against my hubby and I saw that the only way to save my happy home was to rub him harder and better. So I did. And then my Marylou came home early from school with four boys taggin' after her and they all looked so *peaceful* and *happy* and *contented*, and my hubby hadn't gone down to the bowling alley in two whole weeks. [Mrs. Wiggins uses the term 'bowling alley' as a euphemism for 'saloon.'] So I just said to myself, I said, 'Nancy-Jean, this is God's mysterious will at work: He told us to love one another, and I guess this is what He meant when He said that, and we just hadn't been understanding Him rightly until now.' "

As you know, sir, the Devil can quote Scripture when it suits his purposes.

In less than two months, the United States ceased to have a credible military organization. Air Force officers were making love in missile silos. Our troops both at home and overseas lost every shred of discipline, and God alone knows what took place aboard our Navy's far-flung ships. The moral Collapse engulfed our entire Nation, reaching up even into the House of Representatives and the Senate. It was unfortunate that Mike Wallace and his camera crew happened to be in the Senate gallery the afternoon that the orgy broke out, but inasmuch as Wallace himself and everyone else in the gallery soon joined in the debauchery, the videotape footage was poorly focused and of minimal quality. At any rate, by the time CBS News decided to show it on television, everyone was much too busy fornicating to watch others doing the same thing.

Only the fact that the Piece Movement spread with the speed of light through Europe, Asia, and Africa has saved our beloved United States from total annihilation at the hands of the Godless Communists. Western Europe fell into a frenzy of lust, especially Italy, where the Leaning Tower of Pisa finally toppled, but no one noticed or cared. The Pope ordered the Vatican sealed off from all outside contact. No one has heard a word from the Vatican for four months now, although there are rumors that certain of the younger Cardinals have been seen along the Via Venetto, dressed in mufti.

The Warsaw Pact nations quickly fell to the Piece Movement, Poland being the first to succumb. According to some journalists, the Movement averted an imminent Russian invasion and thus saved the Poles from further repression. Martial law collapsed overnight (literally) in Poland, and the Russian troops assigned to crush Polish resistance were soon grappling with other matters. Tanks became bordellos, heavy artillery pieces became symbols of the new Movement, and were soon decorated with flowers by smiling Polish women and laughing Russian soldiers.

Despite every precaution, Russia itself fell to the onslaught. Reliable intelligence reports confirm that the sudden deaths of eight Politburo members (average age, seventy-three) can be attributed to the Movement. The USSR is in chaos, but the Russians do not seem to care.

Even China, long a model of organized patience, has

gone wild. Someone in Beijing found a maxim of Confucius which, roughly translated, means, ''If you can't beat them, join them.'' Seismographs as far away as San Francisco have borne vivid testimony to the vigor with which a billion Chinese are copulating.

Australia was the lone holdout, and I must confess that for several weeks I was tempted to emigrate Down Under. Separated from the rest of the world by the purifying ocean, this huge island continent remained steadfastly immune to the Piece Movement, mainly (I am told) because the average Australian male is inordinately shy of women and prefers to drink beer in the company of his fellow men, talking about sports rather than sex.

Unfortunately, a female American tourist—no doubt an *agent provocateur*—found the chink in the Aussie armor. She put the proposition in sporting terms. She bet the captain of the Australian Americas Cup yacht crew that his team could not equal the endurance record set recently by the crew of the American yacht, *Pulsar*. The Aussies accepted her challenge, although no one seems to know if they won the bet or not. No one has seen any of them since that fateful day.

However, once the average Australian male understood that the national honor was at stake, they leaped into the action with typical Australian enthusiasm. Sales of Forster's Lager have fallen nearly to zero, and Australian women are raising funds to erect a monument to the Unknown American Tourist.

That is the whole sad story. A complete moral Collapse, everywhere in the world. True, there are no viable armies, navies, air forces, or nuclear strike units anywhere on the globe anymore. There is no threat of war. People everywhere are concentrating whatever energies they have left, after fornicating all night, to harvest record crops of food— although the food is merely to keep them nourished enough to continue their eternal lechery.

The world is at peace. Everyone seems deliriously happy. But what good is the world if we have lost our immortal souls? My own dear wife has disappeared into the suburban warrens of Alexandria. Her last words to me were, "Josh, you're a party-poop!" I have sent out teams of investigators to locate her. None of them have returned. One was polite enough to send his badge and tape recorder back to the Agency, by mail. No return address.

The American economy, like most industrial economies, is flourishing. Industrial production seems to have benefitted from the Collapse. Retail sales of almost everything except guns are up: especially flowers, candy, and birth control devices. The Moral Majority has simply disappeared from the land. Yet, strangely, church attendance is increasing. However, the last minister to preach a sermon about the Sins of the Flesh was laughed out of his pulpit.

I must add, sir, that the rumors you may have heard about your own wife are entirely false. After very careful investigation, I can happily assure you that she has remained steadfastly true to you and you alone. I know that she gave away the pistol that she formerly kept on her person, but there appears to be no need for weapons anymore. Alas, why protect our bodies when we have already sold our souls? (Not that your wife has sold her soul, you understand. I merely meant that the incidence of violent crime has dropped to an undetectably low level. No one feels threatened anymore.)

The appropriate agencies are still searching for Ms. Morganthaler, but I do not hold out much hope for finding her. Most of the agents we have sent out have either disappeared or resigned.

I have no further desires now except to return to my ancestral home in the beloved green hills of Kentucky. A distant grand-niece of mine from back in Christian County has volunteered to drive me home this coming weekend.

She is a comely young thing, and she has given me great comfort during the past few trying weeks.

She asked me if she could bring a few of her girl friends with her. There is plenty of room in the car. Therefore, I respectfully request to be relieved of my duties to you, sir, so that I can retire to my home, far from the turmoil of this modern world, to spend my remaining days in peace and contentment, as best I can.

Out of Time

The first day of the trial, the courtroom had been as hectic as a television studio, what with four camera crews and all their lights, dozens of reporters, all the extra cops for security, and just plain gawkers. But after eight months, hardly any onlookers were there when Don Carmine Lombardo had his heart attack.

The *cappo di tutti cappi* for the whole New England region clawed at his chest and made a few gasping, gargling noises in the middle of his brother-in-law's incredibly perjured testimony, struggled halfway out of his chair, then collapsed across the table in front of him, scattering the notes and depositions neatly laid out by his quartet of lawyers as he slid to the floor like a limp sack of overcooked spaghetti.

The rumor immediately sprang up that his brother-in-law's testimony, in which he described the Don as a God-fearing family man who had become immensely wealthy merely by hard work and frugality, brought down the

vengeance of the Lord upon the old man. This is probably
not true. The heart attack was no great surprise. Don
Carmine was almost eighty, grossly overweight, and given
to smoking horrible little Sicilian rum-soaked cigars by the
boxful.

The most gifted and expensive physicians in the Western world were flown to Rhode Island in the valiant attempt to save the Don's life. Tenaciously, the old man
hung on for six days, then, like the God he was said to
have feared, he relaxed on the seventh. He was declared
dead jointly by the medical team, no single one of them
wishing to take the responsibility of making the announce-
ment to the stony-eyed men in their perfectly-tailored silk
suits who waited out in the hospital's corridors, eating
pizzas brought in by muscular errand boys and conversing
in whispered mixtures of Italian and English.

But Don Carmine did not die before issuing orders that
his body be preserved in liquid nitrogen. Perhaps he truly
did fear God. If there was any chance that he could survive
death, he was willing to spend the money and take the
risk.

"What is this cryo . . . cryology or whatever the hell
they call it?" snarled Angelo Marchetti. He was not angry.
Snarling was his normal mode of conversation, except
when he did get angry. Then he bellowed.

"Cryonics," said his lawyer, Pat del Vecchio.

"They froze him in that stuff," Marchetti said. "Like
he was a popsickle."

Del Vecchio was a youngster, one of the new breed of
university-trained legal talents that was slowly, patiently
turning the Mob away from its brutal old ways and toward
the much more profitable pursuits of computer crime and
semi-legitimate business. There was far more money to be
made, at far less risk, in toxic waste disposal than in
narcotics. Let the Latinos cut each other up over the drug
trade. Let one state after another legalize gambling. Del

Vecchio knew the wave of the future: more money was stolen with a few touches of the fingers on the right computer keyboard than with all the guns the old-timers liked to carry.

Marchetti was one of the last surviving old-timers among the New England families. Bald, built like a squat little fireplug with a glistening, narrow-eyed bullet head stuck atop it, he had been a bully all his life. Once he cowed men with his fists. Now he used the threat of his powerful voice, and the organization behind him, to make men do his will. He had inherited Don Carmine's empire, but the thought that the Don might come back some day bothered him.

He sat on the patio of his luxurious home in Newport, gazing out at the lovely seascape formed by Narragansett Bay. The blue waters were dotted by dozens of white sails; the blue sky, by puffy white clouds. Marchetti often spent the afternoon out here, relaxing on his lounge chair, ogling the girls in their bathing suits through a powerful pair of binoculars. He was not oblivious to the fact that the great robber barons of the previous century had built their summer retreats nearby. The thought pleased him. But today he was worried about this scientific miracle called cryonics.

"I mean, is the old Don dead or ain't he?"

Del Vecchio, lean and dapper in a sharply-cut double-breasted ivory blazer and dark blue slacks, assured Marchetti, "He's legally, medically, and really dead."

Marchetti scowled suspiciously. "Then why didn't he wanna be buried?"

With great patience, del Vecchio explained that while the old man was clinically dead, there were some scientists who believed that perhaps in some far-distant future it might be possible to cure the heart problem that caused the death. So Don Carmine had himself frozen, preserved in liquid nitrogen at the temperature of 346 degrees below zero Fahrenheit.

"Christ, that's cold!" Marchetti growled.

At that temperature, del Vecchio said, the old man's body would be perfectly preserved for eternity. As long as the refrigerator wasn't turned off.

"And if the scientists ever find a way to fix what killed him, they can thaw him out and bring him back to life," the young lawyer concluded.

Marchetti squinted in the sunlight, his interest in the sailboats and even the bathing beauties totally gone now.

"Maybe," he said slowly, "somebody oughtta pull the plug out of that icebox." He pronounced the word in the old neighborhood dialect: *i-sa-bocks*.

Del Vecchio smiled, understanding his boss's reluctance to return the New England empire to a newly-arisen Don Carmine.

"Don't worry," he soothed. "There's one great big loophole in the situation."

"Yeah? What?"

"Nobody knows how to defrost a corpse, once it's been frozen. Can't be done without breaking up the body cells. Try to defrost Don Carmine and you'll kill him."

Marchetti laughed, a hearty, loud, blood-chilling roar. "Then he'll be twice as dead!" He laughed until tears streamed down his cheeks.

The years passed swiftly, too swiftly and too few for Angelo Marchetti. Despite del Vecchio's often-repeated advice that he get into the profits that can be skimmed from legalized casino gambling and banking, Marchetti could not change his ways. But the law enforcement agencies of the federal government were constantly improving their techniques and inevitably they caught up with him. Marchetti (he never thought to have himself styled "Don Angelo") was brought to trial to face charges of loan-sharking, tax evasion, and—most embarrassing of all—endangering the public health by improperly disposing of toxic wastes. One of the companies that del Vecchio had urged him to buy through a dummy corporation had gotten caught dumping chemical sludge into a public storm sewer.

Thirty pounds heavier than he had been the year that Don Carmine died, Marchetti sat once again on the patio behind his mansion. The binoculars rested on the flagstones beside his lounge chair; they had not been used all summer. Marchetti's eyesight was not what it once was, nor was his interest in scantily-clad young women. He lay on the lounge chair like a beached white whale in size 52 plaid bathing trunks.

"They've got the goods," del Vecchio was saying, gloomily.

"Ain't there nothin' we can do?"

Standing over his boss's prostrate blubber, the lawyer looked even more elegant that he had a few years earlier. Still lean and trim, there were a few lines in his face now that might have been wisdom, or debauchery, or both. He was deeply tanned, spending almost all his time under the sun, either during the New England summer or the Arizona and California winter. He even had a sunlamp system installed over his bed, encircling the smoked mirror on the ceiling.

"We've tried everything from change-of-venue to bribery," del Vecchio said. "Nothing doing. Uncle Sam's got your balls in a vise."

"How about putting some pressure on the witnesses?" Marchetti growled. "Knock off one or two and the rest'll clam up."

Del Vecchio shook his head. "Most of the 'witnesses' against you are computer records, tapes, floppy disks. The F.B.I. has them under tight security, and they've made copies of them, besides."

Marchetti peered up at his lawyer. "There's gotta be *something* you can do. I ain't goin' to jail—not while you're alive."

A hint of surprise flashed in del Vecchio's dark eyes for a moment, but Marchetti never saw it, hidden behind the lawyer's stylish sunglasses. Del Vecchio recognized the threat in his employer's words, but what shocked him was that the old man was getting desperate enough to make such a threat. Soon he would be lashing out in blind anger, destroying everything and everyone around him.

"There is one thing," he said slowly.

"What? What is it?"

"You won't like it. I know you won't."

"What the hell is it?" Marchetti bellowed. "Tell me!"

"Freezing."

"What?"

"Have yourself frozen."

"Are you nuts? I ain't dead!"

Del Vecchio allowed a slight smile to cross his lips. "No, but you could be."

Actually, the plan had been forming in his mind since Don Carmine's immersion in the gleaming stainless steel tank full of liquid nitrogen. Even then, del Vecchio had thought back to his college days when, as an agile young undergraduate, he had been a star on the school's fencing team. He remembered that there were strict rules of procedure in foil fencing, almost like the fussy rules of procedure in a criminal court. It was possible for a fencer to score a hit on his opponent, but have the score thrown out because he had not followed the proper procedure.

"Out of time!" he remembered his fencing coach screaming at him. "You can't just stab your opponent whenever the hell you feel like it! You've got to establish the proper right-of-way, the proper timing. You're out of time, del Vecchio!"

He realized that Marchetti was glowering at him. "Whattaya mean I could be dead?"

With a patient sigh, del Vecchio explained, "We've gotten your case postponed three times because of medical excuses. Dr. Brunelli has testified that you've got heart and liver problems."

"Fat lot of good that's done," Marchetti grumbled.

"Yeah, but suppose Brunelli makes out a death certificate for you, says you died of a heart attack, just like old Don Carmine."

"And they put somebody else into the ground while I take a vacation in the old country?" Marchetti's face brightened a little.

"No, that won't work. The law enforcement agencies are too smart for that. You'd be spotted and sent back here."

"Then what?"

"We make you clinically dead. Brunelli gives you an injection . . ."

"And kills me?" Marchetti roared.

Del Vecchio put his hands up, as if to defend himself. "Wait. Hear me out. You'll be clinically dead. We'll freeze you for a while. Then we'll bring you back and you'll be as good as ever!"

Marchetti scowled. "How do I know I can trust you to bring me back?"

"For God's sake, Angelo, you've been like a father to me ever since my real father died. You can trust me! Besides, you can arrange for a dozen different guys to see to it that you're revived. And a dozen more to knock me off if I try to keep you frozen."

"Yeah . . . maybe."

"You won't only be clinically dead," del Vecchio pointed out. "You'll be *legally* dead. Any and all charges against you will be wiped out. When you come back, legally you'll be a new person. Just like a baby!"

"Yeah?" The old man broke into a barking, sandpaper laugh.

"Sure. And just to make sure, we'll keep you frozen long enough so that the statute of limitations runs out on all the charges against you. You'll come out of that freezer free and clear!"

Marchetti's laughter grew louder, heartier. But then it abruptly stopped. "Hey, wait. Didn't you tell me that nobody knows how to defrost a corpse? If they try to thaw me out it'll kill me all over again!''

"That's all changed in the past six months," del Vecchio said. "Some bright kid down at Johns Hopkins thawed out some mice and rabbits. Then a couple weeks ago a team at Pepperdine brought back three people, two men and a woman. I hear they're going to thaw Walt Disney and bring him back pretty soon."

"What about Don Carmine?" asked Marchetti.

The lawyer shrugged. "That's up to you."

Without an instant's hesitation, Marchetti ran a stubby forefinger across his throat.

Del Vecchio had every intention of honoring his commitment to Marchetti. He really did. The fireplug-shaped old terror had truly been like a father to the younger man, paying his way through college and even law school after del Vecchio's father had been cut down in the line of duty one rainy night on the street outside a warehouse full of Japanese stereos and television sets.

But one thing led to another as the years rolled along. Del Vecchio finally married and started to raise a family. More and more of the Mob business came under his hands, and he made it prosper better than ever before. The organization now owned banks, resort hotels and other legitimate businesses. As well as state legislators, judges, and half-a-dozen Congressmen. Violent crime was left to the disorganized fools. Del Vecchio's regime was marked by peace, order, and upwardly-spiraling profits.

One after another, Marchetti's lieutenants came to depend on him. Del Vecchio never demanded anything as archaic and embarrassing as an oath of fealty, kissing the hand, or other ancient prostrations. But the lieutenants, some of them heavily-built narrow-eyed thugs, others more lean and stylish and modern, all let it be known, one way or the other, that to revive Marchetti from his cryonic slumber would be a terrible mistake.

So Marchetti slept. And del Vecchio saw his empire grow more prosperous.

But owning legitimate banks and businesses does not make one necessarily honest. Del Vecchio's banks often made highly irregular loans, and sometimes collected much higher interest than permitted by law. On rare occasions, the interest was collected only after brutal demonstrations of force. There were also some stock manipulations that finally attracted the attention of the Securities and Exchange Commission, and a string of disastrous fires in Mob-owned hotels that were on the verge of bankruptcy.

And even the lackadaisical state gambling commission roused itself when the federal income tax people started investigating the strange phenomenon of certain gambling casinos that took in customers by the millions, yet somehow failed to show a profit on their books.

Once he realized that there was no way out of the mounting legal troubles facing him, del Vecchio decided to take his own advice. Carefully, he began to create a medical history for himself that would end in clinical death and cryonic immersion. He explained what he was doing to his most trusted lieutenants, told them that he would personally take the blame and the legal punishment for them all, allowing them to elect a new leader and go on operating as before once he was declared dead. They expressed eternal gratitude.

But del Vecchio knew perfectly well how long eternal gratitude lasted. So he sent his wife and their teenaged children to live in Switzerland, where most of his personal fortune had been cached with the gnomes of Zurich. He gave his wife painfully detailed instructions on when and how to revive him.

"Fifteen years will do it," he told her. "Can you wait for me that long?"

She smiled limpidly at him, threw her arms around his neck and kissed him passionately. But she said, "I'll only be fifty-eight when you get out."

Del Vecchio wondered if she knew about his playmates in Boston. He realized he would still be his current age, forty-seven, when he was thawed back to life. There would be plenty of other women to play with. But would his wife remain faithful enough to have him revived? To make doubly certain of his future, he flew to Zurich and had a very tight legal contract drawn by the bank which held his personal fortune. The gnomes would free him, if no one else would. Otherwise his money would be donated to charity and the bank would lose control of it.

"What you're doing may be legal, Del, but it's damned immoral."

Del Vecchio was having dinner with one of the federal district attorneys who was prosecuting one of the innumerable current cases against him. They were old friends, had been classmates at law school. The fact that they were on opposite sides of the case did not bother either of them; they were too professional to allow such trivialities to get in the way of their social lives.

"Immoral?" Del Vecchio shot back. "What do I care about that? Morality's for little guys, for people who've got no muscle, no backbone. You worry about morality, I'm worrying about spending the rest of my life in jail."

They were sitting at a small corner table in a quiet little restaurant in downtown Providence, barely a block from the federal courthouse, a place frequented almost exclusively by lawyers who never lifted an eyebrow at a defendant buying dinner for a prosecuting attorney. After all, prosecuting attorneys rarely made enough money to afford such an elegant restaurant; candlelight and leather-covered wine lists were not for the protectors of the public, not on the salaries the public allowed them.

"If the jury finds you guilty, the judge has to impose the penalty," the district attorney said, very seriously.

"Jury," del Vecchio almost spat. "Those twelve *chidrools*! I'm supposed to be tried by a jury of my peers, right? That means my equals, doesn't it?"

The district attorney frowned slightly. "They are your equals, Del. What makes you think . . ."

"My equals?" del Vecchio laughed. "Do you really think those unemployed bums and screwy housewives are my equals? I mean, how smart can they be if they let themselves get stuck with jury duty?"

The attorney's frown deepened. His name was Christopher Scarpato. He had gone into the profession of law because his father, a small shopkeeper continually in debt to bookmakers, had insisted that his son learn how to outwit the rest of the world. While Chris was working his way through law school, his father was beaten to death by a pair of overly-zealous collection agents. More of a plodder than a brilliant student, Chris was recruited by the Department of Justice, where careful, thorough groundwork is more important than flashy public relations and passionate rhetoric. Despite many opportunities, he had remained honest and dedicated. Del Vecchio found that charming, even noteworthy, and felt quite superior to his friend.

"And what makes you think they'll find me guilty?" asked del Vecchio, just a trifle smugly. "They're stupid, all right, but can they be *that* stupid?"

Scarpato finally realized he was being baited. He smiled one of his rare smiles, but it was a sad one. "They'll find you guilty, Del. They've got no choice."

Del Vecchio's grin faded. He looked down at his plate of pasta, then placed his fork on the damask tablecloth alongside it. "I got no appetite. Haven't been feeling so good."

With a weary shake of his head, Chris replied, "You don't have to put on the act for me, Del. I know what you're going to do."

"What do you mean?"

"You're going to get some tame doctor to pronounce you dead and then have yourself frozen. Just like Marchetti."

Del Vecchio tried to look shocked, but instead he broke into a grin. "Is there anything illegal about dying? Or being frozen?"

"The doctor will be committing a homicide."

"You'll have to prove that."

Scarpato said, "It's an attempt to evade the law. That's immoral, even if it's not illegal—yet."

"Let the priests worry about morality," del Vecchio advised his old friend.

"You should worry about it," said Scarpato. "You've turned into an asocial menace, Del. When we were in school, you were an okay kind of guy. But now . . ."

"What, I'm going to lose my soul?"

"Maybe you've already lost it. Maybe you ought to be thinking about how you can get it back."

Del Vecchio grinned at him. "Listen, Chris: I don't give a damn about souls. But I'm going to protect my body, you can bet. You won't see me in jail, old buddy. I'm going to take a step out of time, and when I come back, you'll be an old man and I'll still be young."

Scarpato said nothing, and del Vecchio knew that he had silenced his friend's attempts at conscience.

Still, that little hint of "yet" that Scarpato had dropped bothered del Vecchio as the days swiftly raced by. He checked every aspect of his plan while his health appeared to deteriorate rapidly: the doctors played their part to perfection, his wife was already comfortably ensconced in Switzerland, the bankers in Zurish understood exactly what they had to do.

Yet as he lay on the clinic table with the gleaming stainless steel cylinder waiting beside him like a mechanical whale that was going to swallow him in darkness, del Vecchio could feel his pulse racing with fear. The last thing he saw was the green-gowned doctor, masked, approaching him with the hypodermic syringe. That, and frigid wisps of vapor wafting up from the tanks of liquid nitrogen. The needle felt sharp and cold. He remembered that parts of Dante's hell were frozen in ice.

When they awoke him, there was a long period of confusion and disorientation. They told him later that it lasted only a day or so, but to del Vecchio it seemed like weeks, even months.

At first he thought something had gone wrong, and they had never put him under. But the doctors were all different, and the room he was in was not the clinic he had known. They kept him in bed most of the time, except when two husky young men came in to force him to get up and walk around the room. Four times around the little hospital room exhausted him. Then they flopped him back on the bed, gave him a mercilessly efficient massage, and left. A female nurse wheeled in his first meal and spoon-fed him; he was too weak to lift his arms.

The second day (or week, or month) Scarpato came in to visit him.

"How do you feel, Del?"

Strangely, the attorney seemed barely to have aged at all. There was a hint of gray at his temples, perhaps a line or two in his face that had not been there before, but otherwise the years had treated him very kindly.

"Kind of weak," del Vecchio answered truthfully.

Scarpato nodded. "That's to be expected, from what the medics tell me. Your heart is good, circulation strong. Everything is okay, physically."

A thought suddenly flashed into del Vecchio's thawing mind. "What are you doing in Switzerland?"

The attorney's face grew somber. "You're not in Switzerland, Del. We had your vat flown back here. You're in New York."

"Wh . . . how . . . ?"

"And you haven't been under for fifteen years, either. It's only three years."

Del Vecchio tried to sit up in the bed, but he was too

weak to make it. His head sank back onto the pillows. He could hear his pulse thudding in his ears.

"I tried to warn you," Scarpato said, "that night at dinner in Providence. You thought you were outsmarting the law, outsmarting the people who make up the law, who *are* the law. But you can't outwit the people for long, Del."

Out of the corner of his eye, del Vecchio saw that the room's only window was covered with a heavy wire mesh, like bars on a jail cell's window. He choked back a shocked gasp.

Scarpato spoke quietly, without malice. "Your cute little cryonics trick forced the people to take a fresh look at things. There've been a few new laws passed since you had yourself frozen."

"Such as?"

"Such as the state has the right to revive a frozen corpse if and when a grand jury feels he's had himself frozen specifically to evade the law."

Del Vecchio felt his heart sink in his chest.

"But once they got that one passed, they went one step further."

"What?"

"Well, you know how the country's been divided about the death penalty. Some people think it's cruel and unusual punishment; others think it's a necessary deterrent to crime, especially violent crime. Even the Supreme Court has been split on the issue."

Del Vecchio couldn't catch his breath. He realized what was coming.

"And there's been the other problem," Scarpato went on, "of overcrowding in the jails. Some judges—I'm sure you know who—even let criminals go free because they claim that putting them in overcrowded jails is cruel and unusual punishment."

"Oh my God in heaven," del Vecchio gasped.

"So—" Scarpato hesitated. Del Vecchio had never seen

his old friend look so grim, so purposeful. "So they've passed laws in just about every state in the union to freeze criminals, just store them in vats of liquid nitrogen. Dewars, they call them. We're emptying the jails, Del, and filling them up again with dewars. They're starting to look like mortuaries, all those stainless steel caskets piled up, one on top of another."

"But you can't do that!"

"It's done. The laws have been passed. The Supreme Court has ruled on it."

"But that's murder!"

"No. The convicts are clinically dead, but not legally. They can be revived. And since the psychologists and sociologists have been yelling for years that crime is a social maladjustment, and not really the fault of the criminal, we've found a way to make them happy."

"I don't see . . ."

Scarpato almost smiled. "Well, look. If you can have yourself frozen because you've just died of a heart ailment or a cancer that medical science can't cure, in the hopes that science will find a cure in the future and thaw you out and make you well again . . . well, why not use the same approach to social and psychological illnesses?"

"Huh?"

"You're a criminal because of some psychological maladjustment," Scarpato said. "At least, that's what the head-shrinkers claim. So we freeze you and keep you frozen until science figures out a way to cure you. That way, we're not punishing you; we're *rehabilitating* you."

"You can't do that! I got civil rights . . ."

"Your civil rights are not being infringed. Once you're found guilty by a jury of your peers you will be frozen. You will not age a single day while in the liquid nitrogen. When medical science learns how to cure your psychological unbalance, you will be thawed, cured, and returned to society as a healthy, productive citizen. We even start a small bank account for you which accrues compound interest, so that you'll have some money when you're rehabilitated."

"But that could be a thousand years in the future!" del Vecchio screamed.

"So what?"

"The whole world could be completely changed by then! They could revive me to make a slave out of me! They could use me for meat, for Chrissakes! Or spare parts!" He was screeching now, in absolute terror.

Scarpato shrugged. "We have no control over that, unfortunately. But we're doing our best for you. In earlier societies you might have been tortured, or mutilated, or even put to death. Up until a few years ago, you would have been sentenced to years and years in prison; a degrading life, filled with violence and drugs and danger. Now— you just take a nap and then someday someone will wake you up in a wonderful new world, completely rehabilitated, with enough money to start a new life for yourself."

Del Vecchio broke into uncontrollable sobs. "Don't. For God's mercy, Chris, don't do this to me. My wife . . . my kids . . ."

Scarpato shook his head. "It's done. Believe me, there's no way I could get you out of it, even if I wanted to. Your wife has found herself a boyfriend in Switzerland, some penniless count or duke or something. Your kids are getting along fine. Your girlfriends miss you, though, from what I hear."

"You sonofabitch! You dirty, scheming . . ."

"You did this to yourself, Del!" Scarpato snapped, with enough power in his voice to silence del Vecchio. "You thought you had found a nice fat loophole in the law, so you could get away with almost anything. You thought the rest of us were stupid fools. Well, you made a loophole, all right. But the people—those shopkeepers and unemployed bums and screwy housewives that you've walked over all your life—they've turned your loophole into a noose. And your neck is in it. Don't blame me. Blame yourself.''

His eyes still flowing tears, del Vecchio pleaded, ''Don't do it to me, Chris. Please don't do it. They'll never wake me up. They'll pull the plug on me . . .''

''Don't think that everyone's as dishonest as you are. The convicts will be kept frozen. It only costs a thousandth of what it costs to keep a man in jail. You'll be safe enough.''

''But they'll thaw me out sometime in the future. I'll be all alone in the world. I won't know anybody. It'll be all strange to me. I'll be a total stranger ... .''

''No you won't,'' Scarpato said, his face grim. ''It's practically certain that Marchetti and Don Carmine will both be thawed out when you are. After all, you're all three suffering from the same dysfunction, aren't you?''

That's when the capillary in del Vecchio's brain ballooned and burst. Scarpato saw his friend's eyes roll up into his head, his body stiffen. He slammed the emergency call button beside the bed and a team of medics rushed in. While Scarpato watched, they declared del Vecchio clinically dead. Within an hour they slid his corpse into a waiting stainless steel cylinder where it would repose until some happier day in the distant future.

''You're out of time now, Del,'' Scarpato whispered as a technician sealed the end of the gleaming dewar. ''Really out of time.''

Science Fiction
and Reality

Once a year, with the regularity of springtime, Sylvia Burack suggests that I write an article for her magazine, The Writer. *She is a remarkable woman and a dear friend, and she always manages to hit upon an intriguing idea that fastens itself inside my brain and refuses to let go until I've completed the requested article. For the prospective writers among us, this essay, thanks to Sylvia Burack, a woman who has spent her life trying to help writers.*

Writers are always urged to base their stories on their own experiences. "Write what you know about," is the watchword. But in science fiction, where the story is inevitably set in a world that does not exist here and now, how can you "write what you know about?"

To make the problem even more confusing, most science fiction stories are written in a very naturalistic, realis-

tic style. Fantastic scenes and incredible deeds are set on
paper in a fashion that's almost journalistic. The "grand old
men" of the field—H. G. Wells and Jules Verne—wrote
with meticulous attention to realistic detail. Modern science
fiction writers lean much more toward Mark Twain and
Ernest Hemingway, stylistically, than they lean toward
Henry James or William Faulkner.

How can you write realistically about things that have
never happened, places that no human eye has ever seen,
times that are yet to come?

Over the many decades of science fiction's existence as
a distinct literary form, science fiction writers have developed skills and techniques that have allowed them to explore the whole wide universe of space and time in stories
that are wholly believable. In fact, in many cases science
fiction stories are more realistic than the neurotic mum-
blings of so-called "contemporary" fiction. (Indeed, this
is one reason why many writers from outside the science
fiction field are using science fiction ideas and techniques
to write their stories today.)

We should pay special attention to six of the techniques
that the science fiction writers have developed. They are:

1. Characterization
2. Extrapolation
3. Research
4. Projection
5. Speculation
6. Consistency

Characterization. Every piece of fiction succeeds or
fails on the strength of the story's characters. Readers
identify with strong, well-defined characters. They tend to
dismiss stories in which the characters are dull or demeaning.

Many science fiction stories have been written in which
the characters play a strictly secondary role to the scientific
or political ideas in the story. For the most part, these are
"gimmick" stories—interesting, but not memorable. The

best science fiction stories, just like the best of any kind of
fiction, present interesting characters who struggle mightily to solve weighty problems.

The best—and easiest—way to make a story realistic is
to people it with realistic characters. Always pattern fictional characters on people you know personally and have
studied firsthand for some time. A painter or a sculptor
uses a model for his work; why shouldn't a writer? Don't
be afraid that your model will recognize him or herself in
the finished story. As you write, the story's characters will
take on their own personalities—each character in the story
will become a blend of several persons you know, plus
your own fictional inventions. People hardly ever recognize themselves in fiction, unless their "portrait" has been
very deliberately made into an exact replica of the model.

Write about people you know, and emotions that you
have personally experienced. If the closest you have been
to the Pentagon is a hike through the woods of Virginia,
don't expect to be able to write realistically about the inner
workings of the men and women in the Pentagon!

In science fiction, the characters are not always human
beings. They can be alien creatures, robots, computers, or
even intelligent dolphins. *But they must behave like humans*, or they will either bore or baffle the reader. Each
character, no matter what he/she/it looks like, must experience human problems and show some semblance of human
emotions. Think of Spock, on TV's classic *Star Trek*
series. He is alien in appearance and most of the time he is
alien in behavior. But underneath it all (and not so deep
that the viewer cannot see it) Spock has human emotions
of loyalty, courage, humor and love.

Arthur C. Clarke made the computer HAL the most
human character of his *2001: A Space Odyssey*. HAL had
great strengths, but he went neurotic, became a murderer,
and was "executed" by the robot-like human astronaut in
the story. Everyone who saw that film felt a pang of regret
as HAL was "turned off."

Robert A. Heinlein—another giant of the field—created

an even more human-like computer in his masterful novel, *The Moon Is a Harsh Mistress*. This computer, nicknamed Mike (after Mycroft, Sherlock Holmes' older brother) led a war of liberation on the Moon, and suffered tragically as a result.

In science fiction, the characters don't all have to look human, but they must behave in human ways. The reader will accept, trust, *believe* a story that has interesting, exciting, believable characters in it.

Extrapolation. Many science fiction stories are triggered when the author asks a question that begins with, "If this goes on . . . ?"

If we use up all the energy fuels on Earth without developing new energy sources to replace them, what happens?

If medical science finds cures for every disease and people begin to live for hundreds or even thousands of years, how does the world change?

If nuclear weapons proliferate to the point where every nation has H-bombs . . .

If computers and automated machinery take over *all* the jobs . . .

If we find intelligent life in space . . .

If we successfully clone human beings . . .

All these "ifs" are the beginnings of valid science fiction stories. Writers have learned to start story ideas perking by taking the world exactly as it is today, and then following one of these "ifs" to the point where an interesting story begins to develop. You may have to extrapolate several centuries into the future. Or only as far as next week.

H. G. Wells established the technique of starting his stories in a completely contemporary setting. Everything quite normal and here-and-now. Then he would add one tiny change to the scene: a time machine, a serum for invisibility, an invasion from Mars. The story then showed how our here-and-now world would alter as a result of this change.

Classic science fiction formula!

Research. No writer knows everything. Especially when

you are dealing with the future, with events that have not happened and places where no human being has set foot, you cannot know enough to build a realistic story entirely out of your imagination.

Fantasies can be written strictly from imagination. But a good science fiction story demands realistic details. If your story is set on one of the moons of Jupiter, you had better know something about the physical conditions of that place, otherwise your story will not ring true. (And there are plenty of science fiction *readers* who will gleefully point out any errors of fact that you may make!)

Once I wanted to write a "man against nature" story—a sort of latter-day Jack London tale—set on the Moon. This was years before the Apollo astronauts landed there, but NASA and the Russians had put enough hardware on the Moon so that it was possible to draw a fairly accurate picture of what conditions there must be.

The story I eventually wrote was titled "Fifteen Miles." Its description of the Moon's surface is valid today, largely because I immersed myself in every available book, report, and photograph of the Moon's surface before I wrote the story.

Research is vital to realism.

It stands to reason that if the best stories come from "writing what you know about," and you want to write stories about places where no one has ever been—then you must at least do enough homework to learn what is known about such places.

Much of the phoniness that is apparent in many science fiction films and television shows stems from the fact that the Hollywood people don't do much research. They think nobody knows or cares about realism in science fiction. That is why their shows inevitably seem hollow and stilted.

Become a thorough researcher. Learn all there is to know about a subject before you write about it. *Then* you can add your own imaginative details to this basic background of fact. This will produce stories that are highly colorful, yet totally believable.

Projection. This is one of the oldest science fiction tricks. Take an episode from history and "project" it into the future.

Isaac Asimov's brilliant *Foundation* series began when Dr. Asimov started thinking about Gibbon's massive *The Decline and Fall of the Roman Empire*. Many of the "fantastic" battles in deep space in E. E. "Doc" Smith's epic novels are based on actual naval battles fought on the oceans of Earth. My own first novel was a "projection" of the conquests of Alexander the Great into an interstellar setting.

Take a bit of history that interests you—the American Revolution, the travels of Marco Polo, the struggles of a great artist—and project them into a futuristic setting. At least you start your story with a strong sense of character and plot. From there on, it's up to you.

Speculation. If extrapolation begins by asking the question, "If this goes on . . . ?" then speculation starts by asking, "What if . . . ?"

What if a new Ice Age begins covering North America with glaciers?

What if flying saucers really are visitors from other worlds?

What if Russia conquers the world? What if *we* do?

At first glance, it might seem that speculation is just the opposite of realism. Certainly, where the techniques of research, extrapolation, and even projection all deal with carefully building up a realistic future scenario on the basis of presently-known facts, the technique of speculation seems to be a wild, blind leap into the unknown.

But speculation is often necessary for a good science fiction story. If your story has *only* carefully-researched facts and small extrapolations into the near future, you may end up with a story that's tame, dull, predictable. And if there's one thing that's death to a story, it is predictability. The reader must be kept guessing, must be surprised and delighted with each turn of the page. Otherwise, the reader stops turning those pages.

Extrapolation is a carefully worked-out step into the future, a step that is solidly based on known facts. Speculation is a longer leap—often into a much more distant future. But even so, speculation can be based on solid grounds, too.

Perhaps another word for speculation might be "intuition." In the early 1940s, when Heinlein was writing the interconnected stories and novels that we now call his Future History Series, he speculated that the United States would put men on the Moon, and then forget about spaceflight for many years; that the period of the 1970s would see such social upheavals that it would be known as "the crazy years;" that a religious dictatorship would rule the U.S. by the end of the twentieth century.

None of these speculations was taken very seriously; they were merely good story material. There was no basis of fact, in the 1940s, on which to base such speculations.

But Heinlein had a good feel for the temper of the American people. We reached the Moon, and then more-or-less forgot about it. The '70s were marked by tremendous social unrest and personal chaos. And who is to say that the current revival of fundamentalist religious fervor will not lead to a religiously-based government in another decade or two?

Speculation, when it is based on keen observation of today's world and an intuitive jump into the future, can help produce realistic science fiction.

Remember this: When experts make predictions of the future, they are almost invariably wrong, simply because they do not dare speculate freely. Only a science fiction writer can make seemingly wild speculations about the future.

Urban planners of the 1880s worried about the growing

number of horses in our cities; speculative writers "predicted" horseless carriages.

Military experts of the 1930s built huge fortifications such as the Maginot Line. Science fiction writers were worrying about the use of nuclear weapons and biological warfare.

Government advisors of the 1950s totally ignored the problems to come from the population explosion; science fiction stories were rife with population explosion problems.

Today's experts worry about energy shortages, while science fiction writers demonstrate that there are enormous sources of energy available from solar power satellites, hydrogen fuels, and nuclear fusion.

Speculation is important to science fiction. But it must be informed speculation, not just wild imaginings. Like the other techniques we have discussed, your speculations must start from a solid grounding in fact.

Consistency. Every story must be internally consistent. There is no surer way to confuse or exasperate a reader than to produce a story in which the parts do not work together to produce a harmonious, believable whole.

You couldn't have an advanced, self-aware computer such as HAL, for example, in a society where there are such energy shortages that people are burning wood to stay warm. You can't have bathing beauties sunning themselves in bikinis on the sands of Mars. You can't solve your hero's problems by suddenly having him discover a magic lamp in the cockpit of his spacecraft.

Such inconsistencies would jar the reader and put an end to his "suspension of disbelief."

Each facet of a story must mesh smoothly with all the other facets. If you'll forgive still another reference to my own work, here's how I used these techniques in my novel, *Millennium:*

Characters: the major character is a former astronaut who is now in command of a U.S. base on the Moon. I have lived and worked with military officers, fliers, and astronauts for many years. I know how they think, talk, act. (At least, I think I do!)

Extrapolation: The U.S. and the Soviet Union have been engaged in a global competition since the end of World War II. *If this goes on,* I asked myself, when both nations have bases on the Moon, what will happen?

Research: A good deal of my non-writing work, and most of my leisure time, was taken up by studying everything available on the nature of the Moon and the technologies that would allow people to live and work there.

Projection: All through history, whenever a colony of any nation has achieved self-sufficiency, that colony has opted for its own independence. So what would happen when the Russian and American bases on the Moon reached physical and economic self-sufficiency? How would they go about obtaining their independence?

Speculation: I assumed that by the end of this century, we would have permanent self-sufficient bases on the Moon. And laser-armed satellites in orbit around the Earth, ready to shoot down ballistic missiles on command from Washington or Moscow.

All these factors worked together, reinforced one another, to produce a story that was internally consistent. If any of these factors had been absent, the story would have been weakened considerably.

There are many kinds of fiction—fantasy, gothic, romance, horror, certain types of detective stories—in which realism is not terribly important. There are even some kinds of science fiction where realism is not vital. But the science fiction that seems to attract the widest audience (and therefore pays best) is the type where realism *is* necessary.

It is never easy to write good fiction, of any kind. But it is perfectly possible to write realistic science fiction if you pay honest attention to the techniques we have discussed here. Imagination is all-important, of course. But for good science fiction, imagination must work in tandem with knowledge.

To Be or Not

The preceding essay dealt with science fiction and reality. Herewith, four works which treat reality in four different ways: four separate facets of the Astral Mirror, so to speak.

"To Be Or Not" pokes a little fun at what passes for creativity out in the semi-sacred hills of Hollywood.

"The Man Who Saw Gunga Din Thirty Times" might not be intelligible, I confess, to anyone who has not seen that motion picture more than once. It is frankly an experimental story, one that shaped itself out of my subconscious as I sat and typed it. Gunga Din, incidentally, is still the best movie Hollywood ever made, the nine-year-old boy inside me keeps on insisting. Cavalry charges, elephants, a temple of gold, villains who are bad, heroes who are good, a great script with terrific lines even for the bad guys, Gary Grant, Victor McLaughlin, and Douglas Fairbanks, Jr. Who could ask for more?

143

Lest you sophisticates out there start smirking, let me tell you that a few years ago, as I watched Gunga Din *for about the fiftieth time in a theater in urbanely sophisticated Greenwich Village, in the romantic scene in which Doug Fairbanks kisses Joan Fontaine so hard that it knocks her hat off, a sigh arose in that darkened theater from the chic, with-it females that was loud enough to hear across the street.*

The System *is a nasty little short-short story, written several years before government agencies started taking the responsibility for deciding who would receive lifesaving kidney dialysis therapy and who would not.*

Cement *is a non-fact article, a silly little idea that just might be true. It is a variant on reality that can be published only within the science fiction genre, because the rest of the publishing world is simply not equipped to deal with such ideas.*

Year: 2007 A.D.
NOBEL PRIZE FOR PHYSICAL ENGINEERING: Albert Robertus Leoh, for application of simultaneity effect to interstellar flight
OSCAR/EMMY AWARD: Best dramatic film, "The Godfather, Part XXVI"
PULITZER PRIZE FOR FICTION: Ernestine Wilson, "The Devil Made Me"

Al Lubbock and Frank Troy shared an office. Not the largest in Southern California's entertainment industry, but adequate for their needs. Ankle-deep carpeting. Holographic displays instead of windows. Earthquake-proof building.

Al looked like a rangy, middle-aged cowboy in his rumpled blue jumpsuit. Frank wore a traditional Wall Street vested suit of golden brown, neat and precise as an accountant's entry. His handsome face was tanned; his body had the trimness of an inveterate tennis player. Al played tennis, too, but he won games instead of losing weight.

The walls of their office were covered with plaques and shelves bearing row after row of awards—a glittering array of silver and gold plated statuettes. But as they slumped in the foam chairs behind their double desk, they stared despondently at each other.

"Ol' buddy," Al said, still affecting a Texas drawl, "I'm fresh out of ideas, dammit."

"This whole town's fresh out of ideas," Frank said sadly.

"Nobody's got any creativity anymore."

"I'm awfully tired of having to write our own scripts," Frank said. "You'd think there would be at least one creative writer in this industry."

"I haven't seen a decent script in three years," Al grumbled.

"Or a treatment."

"An *idea*, even." Al reached for one of his nonhallucinogenic cigarettes. It came alight the instant it touched his lips.

"Do you suppose," he asked, blowing out blue smoke, "that there's anything to this squawk about pollution damaging people's brains?"

Frowning, Frank reached for the air-circulation control knob on his side of the desk and edged it up a bit. "I don't know," he answered.

"It'd effect the lower income brackets most," Al said.

"That *is* where the writers come from," Frank admitted slowly.

For a long moment they sat in gloomy silence.

"Damn!" Al said at last. "We've just *got* to find some creative writers."

"But where?"

"Maybe we could make a few . . . you know, clone one of the old-timers who used to be good."

Frank shook his head carefully, as if he was afraid of making an emotional investment. "That doesn't work. Look at the Astaire clone they tried. All it does is fall down a lot."

"Well, you can't raise a tap dancer in a movie studio," Al said. "They should have known that. It takes more than an exact copy of his genes to make an Astaire. They should have reproduced his environment, too. His whole family. Especially his sister."

"And raised him in New York City during World War I?" Frank asked. "You know no one can reproduce a man's whole childhood environment. It just can't be done."

Al gave a loose-jointed shrug. "Yeah. I guess cloning won't work. That Brando clone didn't pan out either."

Frank shuddered. "It just huddles in a corner and picks its nose."

"But where can we get writers with creative talent?" Al demanded.

There was no answer.

Year: 2012 A.D.
NOVEL PRIZE FOR SCIENCE AND/OR MEDI-
CINE: Jefferson Muhammed X, for developing
technique of re-creating fossilized DNA
OSCAR/EMMY/TONY AWARD: Best entertain-
ment series, "The Plutonium Hour"
PULITZER PRIZE FOR FICTION OR DRAMA:
No award

It was at a party aboard the ITT-MGM orbital station that Al and Frank met the real estate man. The party was floating along in the station's zero-gravity section, where the women had to wear pants but didn't need bras. A thousand or so guests drifted around in three dimensions, sucking drinks from plastic globes, making conversation over the piped-in music, standing in midair up, down, or sideways as they pleased.

The real estate man was a small, owlish-looking youngster of thirty, thirty-five. "Actually, my field is astrophysics," he told Al and Frank. Both of them looked quite distinguished in iridescent gold formal suits and stylishly graying temples. Yet Al still managed to appear slightly mussed, while Frank's suit had creases even on the sleeves.

"Astrophysics, eh?" Al said, with a happy-go-lucky grin. "Gee, way back in college I got my Ph.D. in molecular genetics."

"And mine in social psychology," Frank added. "But there weren't any jobs for scientists then."

"That's how we became TV producers," Al said.

"There still aren't any jobs for scientists," said the astrophysicist-real estate man. "And I know all about the two of you. I looked you up in the *IRS Who's Who*. That's why I inveigled my way into this party. I just *had* to meet you both."

Frank shot Al a worried glance.

"You know the Heinlein Drive has opened the stars to humankind," asked the astro-realtor rhetorically. "This means whole new worlds are available to colonize. It's the biggest opportunity since the Louisiana Purchase. Dozens of new Earthlike planets, unoccupied, uninhabited, pristine! Ours for the taking!"

"For a few billion dollars apiece," Frank said.

"That's small potatoes for a whole world!"

Al shook his head, a motion that made his whole weightless body start swaying. "Look fella . . . we're TV producers, not land barons. Our big problem is finding creative writers."

The little man clung to Al tenaciously. "But you'd have a whole new *world* out there! A fresh, clean, unspoiled new world!"

"Wait a minute," Frank said. "Psychologically, . .

maybe a new world is what we need to develop new writers.''

"Sure,'' the astro-realtor agreed.

A gleam lit Al's eye. ''The hell with new writers. How about re-creating old writers?''

"Like Schulberg?''

"Like Shakespeare.''

> Year: 2037 A.D.
> NOBEL PRIZE FOR SCI-MED: Cobber McSwayne, for determining optimal termination time for geriatrics patients
> OSCAR/EMMY/TONY/HUGO/EDGAR/ET AL. AWARD: The California Earthquake
> PULITZER PRIZE FOR WRITING: Krissy Jones, "Grandson of Captain Kangaroo''

Lubbock & Troy was housed in its own satellite now. The ten-kilometer-long structure included their offices, living quarters, production studios, and the official Hollywood Hall of Fame exhibit hall. Tourists paid for the upkeep, which was a good thing because hardly anyone except children watched new dramatic shows.

"Everything's reruns,'' Frank complained as he floated weightlessly in their foam-walled office. He was nearly sixty years old, but still looked trim and distinguished. Purified air and careful diet helped a lot.

Al looked a bit older, a bit puffier. His heart had started getting cranky, and the zero-gravity they lived in was a necessary precaution for his health.

"There aren't any new ideas,'' Al said from up near the office's padded ceiling. ''The whole human race's creative talents have run dry.'' His voice had gotten rather brittle with age. Snappish.

"I know I can't think of anything new anymore,'' Frank said. He began to drift off his desk chair, pushed himself down and fastened the lap belt.

"Don't worry, ol' buddy. We'll be hearing from New Stratford one of these days."

Frank looked up at his partner. "We'd better. The project is costing us every cent we have."

"I know," Al answered. "But the Shakespeare's World exhibit is pulling in money, isn't it? The new hotels, the entertainment complex . . ."

"They're all terribly expensive. They're draining our capital. Besides, that boy in New Stratford is a very expensive proposition. All those actors and everything."

"Willie?" Al's youthful grin broke through his aging face. "He'll be okay. Don't worry about him. I supervised that DNA reconstruction myself. Finally got a chance to use my ol' college education."

Frank nodded thoughtfully.

"That DNA's perfect," Al went on, "right down to the last hydrogen atom." He pushed off the ceiling with one hand and settled slowly down toward Frank, at the desk. "We've got an exact copy of William Shakespeare—at least, genetically speaking."

"That doesn't guarantee he'll write Shakespeare-level plays," Frank said. "Not unless his environment is a faithful reproduction of the original Shakespeare's. It takes an *exact* reproduction of both genetics and environment to make an exact duplicate of the original."

"So?" Al said, a trifle impatiently. "You had a free hand. A whole damned planet to play with. Zillions of dollars. And ten years' time to set things up."

"Yes, but we knew so little about Shakespeare's boyhood when we started. The research we had to do!"

Al chuckled to himself. It sounded like a wheezing cackle. "Remember the look on the lawyers' faces when we told 'em we had to sign the actors to lifetime contracts?"

Frank smiled back at his partner. "And the construction crews, when they found out that their foremen would be archeologists and historians?"

Al perched lightly on the desk and worked at catching

his breath. Finally he said, more seriously, "I wish the kid would hurry up with his new plays, though."

"He's only fifteen," Frank said. "He won't be writing anything for another ten years. You know that. He's got to be apprenticed, and then go to London and get a job with. . . ."

"Yeah, yeah." Al waved a bony hand at his partner.

Frank muttered, "I just hope our finances will hold out for another ten years."

"What? Sure they will."

Frank shrugged. "I hope so. This project is costing us every dollar we take from the tourists on Shakespeare's World, and more. And our income from reruns is dropping out of sight."

"We've got to hang on," Al said. "This is bigger than anything we've ever done, ol' buddy. It's the biggest thing to hit the industry since . . . since 1616. New plays. New originals, written by Shakespeare. Shakespeare! All that talent and creativity working for us!"

"New dramatic scripts." Frank's eyes glowed. "Fresh ideas. Creativity reborn."

"By William Shakespeare," Al repeated.

Year: 2059 A.D.
NOBEL PRIZE FOR THINKING: Mark IX of
Tau Ceti Computer Complex, for correlation of
human creativity index with living space
ALL-INCLUSIVE SHOWBIZ AWARD: *The Evening News*
PULITZER PRIZE FOR REWRITING: *The Evening News*

Neither Al nor Frank ever left their floater chairs anymore, except for sleeping. All day, every day, the chairs buoyed them, fed them intravenously, monitored their aging bodies, pumped their blood, worked their lungs, reminded them of memories that were fading from their minds.

Thanks to modern cosmetic surgery their faces still looked reasonably handsome and taut. But underneath their colorful robes they were more machinery than functional human bodies.

Al floated gently by the big observation port in their old office, staring wistfully out at the stars. He heard the door sigh open and turned his chair slowly around.

There was no more furniture in the office. Even the awards they had earned through the years had been pawned to the Hall of Fame, and when their creditors took over the Hall, the awards went with everything else.

Frank glided across the empty room in his chair. His face was drawn and pale.

"They're still not satisfied?" Al asked testily.

"Thirty-seven grandchildren, between us," Frank said. "I haven't even tried to count the great-grandchildren. They all want a slice of the pie. Fifty-eight lawyers, seventeen ex-wives . . . and the insurance companies! They're the worst of the lot."

"Don't worry, ol' buddy. They can't take anything more from us. We're bankrupt."

"But they still . . ." Frank's voice trailed off. He looked away from his old friend.

"What? They still want more? What else is there? You haven't told them about Willie, have you?"

Frank's spine stiffened. "Of course not. They took Shakespeare's World, but none of them know about Will himself, and his personal contract with us."

"Personal *exclusive* contract."

Frank nodded, but said, "It's not worth anything, anyway. Not until he gets some scripts to us."

"That ought to be soon," Al said, forcing his old optimistic grin. "The ship is on its way here, and the courier aboard said he's got ten plays in his portfolio. Ten plays!"

"Yes. But in the meantime . . ."

"What?"

"It's the insurance companies," Frank explained. "They claim we've both exceeded McSwayne's Limit and we ought to be terminated."

"Pull our plugs? They can't force . . ."

"They can, Al. I checked. It's legal. We've got a month to settle our debts, or they turn off our chairs and . . . we die."

"A month?" Al laughed. "Hell, Shakespeare's plays will be here in a month. Then we'll show 'em!"

"If . . ." Frank hesitated uncertainly. "If the project has been a success."

"A success? Of course, it's a success! He's writing plays like mad. Come on, ol' buddy. With your reproduction of his environment and my creation of his genes, how could he be anybody else except William goddam' Shakespeare? We've got it made, just as soon as that ship docks here."

The ship arrived exactly twenty-two days later. Frank and Al were locked in a long acrimonious argument with an insurance company's computer-lawyer over the legal validity of a court-ordered termination notice, when their last remaining servo-robot brought them a thick portfolio of manuscripts.

"Buzz off, tin can!" Al chortled happily and flicked the communicator switch off before the computer could object.

With trembling hands, Frank opened the portfolio. Ten neatly bound manuscripts floated out weightlessly. Al grabbed one and opened it. Frank took another one.

"Henry VI, Part One."

"Titus Andronicus!"

"The Two Gentlemen from Verona . . ."

Madly they thumbed through the scripts, chasing them all across the weightless room as they bobbed and floated through the purified air. After fifteen frantic minutes they looked up at each other, tears streaming down their cheeks.

"The stupid sonofabitch wrote the same goddam' plays all over again!" Al bawled.

"We reproduced him exactly," Frank whispered, aghast. "Heredity, environment . . . exactly."

Al pounded the communicator button on his chair's armrest.

"What . . . what are you doing?" Frank asked.

"Get me the insurance company's medics," Al yelled furiously. "Tell 'em to come on up here and pull my goddam' plug!"

"Me too!" Frank shouted with unaccustomed vehemence. "And tell them not to make any clones of us, either!"

The Man Who Saw
Gunga Din Thirty Times

Nosing the car through the growling traffic down Memorial Drive, autos clustered thick and sullen as Bombay thieves, the Charles River looking clear in the morning sunlight, the golden dome of the Capitol sparkling up on Beacon Hill, the sky a perfect Indian blue.

The temple of gold.

—What?—

Charlie's a perfect Higgenbottom type: capable in a limited way, self-centered, basically stupid.

The golden temple, I repeat.

—Oh, the Capitol. It's a wonder the goddam politicians haven't stolen *that* yet—

A Fiat bulging with bearded Harvard Square types cuts in front of us. I hit the brakes and Charlie lurches and grumbles—goddam hippies. They oughtta get a job—

They're in the morning traffic. Maybe they have jobs.

—Yeah. Undercutting some guy who's been working twenty years and has a family to support—

It was on the Late Show again last night, did you see it?
—See what?—

Gunga Din. The movie. Cary Grant. Doug Fairbanks, Jr., Victor McLaglen . . .

—What? They have that on again?—

It's the best movie Hollywood ever made. It has everything: golden temple, elephants, cavalry charges, real heroes. They don't make movies like that any more. Can't.

—They must have it on the Late Show every week—

No, it's been months since they showed it. I check *TV Guide* every week to make sure.

Charlie looks a little surprised, startled. Just like Higgenbottom when Cary Grant dropped that kilted Scottie corporal out the window.

I'll bet I've seen that movie thirty times, at least. I know every line of it, just about. They cut it terribly on television. Next time there's a Cary Grant film festival in New York I'm going down to see it. All of it. Without cuts.

Charlie says nothing.

We inch along, crawling down the Drive as slowly as the waterboy himself. I can see him, old Sam Jaffe all blacked over, heavy goatskin waterbag pulling one shoulder down, twisting his whole skinny body. White turban, white breechcloth. Staggering down the grassy walk alongside the Drive, keeping pace with us. If they made the movie now, they'd have to use a real Negro for the part. Or an Indian. For the guru's part, too. No Eduardo Cianelli.

We turn off at the lab. There are guards at the gates and more guards standing around in the parking lot. The lab building is white and square and looming, like Army headquarters—an oasis of science and civilization in the midst of the Cambridge slum jungles.

Even in uniform the guards look sloppy. They ought to take more pride in themselves. We drive past them slowly, like the colonel reviewing the regiment. The regimental band is playing *Bonnie Charlie*. The wind is coming down crisply off the mountains, making all the pennants flutter.

—Stockholders' meeting today. They're worried about some of these student protesters kicking up a rumpus.—

McLaglen would straighten them out. That's what they need, a tough sergeant major.

This time Charlie really looks sour.—McLaglen! You'd better come back into the real world. It's going to be a long day.—

For you, I say to myself. Accountant, paper shuffler. Money juggler. The stockholders will be after you. Not me. They don't care what I do, as long as it makes money. They don't care who it kills, as long as it works right and puts numbers in the right columns of your balance sheets.

The air-conditioning in my office howls like a wind tunnel. It's too cold. Be nice to have one of those big lazy fans up on the ceiling.

—Got a minute?—

Come on in, Elmer. What's the matter, something go wrong downstairs?

—Naw, the lab's fine. Everything almost set up for the final series. Just got to calibrate the spectrometer.—

But something's bothering you.

—I was wondering if I could have some time off to attend the stockholders' meeting—

Today? I didn't know you were a stockholder.

—Five shares.—

He's black. He's always seemed like a good lab technician, a reasonable man. But could he be one of them?

—I never been to a stockholders' meeting.—

Oh sure. You can go. But . . . we're not allowed to talk about PMD. Understand?

—Yeah, I know.—

Not that it's anything we're ashamed of—military security.

—Yeah I know.—

Good military form. Good regimental attitude. We've got to stand together against the darkness.

Elmer nods as he leaves, but I don't think he really

understands. When the time comes, when the Thugees rise in rebellion, which side will he join?

I wonder how I'd look in uniform? With one of those stiff collars and a sergeant's stripes on my sleeves. I'm about as tall as Grant, almost. Don't have his shoulders, though. And this flabby middle—ought to exercise more.

Through my office window I can see the world's ugliest water tower, one of Cambridge's distinguishing landmarks. Mountains, that's what should be out there. The solid rock walls of the Himalayas. And the temple of gold is tucked in them somewhere. Pure gold! Din was telling the truth. It's all gold. And I'm stuck here, like Cary Grant in the stockade. Get me out of here, Din. Get me out.

—Please, sahib, don't take away bugle. Bugle only joy for poor *bhisti*.—

He only wants to be one of us. Wants to be a soldier, like the rest of us. A bugler. McLaglen would laugh at him. Fairbanks would be sympathetic. Let him keep the bugle. He's going to need it.

—Tonight, when everyone sleeping. I go back to temple.—

Not now, Din. Not now. Got some soldiering to do. Down in the lab. Test out the new batch of PMD. A soldier's got to do his duty.

The phone. Don't answer it. It's only some civilian who wants to make trouble. Leave it ringing and get down to the lab. Wife, sister, mother, they're all alike. Yes, I'm a man, but I'm a soldier first. You don't want a man, you want a coward who'd run out on his friends. Well, that's not me and never was . . . No, wait—that's Fairbanks' speech. He's Ballantine. And who was the girl? Olivia de Haviland or her sister?

The halls are crawling with stockholders. Fat and old. Civilians. Visiting the frontier, inspecting the troops. We're the only thing standing between you and the darkness, but you don't know it. Or if you do, you wouldn't dare admit it.

The lab's always cold as ice. Got to keep it chilled down. If even a whiff of PMD gets out . . .

Elmer, hey, why isn't the spectrometer ready to go?

—You said I could go to the stockholders' meeting.—

Yes, but we've still got work to do. When does the meeting start?

—Ten sharp.—

Well, we've still got lots of time . . .

—It's ten of ten.—

What? Can't be . . . Is that clock right?

—Yep.—

He wouldn't have tampered with the clock; stop being so suspicious. O.K., go on to the meeting. I'll set it up myself.

—O.K., thanks.—

But I'm not by myself, of course. Good old grinnin' gruntin' Gunga Din. You lazarushin leather Gunga Din. He's not much help, naturally. What does an actor know about biochemistry? But he talks, and I talk, and the work gets done.

—Satisfactory, sahib?—

Very regimental, Din. Very regimental.

He glows with pride. White teeth against black skin. He'll die for us. They'll kill him, up there atop the temple of gold. The Thugees, the wild ones. The cult of death, worshippers of heathen idols. Kali, the goddess of blood.

Up to the roof for lunch. The stockholders are using the cafeteria. Let them. It's better up here, alone. Get the sun into your skin. Let the heat sink in and the glare dazzle your eyes.

My god, there they are! The heathens, the Thugees. Swarms of them grumbling outside the gate. Dirty, unkempt. Stranglers and murderers. Already our graves are dug. Their leader, he's too young to be Cianelli. And he's bearded; the guru should be clean-shaven. The guards look scared.

He's got a bullhorn. He's black enough to be the guru,

all right. What's he telling the crowd? I know what he's saying, even though he tries to disguise the words. Cianelli didn't hide it, he said it straight out: Kill lest you be killed yourselves. Kill for the love of killing. Kill for the love of Kali. Kill! Kill! Kill!

They howl and rush the gate. The guards are bowled over. Not a chance for them. The swarming heathen boil across the parking lot and right into the lab building itself. They're all over the place. Savages. I can smell smoke. Glass is shattering somewhere down there. People screaming.

One of the guards comes puffing up here. Uniform torn and sweaty, face red.

—Hey, Doc, better get down the emergency stairs right away. It ain't safe up here. They're burning your lab.—

I'm a soldier of Her Majesty the Queen. I don't bow before no heathen!

His eyes go wide. He's scared. Scared of rabble, of heathen rabble.

—I'll . . . I'll get somebody to help you, Doc. The fire engines oughtta be here any minute.—

Let him run. We can handle it. The Scotties will be here soon. I can hear their bagpipes now, or is it just the heat singing in my ears?

They'll be here. Get up on top of the temple dome, Din. Warn them. Sound your trumpet. The colonel's got to know! These dark incoherent forces of evil can't be allowed to win. You know that. Snake worshippers, formless, nameless shadows of death. The Forces of Light and Order have to win out in the end. Western organization and military precision always triumph. It will kill you, Din, I know. But that's the price of admission. We'll make you an honorary corporal in the regiment, Din. Your name will be written on the rolls of our honored dead.

They're coming; I know they're coming. The whole bloomin' regiment! Climb the golden dome and warn them. Warn them. Warn them!

The System

"Not just research," Gorman said, rocking smugly in his swivel chair, "*Organized* research."

Hopler, the cost-time analyst, nodded agreement.

"Organized," Gorman continued, "and carefully controlled—from above. The System—that's what gets results. Give the scientists their way and they'll spend you deaf, dumb, and blind on butterfly sex-ways or sub-subatomic particles. Damned nonsense."

Sitting on the front inch of the visitor's chair, Hopler asked meekly, "I'm afraid I don't see what this has to do . . ."

"With the analysis you turned in?" Gorman glanced at the ponderous file that was resting on a corner of his desk. "No, I suppose you don't know. You just chew through the numbers, don't you? Names, people, ideas . . . they don't enter into your work."

With an uncomfortable shrug, Hopler replied, "My job

is economic analysis. The System shouldn't be biased by personalities . . .''

"Of course not."

"But now that it's over, I would like to know . . . I mean, there've been rumors going through the Bureau."

"About the cure? They're true. The cure works. I don't know the details of it," Gorman said, waving a chubby hand. "Something to do with repressor molecules. Cancerous cells lack 'em. So the biochemists we've been supporting have found out how to attach repressors to the cancer cells. Stops 'em from growing. Controls the cancer. Cures the patient. Simple . . . now that we can do it."

"It . . . it's almost miraculous."

Gorman frowned. "What's miraculous about it? Why do people always connect good things with miracles? Why don't you think of cancer as a miracle, a black miracle?"

Hopler fluttered his hands as he fumbled for a reply.

"Never mind," Gorman snapped. "This analysis of yours. Shows the cure can be implemented on a nationwide basis. Not too expensive. Not too demanding of trained personnel that we don't have."

"I believe the cure could even be put into worldwide effect," Hopler said.

"The hell it can be!"

"What? I don't understand. My analysis . . ."

"Your analysis was one of many. The System has to look at all sides of the picture. That's how we beat heart disease, and stroke, and even highway deaths."

"And now cancer."

"No. Not cancer. Cancer stays. Demographic analysis knocked out all thoughts of using the cure. There aren't any other major killers around anymore. Stop cancer and we swamp ourselves with people. So the cure gets shelved."

For a stunned instant, Hopler was silent. Then, "But . . . I *need* the cure!"

Gorman nodded grimly. "So will I. The System predicts it."

Cement

Professor Uriah K. Pencilbeam, an obscure anthropologist from a virtually unknown small college in (where else?) southern California, has announced a theory that has sent shock waves throughout the myriad worlds of science, government, and industry.

"I don't believe a word of it," says Tony ("Slug") Solazzo, one of Los Angeles' leading building contractors. "This professor don't know what he's talking about."

But the head of the anthropology department of a prestigious Ivy League university has said of Pencilbeam's theory, "He's explained it all. There's nothing left for the rest of us to do except fill in a few of the details." The Ivy League anthropologist refused to allow his name to be used.

Briefly stated, Pencilbeam's theory is this: Governments exist for the benefit of building contractors. Indeed, Pencilbeam insists that governments were originally created, back in the Old Stone Age, so that building contractors could flourish.

As the professor himself puts it, "If it means pouring cement, a government will do it. If it doesn't mean pouring cement, a government *might* do it, but the chances are much slimmer."

In his startling research paper, which is already rumored to be in line for a Pulitzer Prize, Pencilbeam gives a long list of examples to bolster his thesis.

Ancient Egypt, he claims, was little more than a few scattered towns strung out along the Nile until the first Pharaoh united the Upper and Lower Kingdoms into a single political entity. Historians and paleontologists have always been puzzled as to the reasons for this sudden unification. Pencilbeam has the answer: the building contractors lobbied for unification so that they could get to build the colossal monuments that we still revere today: the pyramids, the sphinx, Cleopatra's Needle, etc.

Pencilbeam points out that the ancient civilization of Sumer, on the plain between the Tigris and Euphrates Rivers in what is now Iraq, was just as old and perhaps even older than Egypt. But they built their cities out of bricks made from dried mud. "No cement, no endurance," Pencilbeam says. The Sumerian civilization decayed while Egypt flourished for thousands of years.

Every conqueror and emperor, from Caesar through Napoleon, was secretly a front man for the construction contractors. Look at the money and effort they lavished on building their capital cities. Caesar was assassinated when he threatened to stop construction of the Circus Maximus, which was suffering from serious cost overruns and labor disputes. Napoleon practically rebuilt all of Paris, except for Montmartre, where the nightclub interests were already firmly entrenched. While his *Grand Armée* was freezing its collective butt in Russia, Napoleon's building contractors were amassing huge fortunes back home.

It is interesting to note that barbarian conquerors such as

Attilla, Genghis Khan, and Tambarlane had no lasting
impact on history despite their extensive conquests. This is
true precisely because they poured no cement, according to
Pencilbeam's theory. They came, they saw, they conquered, but they did not build any public monuments,
bridges, highways or condominium complexes. In Pencilbeam's view, one way to delineate a barbarian from a true
empire-builder is to look at the state of the construction
industry during a man's reign. Contrast Genghis Khan,
who conquered everything from the coast of China to the
Danube River, with Cecil Rhodes, the Victorian Englishman
who dreamed of a railroad from Cape Town to Cairo. How
many Khan Scholarships are there in the world today?

Pencilbeam's theory even explains much of recent and
current history. Adolph Hitler would have been the great-
est ruler of all time, considering the amount of cement he
expended on bunkers, pillboxes, tank traps, bomb shelters,
etc. Fortunately for the Allies, brilliant military thinkers
hit upon the idea of demolishing those constructions by
aerial bombardment and, also by bombing night and day,
preventing the Nazis from erecting new constructions. Unable to pour cement effectively, Nazi Germany eventually
collapsed.

In the United States it has long been known that if a
state or local government can start a construction project,
it will. Traditionally, the federal government's role has
been limited to constructing Post Offices and interstate
highways, except for Washington, D.C., where the amount
of cement used is obvious even to the most casual visitor.
(*Vide* the Washington Monument, the new Metro, *et al.*)

Even the US space program is no exception to Pencilbeam's penetrating theory. NASA was at its prime, with
virtually unlimited funding, in the 1960s when the space
agency was pouring megatonnages of cement for its facilities at Cape Canaveral, Houston, and elsewhere. Once
those facilities were built, once the cement hardened,
NASA's funding woes began. Not even the Space Shuttle

(which uses practically no cement at all) has significantly brightened NASA's funding picture.

Every valid scientific theory must be able to predict new phenomena, as well as explaining old ones. Pencilbeam points out that the MX missile program, which will require the expenditure of huge amounts of cement wherever and however the missiles are ultimately based, will certainly pass Congressional muster and go on to full-scale construction. Of course, the Russians—who are probably slightly ahead of the US in the cement race—might revert to the World War II tactic of demolishing the cement sites and establishing their own construction industry as supreme in the world.

If they do, Pencilbeam insists, the survivors of the nuclear exchange will undoubtedly start right in where civilization began: pouring cement and pressuring the government for bigger construction contracts.

Building a Real World

In addition to being a writer, lecturer, and retired editor, I am also a space activist. I believe firmly that humankind's expansion into space is not only exciting and beneficial, it is necessary for the survival of the species. I wrote a book on the subject, called The High Road. *I have also joined several space-activism organizations, and in 1983 was elected the president of the oldest of them, the National Space Institute. Back in 1980, when I was asked to be Guest of Honor at the Philadelphia Science Fiction Society's annual conference, Philcon 80, it occurred to me that although science fiction fans love to read about space travel, relatively few of them were actively working in the real world to strengthen the space program. I wrote this speech, which was later adapted into magazine form and published in* Analog.

Frankly, I'm afraid that there are still too many science fiction fans sitting on their duffs reading about the future instead of working to help make it come true.

My text today is from the Gospel according to St. Matthew, Chapter 5, Verse 13: "Ye are the salt of the earth; but if the salt has lost his savor, wherewith shall it be salted?"

We all love this thing we call science fiction. No two of us agree as to just what, exactly, science fiction is—but whatever it is, we agree that we love it.

Perhaps too much. After all, there is a big, brawling world out there that desperately needs men and women of vision, and vigor, and courage. Yet it is awfully tempting to remain here in our snug little world of science fiction and hope that the outside world leaves us alone.

When I first came into science fiction, writers and fans alike bemoaned the fact that we were in a literary ghetto. Science fiction was ignored by the general reading public, despised by the critics, and treated by the publishers as something between a narcotics addiction and a social disease.

Through the decades of the 1960s and 1970s, many writers struggled to break down the old ghetto walls. So did a few fans. Gradually, brick by stubborn brick, the walls did come down.

An enormous part of that success was due to two men whom we seldom think of as science fiction writers: Gene Roddenberry and George Lucas. *Star Trek* created a huge audience for science fiction among people who had never read a science fiction story in their lives. *Star Wars* cashed in on that audience—and made it even bigger.

Shallow as *Star Wars* was, as science fiction, it was a profound message to the men who make the money decisions in New York and Hollywood. The old ghetto walls were finally leveled by outsiders who came to us searching for gold.

Much of what those outsiders have created is unpalatable to the majority of us who have spent our lives in science fiction.

Frankly, I am appalled to see motion picture producers sinking twenty, thirty, forty million dollars into tripe such as *Close Encounters of the Third Kind,* or *Alien.* The motion picture version of *Star Trek* was not as good as the average segment of the TV series, despite the money and talent that was lavished on it. And Disney's *Black Hole* was an exercise in frustration for all concerned, especially the audience.

In the world of the printed word, we have seen the mainstream picking up a number of science fiction ideas and themes, and using them in mainstream novels that have little to do with science fiction.

Try reading a Robert Ludlum novel, or any of a dozen books that have been on the best seller lists this year, such as *The Third World War.* The scenarios, the plot techniques, the trick of presenting future events as past history, all these have been lifted bodily from science fiction.

Most of these books would not have been published at all five or ten years ago, because the publishers would have considered them too "far out." Or, if they were published, they would have been labeled Science Fiction and sold to us in the ghetto, while the multi-million-dollar mainstream market totally ignored them.

The only thing that the mainstream has not lifted from science fiction has been the science fiction writers. With the exception of Frank Herbert's *Dune* novels and Robert Heinlein's newest work, no science fiction writer has ever received the backing from a publisher that is necessary to reach the exalted level of Best Sellerdom.*

Of course, Heinlein's *Stranger in a Strange Land* has sold millions of copies. So have several other science fiction novels. But only over a period of many years. Movie tie-ins sell fast and furiously, but it is difficult to rank them as science fiction novels.

On the magazine front, there is good news and bad news.

---

*Happily, this situation has improved greatly since 1980.

The good news, I say unabashedly, is *Omni*. For some strange reason, I'm rather partial to that magazine.

Omni is selling close to one million copies per month. It has nearly 200,000 paid subscriptions. Readership surveys by independent organizations such as Yankelovich, Skelley, and White report that *Omni* has at least four million readers each month.

In short, *Omni* is doing quite well, despite the persistent rumors of catastrophe that I hear at science fiction conventions. Two months after the magazine started, some fans were claiming that it was going to fold up. Two weeks after I became the Executive Editor, I heard a rumor that I had walked off the job. It's as if some fans *want* *Omni* to fail, because they cannot stand the idea of a magazine that contains science fiction making a major success out there in the real world.

Less good is the situation with the other science fiction magazines.

Analog has been sold to Davis Publications. While this is probably a good thing for *Analog* in the long run, because Davis is much more interested in the magazine than Condé Nast ever was, it is a disappointment because it means that one of the most powerful magazine publishers in the nation still cannot see the value of science fiction.

Isaac Asimov's Science Fiction Magazine is doing very well, and George Scithers picked up his second well-earned Hugo in three years at Noreascon II. But frankly, the magazine is aimed at such a juvenile audience that an old-timer like me finds it rather uninteresting most of the time.

The Magazine of Fantasy and Science Fiction seems to be going along its literate way, still the darling of Charlie Brown's readers, but virtually unchanging, year by year. *Galaxy* and *Amazing* have been in deep trouble for years, and *Galileo*—the most interesting of the newcomers—has also run into serious financial problems.

If history has taught us anything, it is that magazines must grow or die. Inflation is constantly driving costs upward. If a magazine that depends almost entirely on its cover price is to stay in business, it must either bring in more customers or raise its cover price. No magazine can continue escalating its price indefinitely, so the long-range goal must be to increase circulation.

Yet the science fiction magazines have been singularly unable to accomplish that task.

I must point out that *Omni*—because it is sold to a much larger readership than the science fiction audience, and because it is heavy with advertising—does not fall into the same category as the "hard-core" science fiction magazines.

Grow or die. The hard-core science fiction magazines are not growing.

Is science fiction itself growing or dying? Most outward signs point toward growth. There are more people attending science fiction conventions than ever before, and more conventions being held. Noreascon II was a well-managed mob scene, with nearly six thousand people in attendance. In fact, the WorldCon now ranks among the top annual conventions held within the United States, which explains why the hotel chains treat fandom with some respect.

Most colleges and universities regularly schedule classes in science fiction. And (God help us all) there are now professorships in science fiction. No one has been able to count the thousands of high schools and junior highs that hold science fiction classes.

Yet, how many of these convention attendees and students and—yes, even *Omni* readers—are truly science fiction fans? Only a small percentage, apparently. The true test of fandom's strength lies in the circulation of the hard-core science fiction magazines and in the sales of science fiction paperbacks. Magazine circulation has grown very little, if any, over the past decade. And paperback book sales have dropped so steeply that heads are rolling all through the book publishing industry.*

More alarming—to me, at least—is that the mental attitude of fandom has not seemed to grow much over the past ten years. Or twenty, for that matter.

I attend conventions year after year and see the same people saying the same things to each other. Some of the faces change, from time to time, but the *ideas*, the *mind-set*, remains the same.

You don't think so? Take a look at the most popular science fiction books of 1980 and compare that list with the best-read books of 1970, or 1960, or even earlier. The same themes, the same characters, with only minor variations.

We pride ourselves on being "the literature of ideas." But too many of us are locked into the past: the future we dream about is a juvenile's dream—a juvenile of 1945, at that.

Instead of stepping into the real world and taking charge of it, as we should be doing, we sit back with still-yet-another version of a Doc Smith epic, or the latest heroic spasms of Conan the Kumquat.

And don't you women snicker at the phallic fantasies of the men. Neither as writers nor as readers have you raised the level of science fiction a notch. Women have written a lot of books about dragons and unicorns, but damned few about future worlds in which adult problems are addressed.

Fandom stays firmly in the vanished remains of the old ghetto, like a tribe that clings to the ruins of an ancient city. We revel over the nonsense regurgitated in fan magazines when we should be pondering the ideas of René Dubos or Hans Bethe.

Now, all of this is fine, if that's what you like. I'd be an ungrateful sonofabitch to insist that you *must* take your

---

*This too has changed for the better.

heads out of those yellowing pages and assume your rightful place in the real world.

The trouble is, you are bright, intelligent, vigorous, capable men and women. The real world needs you, needs your intelligence and dedication, and needs it *now*. There are not many like you. As Cyril Kornbluth pointed out in "The Marching Morons," there are more idiots out there than geniuses. By far.

I can't force you to become active in the world beyond the science fiction ghetto, so I've got to convince you that you should. The place where you are most needed, where you can make the most important contribution, is in the space program.

In the beginning was the Word, and the Word was Arthur C. Clarke's . . . and Robert A. Heinlein's . . . and Willy Ley's . . . and the words of many other writers.

When I first started reading science fiction, "flying to the Moon" was a popular way of saying that something is impossible. "Harry Truman has as much chance of beating Tom Dewey as he has of flying to the Moon." Hearty laugh.

But the poets of that era—the science fiction writers— dreamed of going to the Moon. Writers such as Ley, and Heinlein, and Clarke showed that it could be done. They convinced the American people that it should be done.

By 1961 we had a President who accepted the challenge and led the American people to the Moon. Some of you may be old enough to remember that in 1961 we were far behind the Russians in space efforts. By 1969, a scant eight years later, we had raced ahead so far, so fast, that the Russians pretended they had never been interested in the Moon at all.

And we believed them! Our space technology reached the Moon so easily that many Americans fell for the delusion that it was all a big public relations stunt.

Even science fiction writers (some of them) thought that the space program had somehow lost its excitement, its romance, its poetry.

What had happened, of course, was that the poets had been shouldered aside by the engineers. Science fiction writers had helped to get the program started, but they could not do the actual technical work. I certainly would not want to ride in a rocket engineered by me! Getting to the Moon required engineers and astronauts, administrators and bureaucrats. Not poets.

So the science fiction writers stood on the sidelines and watched. Some refused to watch. Some became antagonistic. Brian Aldiss complained bitterly that American science fiction writers were ''sucking up to NASA'' and that this was ruining American science fiction. Barry Malzberg, on hearing that Spiro Agnew was in favor of going on to Mars, castigated the whole space program and everyone in it as tools of repression.

These were foolish statements, made under the passions of the moment. There is an old Russian story about a fox and a sparrow and a pile of manure that ends with the moral: It's not always your enemies who put you in it, and it isn't always your friends who get you out of it, but if you're in it up to your neck the least you can do is keep your big mouth shut!

Because of the general backlash against space—a punishment, mind you, for being successful—the Nixon Administration was able to slice away at NASA's funding. While Nixon himself smilingly greeted the first astronauts to return from the Moon, his White House aides were cutting the throat of the Apollo program. Apollo did not die; it was foully murdered.

If we had used our space capabilities through the decade of the 1970s as we had originally planned to, we would today be beaming energy from space to the Earth. We would be preparing to mine the Moon and the asteroids for the megatonnages of natural resources that have been waiting there untouched for four and a half billion years.

Instead, we have allowed our ambitions in space to dwindle to almost nothing. And our national economy, our prestige, our power, our standard of living, our own self-respect, have all dwindled equally over the past decade.

Enemies of the space program say we should not spend so much money on space, as if we take cartloads of greenbacks up in rockets and leave them on the Moon. We do not spend a lot of money on the space program. I know that NASA's budget of $5 billion per year looks huge. But consider the job that needs to be done.

Consider the fact that the Department of Defense spends $5 billion every two weeks. And the Department of Health and Human Services spends that much every nine days. Consider the fact that we, you and I, spend $7.5 billion per year on pizza, $18 billion on cigarettes, $40 billion on booze, and God knows how much on pot.

During the course of the Apollo program we spent $23 billion to reach the Moon. We got in return, not merely a few hundred pounds of rocks, but the team and the technology that can take us anywhere in the solar system that we wish to travel. During those same years the Federal government spent more than $500 billion on programs to help the poor. Who has been helped? There are more poor today than there were when those programs began. And the gap between rich and poor has widened, not narrowed.

Make no mistake about it. We need the energy and the natural resources that exist in space. Today, the world's population is almost 4.5 billion. By the end of this century it will be at least 6 or 7 billion. Can you imagine the social turmoil, the political conflicts, the terrorism and wars of a world twice as crowded as we are today? A world with fewer natural resources, less food, less energy?

We must reach out to the wealth that waits in space and bring it safely here to Earth, to make everyone richer. Not a welfare system, where we slice a finite-sized pie of resources into smaller and constantly-smaller pieces until everyone starves. That is the politics of scarcity. It leads only to doom.

We have at our fingertips a new bonanza that will give us a hugely larger pie, so that everyone can share in abundance.

And that is why you are needed.

Science fiction fans can see the future more clearly than politicians and businessmen. It is up to you to convince them that our future lies in space.

"Ye are the light of the world . . . but men do not light a candle and put it under a bushel . . . let your light so shine before men, that they may see your good works . . ."

All around this country, grass roots organizations are forming to support a stronger, more effective space program. These groups include the National Space Institute, the L-5 Society, the Planetary Society, the AIAA, the AAS, and many others.

I urge you to join these groups, to use your energy and intelligence—and your experience in organization—to help these grass-roots groups to build a powerful voice in favor of a truly vigorous space program.

And more.

Twenty years ago, the environmental movement was as small and scattered as the space movement is today. Now the environmentalists are a powerful political force. Unfortunately, most environmentalists tend to look at the space program with suspicion, if not outright hostility. This is a tragedy for both sides, because the long-range goal of both sides is exactly the same: we both want a clean, green, safe planet Earth, a homeworld for humankind that is a good place to live on.

We must bridge these gaps of mistrust and misunderstanding between the environmentalists and the space enthusiasts. We must prove to our political and business leaders that either we reach into space or we collapse here on Earth and sink into decay.

You can help.

It is time you lifted your faces from those fantasies of the future and got to work here in the present. We build our future by what we do—or fail to do—today. Now. Here.

The future begins today. Let us build together the kind of future that we all want to live in. And let us start *now*.

It's Right Over
Your Nose

I do a good deal of lecturing around the country, on a number of topics. I like to spring this one on astronomy groups. It's an old conundrum among astronomers and cosmologists: "If the universe truly holds many intelligent life forms, why have we not found any evidence of their existence?" This essay shows that we have. It takes a fairly detailed understanding of modern astronomy to find the weak points in my argument. Sometimes, I almost convince myself!

All right, so we believe that there could be older, smarter races out among the stars. Maybe they've even visited here. Perhaps they're watching us with some gentle amusement as we sweat over our dinky little shuttle missions and Voyager probes.

When are we going to get some evidence about these

alien races—some cold, hard facts that show they really exist?

Many astronomers and cosmologists will give you statistics. They'll state that out of the billions and billions of stars in the universe, even if intelligent races arose on only one out of every hundred billion, there would still be a huge number of intelligent aliens out there. But we're not interested in statistics and speculation now. We're after *evidence*—something we see, hear, taste, touch, or smell.

And we want the evidence now, for us, not our descendants.

For years, astronomers have searched the stars for intelligent signals with radio telescopes. There are a hundred billion stars in the Milky Way galaxy. Unless intelligence is *very* commonplace, the chances of getting to chat with alien creatures on the radio during our own lifetimes are very slim at best.

All right. Somebody's out there—we hope. But probably not close enough to reach by interstellar phone. So we run smack into the starflight problem again. If we have any hope of seeing or hearing them, either they have to get close enough to make at least a radio contact or we have to go out and find them.

Maybe they are out there, flitting around among the stars, but we just don't know it. Maybe we've actually seen their starships without realizing it. What would a starship look like, from Earth?

Let's try to construct a starship mentally and see if we can find anything in the heavens that fits the description. After all, we have some fairly decent telescopes and radio receivers. Maybe, if we know what to look for, we can come up with a hunk of evidence that shows they're really out there.

We must assume that interstellar ships will be propelled by some form of rockets. We're forced into this. No other propulsion system that we know of today can move a vehicle through space. Except solar sailing, in which you allow the minuscule pressure of starlight to push you along. But solar sailing is incredibly slow. It would take a ship hundreds of years to get from here to Pluto. Count it out as an interstellar propulsion system.

Perhaps a starship would have some form of propulsion that we don't know about—antigravity, or something equally far out. But if we don't know how it works, we don't know what to look for. There could be a sky full of such ships and we'd never realize it.

So we'll have to live with rockets.

Dr. Edward Purcell, a Nobel laureate in physics from Harvard University, tackled the very same problem some years ago. He worked out the mathematical foundations for interstellar flight; it is published in a book called *Interstellar Communications* (1963). But Dr. Purcell did the job in order to show that interstellar flight is not only impossible, it's hogwash—pure and unadulterated!

He first pointed out that the best you could hope for was a speed of about 99 percent of the speed of light. Fine, we can accept that. As we saw in "Starflight," relativity theory shows that you can't go faster than light, but at speeds close to light speed there's a time-stretching effect that allows you to cover enormous distances while hardly aging a moment. Combine that with cryogenically suspended animation during the dull portions of the trip, and you've got the possibility of exploring practically the whole known universe within a human lifetime.

But how do you get to that speed? Purcell showed that if you use nuclear fusion engines—even fusion engines that are 100 percent efficient—the rocket ship needs about 1.6 billion tons of propellant for every ton of payload. Billion. A bit uneconomical.

So Purcell looked into the possibilities of using an anti-matter drive for the rocket.

Antimatter was first predicted theoretically, and then discovered in experiments involving huge particle accelerators—"atom smashers" such as cyclotrons and synchrotrons. Whereas a normal electron has a negative electrical charge, an antielectron has a positive charge and is called a *positron*. A normal proton carries a positive charge, an antiproton is negative. For every normal type of subatomic particle there is an antiparticle.

Antimatter has the interesting property of reacting violently when it contacts normal matter. Both the normal matter and antimatter are completely annihilated and transformed into energy.

In contrast, our hydrogen fusion reaction turns only 0.7 percent of the original hydrogen's matter into energy. A matter-antimatter collision turns 100 percent of the material into energy.

So Purcell examined the possibilities of using matter-antimatter reactions to drive a starship. He found that you need "only" 40,000 tons of propellant—half of it antimatter—for every ton of payload.

But two other problems arise. First: how do you hold antimatter? It can't touch any normal matter, or *boom!* Perhaps a strong magnetic field—a "magnetic bottle"—could do it. Second, the rocket exhaust of an antimatter drive would pour out some 10^{18} watts of gamma rays. That's a billion billion watts of gamma radiation. This is more energy than the Sun lavishes on our Earth—and sunlight is far more gentle than gamma radiation. If you turned on that kind of engine, you'd bake Earth—or whatever planet you're close to—to a fine dead ash.

Purcell concludes, "Well, this is preposterous. . . . And remember, our conclusions were forced on us by the elementary laws of mechanics."

Preposterous? That's his opinion. It would have been Leif Ericson's opinion if one of his Viking cohorts had shown him the blueprints for a nuclear submarine. It would have been Orville Wright's opinion if he had seen sketches of a swing-wing supersonic jet plane.

All that Purcell's equations really show is that starships

should be bulky—huge. And as for radiating 10^{18} watts—
marvelous! That kind of light bulb should be visible over
long distances and help us to find starships, if they're out
there. It's probably safe to assume that anyone smart
enough to build a starship might also be smart enough to
coast away from planetary neighborhoods before lighting
up his main engines.

And, of course, the Bussard interstellar ramjet gets
around the propellant problem almost entirely.

But there's another consideration that leads to the conclusion that *anyone's* starship is going to be huge—the
time problem.

All starflights are going to be one-way trips, in a sense.
Thanks to the time-dilation effect at near the speed of
light, you can cover thousands of light-years in the subjective twinkling of an eye, but when you return to your
home world, thousands of years will have elapsed there.
Even in a very, *very* stable society, things would have
changed so much that you'd be out of place. And even if
your friends have tremendous life-spans, either they would
be so different from you when you return as to be virtual
strangers or they would be the biggest bores in the galaxy.
People change, and cultures change, over the millennia.

So interstellar voyages are going to be one-way voyages, in effect—unless our concept of the universe is
glaringly wrong.

This means that a starship will become all the home that
its crew ever knows. Which, in turn, means that the crew's
family is going to be aboard. The ships will be little cities
of their own—and maybe not so little, either. For just as
the Old Testament patriarchs begat new generations, interstellar families are going to grow.

Several thinkers have mentioned in the past that a
hollowed-out asteroid might make a good spaceship. Why
not consider a larger body, something the size of the Moon
or Mars? There would be plenty of room for families and

cargo, and lots of hydrogen fuel locked away in the planet's bulk. All the natural resources of a full-sized world would be right there. Sure, the planet-ship would be getting smaller all the time, but you could probably pick up other unpopulated chunks in your travels. In fact, the moons of ice-giant planets such as Jupiter might well be perfect fuel tanks for interstellar ships—little more than fat balls of hydrogen ice.

The starship crew would have to live underground when they're in between stars, but they'd have to live indoors in a factory-built ship anyway. At least, on a reasonable-sized planet, when they got close enough to a warm star they could come outdoors just as soon as their atmosphere thawed out.

The propulsion system that pushes a moderate-sized planet through interstellar space at relativistic speeds (close to light speed) would have to be so powerful that it boggles the imagination. As we've already seen, it staggered at least one Nobel Prize winner. But it's not beyond the known laws of physics! Certainly, we can't build such a rocket engine now; but there's no fundamental law of physics that says it's impossible to build such an engine.

All right, now we know what to look for. At least, we think we know one of the things that we might want to look for. Is there anything resembling a planet-sized starship, using fusion or antimatter rockets, within sight of our telescopes?

Well, what would it look like through a telescope?

Most likely, what we'd see would not be the ship itself, but its exhaust plume, a huge, hot glob of ionized gas, which physicists call a *plasma*. The plasma would expand from the ship's rocket nozzles to enormous dimensions in the hard vacuum of interstellar space. The plasma would be moving at speeds close to that of light, and so would show huge red shifts. And, unlike any natural heavenly body, the plasma exhaust might fluctuate unpredictably as the ship changed course or speed.

Over the past two dozen years, the entire astronomical community has gone out of its head trying to figure out what the "quasi-stellar objects," or quasars, might be.

Quasars show enormous red shifts, amounting to speeds of close to 90 percent of the speed of light. Because of these red shifts, astronomers at first thought that the quasars were out at the farthest edges of the observable universe, and their red shifts are caused by the general expansion of the universe.

But quasars twinkle! Some of them brighten and dim over the course of a year or two, others in several weeks or days. A few have been seen to change brightness within a few minutes.

Partly because of this twinkling, many astronomers have leaned toward the idea that the quasars are relatively close by, perhaps not far from the Milky Way galaxy, perhaps actually within it. However, most of the evidence available points to the conclusion that the quasars are at least some distance outside the Milky Way, probably on the order of a hundred million light-years distant. This is still "local," compared to the "cosmological" distances of billions of light-years that were originally assigned to them.

The quasars are apparently composed of very hot gases, plasmas, that are strongly ionized at temperatures of some 30,000 degrees Kelvin. The actual size of the quasars is not yet known. If they're cosmologically distant, then they must be close to the sizes of galaxies. But if they're close to the Milky Way or even inside it, they could be as small as star clusters or even smaller.

Neither cosmologists, astronomers, nor physicists have been able to explain what produces the titanic power output of the quasars. Their light and radiowave emissions are beyond anything that known natural physical processes can explain. Ordinary physical processes, such as the hydrogen fusion reactions that power the stars, just won't fill the bill. Something else must be burning inside the quasars. A few scientists have suggested matter-antimatter reactions.

Could the quasars be powered by fusion reactors of the type that we would build someday to drive starships? They would run much hotter than the fusion reactions that power the stars. Or might the quasars truly be driven by antimatter reactions?

But if the quasars are starships, and what we're seeing is part of the normal interstellar traffic of the Milky Way galaxy, how come all we see are *red-shifted* quasars? A red shift means the object is moving away from us. Why don't we see any blue-shifted quasars, that is, starships heading toward us?

Maybe we don't see blue shifts because we're out toward the galaxy's edge, and most of the starship traffic is in the star-rich central regions. More likely, though, the answer is that such blue shifts would be very difficult to detect on Earth.

The plasma of the quasars, whether they are the exhausts of starship rockets or not, are inherently very hot, and very blue in color—ranging into the ultraviolet. Most UV wavelengths don't get through our atmosphere—the ozone layers up high in our atmosphere filter out almost all ultraviolet. Only a little UV gets through, and that's what suntans us.

The reason we can see any quasars at all is that their enormous red shifts move the ultraviolet radiation down into the wavelengths of visible light, which do penetrate our atmosphere quite nicely.

Now, a blue-shifted quasar would have its light shifted the other way—from blue and ultraviolet into the far UV, X-ray, and gamma ray wavelengths. None of these wavelengths gets through our atmosphere. So blue-shifted quasars would be quite invisible to us—from the ground. Special ultraviolet detectors placed aboard some of our orbiting astronomical satellites, however, have picked up many, many UV objects that are entirely new to the ground-dwelling astronomers. Could they be blue-shifted quasars? Starships heading our way?

And if they are, should we be doing something to attract their attention?

The Perfect Warrior

*This story has two separate origins, which came to-
gether to form the novelet and, eventually, a full-sized
novel.*

*One origin was Myron R. Lewis, a friend and co-worker
at the Avco Everett Research Laboratory, back in the
1960s. (Was it really twenty years ago? Gad!) Myron
invented the Dueling Machine, and together we plotted out
the story that became* The Perfect Warrior. *I did the
writing, as I had on an earlier tale we had thrashed out
together,* Men of Good Will.* *Little did either of us
realize, back then, that we had "invented" a kind of video
game; nor did we foresee that the room-filling gadgetry of
the Dueling Machine could be shrunk down to desktop size
within little more than a decade.*

*See my story collection, *Escape Plus*, published by Tor Books.

The other source for this story was a nagging "What if?" question that had been preying on my mind for many, many years: What if Winston Churchill had been Prime Minister of Britain in 1938, rather than Neville Chamberlain? Could World War II have been averted if doughty old Winnie had been there to face up to Hitler, rather than the appeasing Chamberlain? The Perfect Warrior *and, later, the novel it gave birth to,* The Dueling Machine, *are my attempt to answer that question.*

I

Dulaq rode the slide to the upper pedestrian level, stepped off and walked over to the railing. The city stretched out all around him—broad avenues thronged with busy people, pedestrian walks, vehicle thoroughfares, aircars gliding between the gleaming, towering buildings.

And somewhere in this vast city was the man he must kill. The man who would kill him, perhaps.

It all seemed so real! The noise of the streets, the odors of the perfumed trees lining the walks, even the warmth of the reddish sun on his back as he scanned the scene before him.

It is an illusion, Dulaq reminded himself, *a clever man-made hallucination. A figment of my own imagination amplified by a machine.*

But it seemed so very real.

Real or not, he had to find Odal before the sun set. Find him and kill him. Those were the terms of the duel. He fingered the stubby cylindrical stat-wand in his tunic pocket. That was the weapon he had chosen, his weapon, his own invention. And this was the environment he had picked: his city, busy, noisy, crowded, the metropolis Dulaq had known and loved since childhood.

Dulaq turned and glanced at the sun. It was halfway

down toward the horizon, he judged. He had about three hours to find Odal. When he did—kill or be killed.

Of course, no one is actually hurt. That is the beauty of the machine. It allows one to settle a score, to work out aggressive feelings, without either mental or physical harm.

Dulaq shrugged. He was a roundish figure, moon-faced, slightly stooped shoulders. He had work to do. Unpleasant work for a civilized man, but the future of the Acquataine Cluster and the entire alliance of neighboring star systems could well depend on the outcome of this electronically synthesized dream.

He turned and walked down the elevated avenue, marveling at the sharp sensation of hardness that met each footstep on the paving. Children dashed by and rushed up to a toyshop window. Men of commerce strode along purposefully, but without missing a chance to eye the girls sauntering by.

I must have a marvelous imagination, Dulaq thought, smiling to himself.

Then he thought of Odal, the blond, icy professional he was pitted against. Odal was an expert at all the weapons, a man of strength and cool precision, an emotionless tool in the hands of a ruthless politician. But how expert could he be with a stat-wand, when the first time he saw one was the moment before the duel began? And how well acquainted could he be with the metropolis, when he had spent most of his life in the military camps on the dreary planets of Kerak, sixty light-years from Acquatainia?

No, Odal would be lost and helpless in this situation. He would attempt to hide among the throngs of people. All Dulaq had to do was to find him.

The terms of the duel restricted both men to the pedestrian walks of the commercial quarter of the city. Dulaq knew the area intimately, and he began a methodical hunt through the crowds for the tall, fair-haired, blue-eyed Odal.

And he saw him! After only a few minutes of walking

down the major thoroughfare, he spotted his opponent, strolling calmly along a crosswalk, at the level below.

Dulaq hurried down the next ramp, worked his way through the crowd, and saw the man again. Tall and blond, unmistakable. Dulaq edged along behind him quietly, easily. No disturbance. No pushing. Plenty of time. They walked along the street for a quarter hour while the distance between them slowly shrank from fifty feet to five.

Finally Dulaq was directly behind him, within arm's reach. He grasped the stat-wand and pulled it from his tunic. With one quick motion he touched it to the base of the man's skull and started to thumb the button that would release the killing bolt of energy . . .

The man turned suddenly. It wasn't Odal!

Dulaq jerked back in surprise. It couldn't be. He had seen his face. It was Odal—and yet this man was definitely a stranger.

He stared at Dulaq as the duelist backed away a few steps, then turned and walked quickly from the place.

A mistake, Dulaq told himself. *You were overanxious. A good thing this is an hallucination, or else the auto-police would be taking you in by now.*

And yet . . . he had been so certain that it was Odal. A chill shuddered through him. He looked up, and there was his antagonist, on the thoroughfare above, at the precise spot where he himself had been a few minutes earlier. Their eyes met, and Odal's lips parted in a cold smile.

Dulaq hurried up the ramp. Odal was gone by the time he reached the upper level. *He could not have gotten far,* Dulaq reasoned.

Slowly, but very surely, Dulaq's hallucination turned into a nightmare. He spotted Odal in the crowd, only to have him melt away. He saw him again, lolling in a small park, but when he got closer, the man turned out to be another stranger. He felt the chill of the duelist's ice-blue eyes on him again and again, but when he turned to find his antagonist, no one was there but the impersonal crowd.

Odal's face appeared again and again. Dulaq struggled through the throngs to find his opponent, only to have him vanish. The crowd seemed to be filled with tall, blond men crisscrossing before Dulaq's dismayed eyes.

The shadows lengthened. The sun was setting. Dulaq could feel his heart pounding within him and perspiration pouring from every square inch of his skin.

There he is! Definitely, positively him! Dulaq pushed through the homeward-bound crowds toward the figure of a tall, blond man leaning against the safety railing of the city's main thoroughfare. It was Odal, the damned, smiling, confident Odal.

Dulaq pulled the wand from his tunic and battled across the surging crowd to the spot where Odal stood motionless, hands in pockets, watching him.

Dulaq came within arm's reach . . .

"TIME, GENTLEMEN. TIME IS UP, THE DUEL IS ENDED."

High above the floor of the antiseptic-white chamber that housed the dueling machine was a narrow gallery. Before the machine had been installed, the chamber had been a lecture hall in Acquatainia's largest university. Now the rows of students' seats, the lecturer's dais and rostrum were gone. The chamber held only the machine, the grotesque collection of consoles, control desks, power units, association circuits, and booths where the two antagonists sat.

In the gallery—empty during ordinary duels—sat a privileged handful of newsmen.

"Time limit is up," one of them said. "Dulaq didn't get him."

"Yes, but he didn't get Dulaq, either."

The first one shrugged. "The important thing is that now Dulaq has to fight Odal on *his* terms. Dulaq couldn't win with his own choice of weapons and situation, so—"

"Wait, they're coming out."

Down on the floor below, Dulaq and his opponent emerged from their closed booths.

One of the newsmen whistled softly. "Look at Dulaq's face . . . it's positively gray."

"I've never seen the Prime Minister so shaken."

"And take a look at Kanus's hired assassin." The newsmen turned toward Odal, who stood before his booth, quietly chatting with his seconds.

"Hm-m-m. There's a bucket of frozen ammonia for you."

"He's enjoying this."

One of the newsmen stood up. "I've got a deadline to meet. Save my seat."

He made his way past the guarded door, down the rampway circling the outer walls of the building, to the portable tri-di transmitting unit that the Acquatainian government had permitted for the newsmen on the campus grounds outside the former lecture hall.

The newsman huddled with his technicians for a few minutes, then stepped before the transmitter.

"Emile Dulaq, Prime Minister of the Acquataine Cluster and acknowledged leader of the coalition against Chancellor Kanus of the Kerak Worlds, has failed in the first part of his psychonic duel against Major Par Odal of Kerak. The two antagonists are now undergoing the routine medical and psychological checks before renewing their duel."

By the time the newsman returned to his gallery seat, the duel was almost ready to begin again.

Dulaq stood in the midst of a group of advisors before the looming impersonality of the machine.

"You need not go through with the next phase of the duel immediately," his Minister of Defense was saying. "Wait until tomorrow. Rest and calm yourself."

Dulaq's round face puckered into a frown. He cocked an eye at the chief meditech, hovering at the edge of the little group.

The meditech, one of the staff that ran the dueling machine, pointed out, "The Prime Minister has passed the examinations. He is capable, within the agreed-upon rules of the contest, of resuming."

"But he has the option of retiring for the day, does he not?"

"If Major Odal agrees."

Dulaq shook his head impatiently. "No. I shall go through with it. Now."

"But—"

The Prime Minister's face suddenly hardened; his advisors lapsed into a respectful silence. The chief meditech ushered Dulaq back into his booth. On the other side of the room, Odal glanced at the Acquatainians, grinned humorlessly, and strode to his own booth.

Dulaq sat and tried to blank out his mind while the meditechs adjusted the neurocontacts to his head and torso. They finished at last and withdrew. He was alone in the booth now, looking at the dead-white walls, completely bare except for the viewscreen before his eyes. The screen finally began to glow slightly, then brightened into a series of shifting colors. The colors merged and changed, swirled across his field of view. Dulaq felt himself being drawn into them gradually, compellingly, completely immersed in them.

The mists slowly vanished, and Dulaq found himself standing on an immense and totally barren plain. Not a tree, not a blade of grass; nothing but bare, rocky ground stretching in all directions to the horizon and disturbingly harsh yellow sky. He looked down and at his feet saw the weapon that Odal had chosen.

A primitive club.

With a sense of dread, Dulaq picked up the club and hefted it in his hand. He scanned the plain. Nothing. No hills or trees or bushes to hide in. No place to run to.

And off on the horizon he could see a tall, lithe figure holding a similar club walking slowly and deliberately toward him.

* * *

The press gallery was practically empty. The duel had more than an hour to run, and most of the newsmen were outside, broadcasting their hastily drawn guesses about Dulaq's failure to win with his own choice of weapon and environment.

Then a curious thing happened.

On the master control panel of the dueling machine, a single light flashed red. The meditech blinked at it in surprise, then pressed a series of buttons on his board. More red lights appeared. The chief meditech rushed to the board and flipped a single switch.

One of the newsmen turned to his partner. "What's going on down there?"

"I think it's all over. . . . Yes, look, they're opening up the booths. Somebody must've scored a victory."

They watched intently while the other newsmen quickly filed back into the gallery.

"There's Odal. He looks happy."

"Guess that means—"

"Good Lord! Look at Dulaq!"

II

Dr. Leoh was lecturing at the Carinae Regional University when the news of Dulaq's duel reached him. An assistant professor perpetrated the unthinkable breach of interrupting the lecture to whisper the news in his ear.

Leoh nodded grimly, hurriedly finished his lecture, and then accompanied the assistant professor to the university president's office. They stood in silence as the slideway whisked them through the strolling students and blossoming greenery of the quietly busy campus.

Leoh remained wrapped in his thoughts as they entered the administration building and rode the lift tube. Finally, as they stepped through the president's doorway, Leoh asked the assistant professor:

"You say he was in a state of catatonic shock when they removed him from the machine?"

"He still is," the president answered from his desk. "Completely withdrawn from the real world. Cannot speak, hear, or even see—a living vegetable."

Leoh plopped down in the nearest chair and ran a hand across his fleshy face. He was balding and jowly, but his face was creased from a smile that was almost habitual, and his eyes were active and alert.

"I don't understand it," he admitted. "Nothing like this has ever happened in a dueling machine before."

The university president shrugged. "I don't understand it either. But, this is your business." He put a slight emphasis on the last word, unconsciously perhaps.

"Well, at least this will not reflect on the university. That is why I formed Psychonics as a separate business enterprise." Then he added, with a grin, "The money was, of course, only a secondary consideration."

The president managed a smile. "Of course."

"I suppose the Acquatainians want to see me?" Leoh asked academically.

"They're on the tri-di now, waiting for you."

"They're holding a transmission frequency open over eight hundred parsecs?" Leoh looked impressed. "I must be an important man."

"You're the inventor of the dueling machine and the head of Psychonics, Inc. You're the only man who can tell them what went wrong."

"Well, I suppose I shouldn't keep them waiting."

"You can take the call here," the president said, starting to get up from his chair.

"No, no, stay there at your desk," Leoh insisted. "There's no reason for you to leave. Or you either," he said to the assistant professor.

The president touched a button on his desk-communicator.

The far wall of the office glowed momentarily, then seemed to dissolve. They were looking into another office, this one on Acquatainia. It was crowded with nervous-looking men in business clothes and military uniforms.

"Gentlemen," Dr. Leoh said.

Several of the Acquatainians tried to answer him at once. After a few seconds of talking together, they all looked toward one of their members—a tall, purposeful, shrewd-faced civilian who bore a neatly-trimmed black beard.

"I am Fernd Massan, the acting Prime Minister of Acquatainia. You realize, of course, the crisis that has been precipitated in my government because of this duel?"

Leoh blinked. "I realize that, apparently, there has been some difficulty with the dueling machine installed on the governing planet of your star cluster. Political crises are not in my field."

"But your dueling machine has incapacitated the Prime Minister," one of the generals bellowed.

"And at this particular moment," the Defense Minister added, "in the midst of our difficulties with the Kerak Worlds."

"If the Prime Minister is not—"

"Gentlemen!" Leoh objected. "I cannot make sense of your story if you all speak at once."

Massan gestured them to silence.

"The dueling machine," Leoh said, adopting a slightly professorial tone, "is nothing more than a psychonic device for alleviating human aggressions and hostilities. It allows two men to share a dream world created by one of them. There is nearly complete feedback between the two. Within certain limits, the two men can do anything they wish within their dream world. This allows men to settle grievances with violence—in the safety of their own imaginations. If the machine is operated properly, no physical or mental harm can be done to the participants. They can alleviate their tensions safely—without damage of any sort to anyone, and without hurting society.

"Your own government tested one of the machines and approved its use on Acquatainia more than three years ago. I see several of you who were among those to whom I personally demonstrated the device. Dueling machines are in use through wide portions of the galaxy, and I am certain that many of you have used the machine. You have, general, I'm sure."

The general blustered. "That has nothing to do with the matter at hand!"

"Admittedly," Leoh conceded. "But I do not understand how a therapeutic machine can possibly become entangled in a political crisis."

Massan said, "Allow me to explain. Our government has been conducting extremely delicate negotiations with the stellar governments of our neighboring territories. These negotiations concern the rearmament of the Kerak Worlds. You have heard of Kanus of Kerak?"

"I recall the name vaguely," Leoh said. "He's a political leader of some sort."

"Of the worst sort. He has acquired complete dictatorship of the Kerak Worlds, and is now attempting to rearm them for war. This is in direct countervention of the Treaty of Acquatainia, signed only thirty Terran years ago."

"I see. The treaty was signed at the end of the Acquataine-Kerak war, wasn't it?"

"A war that we won," the general pointed out.

"And now the Kerak Worlds want to rearm and try again," Leoh said.

"Precisely."

Leoh shrugged. "Why not call in the Star Watch? This is their type of police activity. And what has all this to do with the dueling machine?"

Massan explained patiently. "The Acquataine Cluster has never become a full-fledged member of the Terran Commonwealth. Our neighboring territories are likewise unaffiliated. Therefore the Star Watch can intervene only if all parties concerned agree to intervention. Unless, of course, there is an actual military emergency. The Kerak Worlds, of course, are completely isolationist—unbound to any laws except those of force.''

Leoh shook his head.

"As for the dueling machine," Massan went on, "Kanus of Kerak has turned it into a political weapon—"

"But that's impossible. Your government passed strict laws concerning the use of the machine; I recommended them and I was in your Council chambers when the laws were passed. The machine may be used only for personal grievances. It is strictly outside the realm of politics.''

Massan shook his head sadly. "Sir, laws are one thing— people are another. And politics consists of people, not words on paper.''

"I don't understand," Leoh said.

Massan explained, "A little more than one Terran year ago, Kanus picked a quarrel with a neighboring star group— the Safad Federation. He wanted an especially favorable trade agreement with them. Their Minister of Trade objected most strenuously. One of the Kerak negotiators—a certain Major Odal—got into a personal argument with the minister. Before anyone knew what had happened, they had challenged each other to a duel. Odal won the duel, and the minister resigned his post. He said that he could no longer effectively fight against the will of Odal and his group . . . he was psychologically incapable of it. Two weeks later he was dead—apparently a suicide, although I have doubts.''

"That's . . . extremely interesting," Leoh said.

"Three days ago," Massan continued, "the same Major Odal engaged Prime Minister Dulaq in a bitter personal argument. Odal is now a military attaché of the Kerak Embassy here. He accused the Prime Minister of cowardice, before a large group at an Embassy party. The Prime Minister had no alternative but to challenge him. And now—''

"And now Dulaq is in a state of shock, and your government is tottering."

Massan's back stiffened. "Our government shall not fall, nor shall the Acquataine Cluster acquiesce to the rearmament of the Kerak Worlds. But"—his voice lowered—"without Dulaq, I fear that our neighboring governments will give in to Kanus's demands and allow him to rearm. Alone, we are powerless to stop him."

"Rearmament itself might not be so bad," Leoh mused, "if you can keep the Kerak Worlds from using their weapons. Perhaps the Star Watch might—"

"Kanus could strike a blow and conquer a star system before the Star Watch could be summoned and arrive to stop him. Once Kerak is armed, this entire area of the galaxy is in peril. In fact, the entire galaxy is endangered."

"And he's using the dueling machine to further his ambitions," Leoh said. "Well, gentlemen, it seems I have no alternative but to travel to the Acquataine Cluster. The dueling machine is my responsibility, and if there is something wrong with it, or with the use of it, I will do my best to correct the situation."

"That is all we ask," Massan said. "Thank you."

The Acquatainian scene faded away, and the three men in the university president's office found themselves looking at a solid wall once again.

"Well," Dr. Leoh said, turning to the president, "it seems that I must request an indefinite leave of absence."

The president frowned. "And it seems that I must grant your request—even though the year is only half-finished."

"I regret the necessity," Leoh said, then, with a broad grin, he added, "My assistant professor, here, can handle my courses for the remainder of the year, very easily. Perhaps he will even be able to deliver his lectures without being interrupted."

The assistant professor turned red.

"Now then," Leoh muttered, mostly to himself, "who is this Kanus, and why is he trying to turn the Kerak Worlds into an arsenal?"

III

Chancellor Kanus, the supreme leader of the Kerak Worlds, stood at the edge of the balcony and looked across the wild, tumbling gorge to the rugged mountains beyond.

"These are the forces that mold men's actions," he said to his small audience of officials and advisors, "the howling winds, the mighty mountains, the open sky and the dark powers of the clouds."

The men nodded and made murmurs of agreement.

"Just as the mountains thrust up from the pettiness of the lands below, so shall we rise above the common walk of men," Kanus said. "Just as a thunderstorm terrifies them, we will make them bend to our will!"

"We will destroy the past," said one of the ministers.

"And avenge the memory of defeat," Kanus added. He turned and looked at the little group of men. Kanus was the smallest man on the balcony: short, spare, sallow-faced; but he possessed piercing, dark eyes and a strong voice that commanded attention.

He walked through the knot of men and stopped before a tall, lean, blond youth in light-blue military uniform. "And you, Major Odal, will be a primary instrument in the first steps of conquest."

Odal bowed stiffly. "I only hope to serve my leader and my worlds."

"You shall. And you already have," Kanus said, beaming. "Already the Acquatainians are thrashing about like a snake whose head has been cut off. Without Dulaq, they have no head, no brain to direct them. For your part in this triumph"—Kanus snapped his fingers, and one of his advisors quickly stepped to his side and handed him a small ebony box—"I present you with this token of the esteem of the Kerak Worlds, and of my personal high regard."

He handed the box to Odal, who opened it and took out a small, jeweled pin.

"The Star of Kerak," Kanus announced. "This is the first time it has been awarded to anyone except a warrior on the battlefield. But then, we have turned their so-called civilized machine into our own battlefield, eh?"

Odal grinned. "Yes, sir, we have. Thank you very much, sir. This is the supreme moment of my life."

"To date, major. Only to date. There will be other moments, even higher ones. Come, let's go inside. We have many plans to discuss . . . more duels . . . more triumphs."

They all filed in to Kanus's huge, elaborate office. The leader walked across the plushly ornate room and sat at the elevated desk, while his followers arranged themselves in the chairs and couches placed about the floor. Odal remained standing, near the doorway.

Kanus let his fingers flick across a small control board set into his desktop, and a tri-dimensional star map glowed into existence on the far wall. As its center were the eleven stars that harbored the Kerak Worlds. Around them stood neighboring stars, color-coded to show their political groupings. Off to one side of the map was the Acquataine Cluster, a rich mass of stars—wealthy, powerful, the most important political and economic power in the section of the galaxy. Until yesterday's duel.

Kanus began one of his inevitable harangues. Objectives, political and military. Already the Kerak Worlds were unified under his dominant will. The people would follow wherever he led. Already the political alliances built up by Acquatainian diplomacy since the last war were tottering, now that Dulaq was out of the picture. Now was the time to strike. A political blow *here*, at the Szarno Confederacy, to bring them and their armaments industries into line with Kerak. Then more political strikes to isolate the Acquataine Cluster from its allies, and to build up subservient states for Kerak. Then, finally, the military blow—against the Acquatainians.

"A sudden strike, a quick, decisive series of blows, and the Acquatainians will collapse like a house of paper. Before the Star Watch can interfere, we will be masters of the Cluster. Then, with the resources of Acquatainia to draw on, we can challenge any force in the galaxy—even the Terran Commonwealth itself!"

The men in the room nodded their assent.

They've heard this story many, many times, Odal thought to himself. This was the first time he had been privileged to listen to it. If you closed your eyes, or looked only at the star map, the plan sounded bizarre, extreme, even impossible. But, if you watched Kanus, and let those piercing, almost hypnotic eyes fasten on yours, then the leader's wildest dreams sounded not only exciting, but inevitable.

Odal leaned a shoulder against the paneled wall and scanned the other men in the room.

There was fat Greber, the vice-chancellor, fighting desperately to stay awake after drinking too much wine during the luncheon and afterward. And Modal, sitting on the couch next to him, was bright-eyed and alert, thinking only of how much money and power would come to him as Chief of Industries once the rearmament program began in earnest.

Sitting alone on another couch was Kor, the quiet one, the head of intelligence, and—technically—Odal's superior. Silent Kor, whose few words were usually charged with terror for those whom he spoke against.

Marshal Lugal looked bored when Kanus spoke of politics, but his face changed when military matters came up. The marshal lived for only one purpose: to avenge his army's humiliating defeat in the war against the Acquatainians, thirty Terran years ago. What he didn't realize,

Odal thought, smiling to himself, was that as soon as he had reorganized the army and reequipped it, Kanus planned to retire him and place younger men in charge. Men whose only loyalty was not to the army, nor even to the Kerak Worlds and their people, but to the chancellor himself.

Eagerly following every syllable, every gesture of the leader was little Tinth. Born to the nobility, trained in the arts, a student of philosophy, Tinth had deserted his heritage and joined the forces of Kanus. His reward had been the Ministry of Education; many teachers had suffered under him.

And finally there was Romis, the Minister of Intergovernmental Affairs. A professional diplomat, and one of the few men in government before Kanus's sweep to power to survive this long. It was clear that Romis hated the chancellor. But he served the Kerak Worlds well. The diplomatic corps was flawless in its handling of intergovernmental affairs. It was only a matter of time, Odal knew, before one of them—Romis or Kanus—killed the other.

The rest of Kanus's audience consisted of political hacks, roughnecks-turned-bodyguards, and a few other hangers-on who had been with Kanus since the days when he held his political monologues in cellars, and haunted the alleys to avoid the police. Kanus had come a long way: from the blackness of oblivion to the dazzling heights of the chancellor's rural estate.

Money, power, glory, revenge, patriotism: each man in the room, listening to Kanus, had his reasons for following the chancellor.

And my reasons? Odal asked himself. *Why do I follow him? Can I see into my own mind as easily as I see into theirs?*

There was duty, of course. Odal was a soldier, and Kanus was the duly-elected leader of the government. Once elected, though, he had dissolved the government and solidified his powers as absolute dictator of the Kerak Worlds.

There was gain to be had by performing well under Kanus. Regardless of his political ambitions and personal tyrannies, Kanus rewarded well when he was pleased. The medal—the Star of Kerak—carried with it an annual pension that would nicely accommodate a family. *If I had one*, Odal thought, sardonically.

There was power, of sorts, also. Working the dueling machine in his special way, hammering a man into nothingness, finding the weaknesses in his personality and exploiting them, pitting his mind against others, turning sneering towers of pride like Dulaq into helpless, whipped dogs—that was power. And it was a power that did not go unnoticed in the cities of the Kerak Worlds. Already Odal was easily recognized on the streets; women especially seemed to be attracted to him now.

"The most important factor," Kanus was saying, "and I cannot stress it overmuch, is to build up an aura of invincibility. This is why your work is so important, Major Odal. You must be invincible! Because today you are the instrument of my own will—and you must triumph at every turn. The fate of your people, of your government, of your chancellor rests squarely on your shoulders each time you step into a dueling machine. You have borne that responsibility well, major. Can you carry it even further?"

"I can, sir," Odal answered crisply, "and I will."

Kanus beamed at him. "Good! Because your next duel—and those that follow it—will be to the death."

IV

It took the starship two weeks to make the journey from Carinae to the Acquataine Cluster. Dr. Leoh spent the time checking over the Acquatainian dueling machine, by direct tri-di beam; the Acquatainian government gave him all the technicians, time, and money he needed for the task.

Leoh spent as much of his spare time as possible with

the other passengers of the ship. He was gregarious, a fine conversationalist, and had a nicely balanced sense of humor. Particularly, he was a favorite of the younger women, since he had reached the age where he could flatter them with his attention without making them feel endangered.

But still, there were long hours when he was alone in his stateroom with nothing but his memories. At times like these, it was impossible not to think back over the road he had been following.

Albert Robertus Leoh, Ph.D., Professor of Physics, Professor of Electronics, master of computer technology, inventor of the interstellar tri-di communications system; and, more recently, student of psychology, Professor of Psychophysiology, founder of Psychonics, Inc., inventor of the dueling machine.

During his earlier years, when the supreme confidence of youth was still with him, Leoh had envisioned himself as helping mankind to spread his colonies and civilizations throughout the galaxy. The bitter years of galactic war had ended in his childhood, and now human societies throughout the Milky Way were linked together—in greater or lesser degree of union—into a more-or-less peaceful coalition of star groups.

There were two great motivating forces at work on those human societies spread across the stars, and these forces worked toward opposite goals. On the one hand was the urge to explore, to reach new stars, new planets, to expand the frontiers of man's civilizations and found new colonies, new nations. Pitted against this drive to expand was an equally powerful force: the realization that technology had finally put an end to physical labor and almost to poverty itself on all the civilized worlds of man. The urge to move off to the frontier was penned in and buried alive under the enervating comforts of civilization.

The result was inescapable. The civilized worlds became constantly more crowded as time wore on. They became jampacked islands of humanity sprinkled thinly across the sea of space that was still full of unpopulated islands.

The expense and difficulty of interstellar travel was often cited as an excuse. The starships *were* expensive: their power demands were frightful. Only the most determined—and the best-financed—groups of colonists could afford them. The rest of mankind accepted the ease and safety of civilization, lived in the bulging cities of the teeming planets. Their lives were circumscribed by their neighbors, and by their governments. Constantly more people crowding into a fixed living space meant constantly less freedom. The freedom to dream, to run free, to procreate, all became state-owned, state-controlled monopolies.

And Leoh had contributed to this situation.

He had contributed his thoughts and his work. He had contributed often and regularly—the interstellar communications system was only one outstanding achievement in a long career of achievements.

Leoh had been nearly at the voluntary retirement age for scientists when he realized what he, and his fellow scientists, had done. Their efforts to make life richer and more rewarding for mankind had made life only less strenuous and more rigid.

And with every increase in comfort, Leoh discovered, came a corresponding increase in neuroses, in crimes of violence, in mental aberrations. Senseless wars of pride broke out between star groups for the first time in generations. Outwardly, the peace of the galaxy was assured; but beneath the glossy surface of the Terran Commonwealth there smoldered the beginnings of a volcano. Police actions fought by the Star Watch were increasing ominously. Petty wars between once-stable peoples were flaring up steadily.

Once Leoh realized the part he had played in this increasingly tragic drama, he was confronted with two emotions—a deep sense of guilt, both personal and professional; and, countering this, a determination to do something, anything, to restore at least some balance to man's collective mentality.

Leoh stepped out of physics and electronics, and entered the field of psychology. Instead of retiring, he applied for a beginner's status in his new profession. It had taken considerable bending and straining of the Commonwealth's rules—but for a man of Leoh's stature, the rules could be flexed somewhat. Leoh became a student once again, then a researcher, and finally a Professor of Psychophysiology.

Out of this came the dueling machine. A combination of electroencephalograph and autocomputer. A dream machine that amplified a man's imagination until he could engulf himself in a world of his own making.

Leoh envisioned it as a device to enable men to rid themselves of hostility and tension, safely. Through his efforts, and those of his colleagues, dueling machines were quickly becoming accepted as devices for settling disputes.

When two men had a severe difference of opinion—deep enough to warrant legal action—they could go to the dueling machine instead of the courts. Instead of sitting helplessly and watching the machinations of the law grind impersonally through their differences, the two antagonists could allow their imaginations free rein in the dueling machine. They could settle their differences personally, as violently as they wished, without hurting themselves or anyone else. On most civilized worlds, the results of properly-monitored duels were acepted as legally binding.

The tensions of civilized life could be escaped—albeit temporarily—in the dueling machine. This was a powerful tool, much too powerful to allow it to be used indiscriminately. Therefore Leoh safeguarded his invention by forming a private company—Psychonics, Inc.—and securing an exclusive license from the Terran Commonwealth to manufacture, sell, install and maintain the machines. His customers were government health and legal agencies; his responsibilities were: legally, to the Commonwealth; morally, to all mankind; and, finally, to his own restless conscience.

The dueling machines succeeded. They worked as well, and often better, than Leoh had anticipated. But he knew that they were only a stopgap, only a temporary shoring of a constantly eroding dam. What was needed, really needed, was some method of exploding the status quo, some means of convincing people to reach out for those unoccupied, unexplored stars that filled the galaxy, some way of convincing men that they should leave the comforts of civilization for the excitement of colonization.

Leoh had been searching for that method when the news of Dulaq's duel against Odal reached him.

Now he was speeding across parsecs of space, praying to himself that the dueling machine had not failed.

The two-week flight ended. The starship took up a parking orbit around the capital planet of the Acquataine Cluster. The passengers transshipped to the surface.

Dr. Leoh was met at the landing disk by an official delegation, headed by Massan, the acting Prime Minister. They exchanged formal greetings there at the base of the ship, while the other passengers hurried by.

As Leoh and Massan, surrounded by the other members of the delegation, rode the slideway to the port's administration building, Leoh commented:

"As you probably know, I have checked through your dueling machine quite thoroughly via tri-di for the past two weeks. I can find nothing wrong with it."

Massan shrugged. "Perhaps you should have checked, then, the machine of Szarno."

"The Szarno Confederation? Their dueling machine?"

"Yes. This morning Kanus's hired assassin killed a man in it."

"He won another duel," Leoh said.

"You do not understand," Massan said grimly. "Major

Odal's opponent—an industrialist who had spoken out against Kanus—was actually killed in the dueling machine. The man is dead!''

V

One of the advantages of being Commander-in-Chief of the Star Watch, the old man thought to himself, is that you can visit any planet in the Commonwealth.

He stood at the top of the hill and looked out over the green tableland of Kenya. This was the land of his birth, Earth was his homeworld. The Star Watch's official headquarters may be in the heart of a globular cluster of stars near the center of the galaxy, but Earth was the place the commander wanted most to see as he grew older and wearier.

An aide, who had been following the commander at a respectful distance, suddenly intruded himself in the old man's reverie.

"Sir, a message for you."

The commander scowled at the young officer. "I gave orders that I was not to be disturbed."

The officer, slim and stiff in his black-and-silver uniform, replied, "Your chief of staff has passed the message on to you, sir. It's from Dr. Leoh, of Carinae University. Personal and urgent, sir."

The old man grumbled to himself, but nodded. The aide placed a small, crystalline sphere on the grass before him. The air above the sphere started to vibrate and glow.

"Sir Harold Spencer here," the commander said.

The bubbling air seemed to draw in on itself and take solid form. Dr. Leoh sat at a desk chair and looked up at the standing commander.

"Harold, it's a pleasure to see you once again."

Spencer's stern eyes softened, and his beefy face broke into a well-creased smile. "Albert, you ancient scoundrel.

What do you mean by interrupting my first visit home in fifteen years?''

"It won't be a long interruption," Leoh said.

"You told my chief of staff that it was urgent," Sir Harold groused.

"It is. But it's not the sort of problem that requires much action on your part. Yet. You are familiar with recent political developments on the Kerak Worlds?''

Spencer snorted. "I know that a barbarian named Kanus has established himself as a dictator. He's a troublemaker. I've been talking to the Commonwealth Council about the advisability of quashing him before he causes grief, but you know the Council . . . first wait until the flames have sprung up, then thrash about and demand that the Star Watch do something!''

Leoh grinned. "You're as irascible as ever."

"My personality is not the subject of this rather expensive discussion. What about Kanus? And what are you doing, getting yourself involved in politics? About to change your profession again?''

"No, not at all," Leoh answered, laughing. Then, more seriously. "It seems as though Kanus has discovered some method of using the dueling machines to achieve political advantages over his neighbors.''

"What?"

Leoh explained the circumstances of Odal's duels with the Acquatainian Prime Minister and Szarno industrialist.

"Dulaq is completely incapacitated and the other poor fellow is dead?" Spencer's face darkened into a thundercloud. "You were right to call me. This is a situation that could easily become intolerable.''

"I agree," Leoh said. "But evidently Kanus has not broken any laws or interstellar agreements. All that meets the eye is a disturbing pair of accidents, both of them accruing to Kanus's benefit.''

"Do *you* believe that they were accidents?"

"Certainly not. The dueling machine cannot cause physical or mental harm . . . unless someone has tampered with it in some way."

"That is my thought, too." Spencer was silent for a moment, weighing the matter in his mind. "Very well. The Star Watch cannot act offically, but there is nothing to prevent me from dispatching an officer to the Acquataine Cluster, on detached duty, to serve as liaison between us."

"Good. I think that will be the most effective method of handling the situation, at present."

"It will be done," Sir Harold pronounced. His aide made a mental note of it.

"Thank you very much," Leoh said. "Now, go back to enjoying your vacation."

"Vacation? This is no vacation," Spencer rumbled. "I happen to be celebrating my birthday."

"So? Well, congratulations. I try not to remember mine," Leoh said.

"Then you must be older than I," Spencer replied, allowing only the faintest hint of a smile to appear.

"I suppose it's possible."

"But not very likely, eh?"

They laughed together and said goodbye. The Star Watch commander tramped through the hills until sunset, enjoying the sight of the grasslands and distant purple mountains he had known in his childhood. As dusk closed in, he told his aide he was ready to leave.

The aide pressed a stud on his belt and a two-place aircar skimmed silently from the far side of the hills and hovered beside them. Spencer climbed in laboriously while the aide remained discreetly at his side. While the commander settled his bulk into his seat, the aide hurried around the car and hopped into his place. The car glided off toward Spencer's personal planetship, waiting for him at a nearby field.

"Don't forget to assign an officer to Dr. Leoh," the commander muttered to his aide. Then he turned and watched the unmatchable beauty of an Earthly sunset.

*   *   *

The aide did not forget the assignment. That night, as Sir Harold's ship spiraled out to a rendezvous with a starship, the aide dictated the necessary order into an autodispatcher that immediately beamed it to the Star Watch's nearest communications center, on Mars.

The order was scanned and routed automatically and finally beamed to the Star Watch unit commandant in charge of the area closest to the Acquataine Cluster, on the sixth planet circling the star Perseus Alpha. Here again, the order was processed automatically and routed through the local headquarters to the personnel files. The automated files selected three microcard dossiers that matched the requirements of the order.

The three microcards and the order itself appeared simultaneously on the desktop viewer of the Star Watch personnel officer. He looked at the order, then read the dossiers. He flicked a button that gave him an updated status report on each of the three men in question. One was due for leave after an extensive period of duty. The second was the son of a personal friend of the local commandant. The third had just arrived a few weeks ago, fresh from the Star Watch Academy on Mars.

The personnel officer selected the third man, routed his dossier and Sir Harold's order back into the automatic processing system, and returned to the film of primitive dancing girls he had been watching before this matter of decision had arrived at his desk.

VI

The space station orbiting around Acquatainia—the capital planet of the Acquataine Cluster—served simultaneously as a transfer point from starships to planetships, a tourist resort, meteorological station, communications center, scientific laboratory, astronomical observatory, medical ha-

ven for allergy-and-cardiac patients, and military base. It
was, in reality, a good-sized city with its own markets, its
own local government, and its own way of life.

Dr. Leoh had just stepped off the debarking ramp of the
starship from Szarno. The trip there had been pointless and
fruitless. But he had gone anyway, in the slim hope that he
might find something wrong with the dueling machine that
had been used to murder a man.

A shudder went through him as he edged along the
automated customs scanners and paper-checkers. What kind
of people could these men of Kerak be? To actually kill a
human being in cold blood; to plot and plan the death of a
fellow man. Worse than barbaric. Savage.

He felt tired as he left customs and took the slideway to
the planetary shuttle ships. Halfway there, he decided to
check at the communications desk for messages. That Star
Watch officer that Sir Harold had promised him a week
ago should have arrived by now.

The communications desk consisted of a small booth
that contained the output printer of a communications computer and an attractive young dark-haired girl. Automation
or not, Leoh thought smilingly, there were certain human
values that transcended mere efficiency.

A lanky, thin-faced youth was half-leaning on the booth's
counter, trying to talk to the girl. He had curly blond hair
and crystal blue eyes; his clothes consisted of an ill-fitting
pair of slacks and tunic. A small traveler's kit rested on the
floor at his feet.

"So, I was sort of, well, thinking . . . maybe somebody
might, uh, show me around . . . a little," he was stam-
mering to the girl. "I've never been, uh, here. . . ."

"It's the most beautiful planet in the galaxy," the girl
was saying. "Its cities are the finest."

"Yes . . . well, I was sort of thinking . . . that is, I
know we just, uh, met a few minutes ago . . . but, well,
maybe . . . if you have a free day or so coming up . . .
maybe we could, uh, sort of . . ."

She smiled coolly. "I have two days off at the end of the week, but I'll be staying here at the station. There's so much to see and do here, I very seldom leave."

"Oh . . ."

"You're making a mistake," Leoh interjected dogmatically. "If you have such a beautiful planet for your homeworld, why in the name of the gods of intellect don't you go down there and enjoy it? I'll wager you haven't been out in the natural beauty and fine cities you spoke of since you started working here on the station."

"Why, you're right," she said, surprised.

"You see? You youngsters are all alike. You never think further than the ends of your noses. You should return to the planet, young lady, and see the sunshine again. Why don't you visit the university at the capital city? Plenty of open space and greenery, lots of sunshine and available young men!"

Leoh was grinning broadly, and the girl smiled back at him. "Perhaps I will," she said.

"Ask for me when you get to the university. I'm Dr. Leoh. I'll see to it that you're introduced to some of the girls and gentlemen of your own age."

"Why . . . thank you, doctor. I'll do it this weekend."

"Good. Now then, any messages for me? Anyone aboard the station looking for me?"

The girl turned and tapped a few keys on the computer's control console. A row of lights flicked briefly across the console's face. She turned back to Leoh:

"No, sir, I'm sorry. No messages and no one has asked for you."

"Hm-m-m. That's strange. Well, thank you . . . and I'll expect to see you at the end of this week."

The girl smiled a farewell. Leoh started to walk away from the booth, back toward the slideway. The young man took a step toward him, stumbled on his own traveling kit, and staggered across the floor for a half-dozen steps before regaining his balance. Leoh turned and saw that the youth's

face bore a somewhat ridiculous expression of mixed inde-
cision and curiosity.

"Can I help you?" Leoh asked, stopping at the edge of
the moving slideway.

"How . . . how did you do that, sir?"

"Do what?"

"Get that girl to agree to visit the university. I've been
talking to her for half an hour, and, well, she wouldn't
even look straight at me."

Leoh broke into a chuckle. "Well, young man, to begin
with, you were much too flustered. It made you appear
overanxious. On the other hand, I am at an age where I
can be strictly platonic. She was on guard against you, but
she knows she has very little to fear from me."

"I see . . . I think."

"Well," Leoh said, gesturing toward the slideway, "I
suppose this is where we go our separate ways."

"Oh, no, sir, I'm going with you. That is, I mean, you
are Dr. Leoh, aren't you?"

"Yes, I am. And you must be . . ." Leoh hesitated.
Can this be a Star Watch officer? he wondered.

The youth stiffened to attention and for an absurd flash
of a second, Leoh thought he was going to salute. "I am
Junior Lieutenant Hector, sir; on special detached duty
from the cruiser SW4-J188, home base Perseus Alpha
VI."

"I see," Leoh replied. "Um-m-m . . . is Hector your
first name or your last?"

"Both, sir."

I should have guessed, Leoh told himself. Aloud, he
said, "Well, lieutenant, we'd better get to the shuttle
before it leaves without us."

They took to the slideway. Half a second later, Hector
jumped off and dashed back to the communications desk
for his travel kit. He hurried back to Leoh, bumping into
seven bewildered citizens of various descriptions and nearly

breaking both his legs when he tripped as he ran back onto the moving slideway. He went down on his face, sprawled across two lanes moving at different speeds, and needed the assistance of several persons before he was again on his feet and standing beside Leoh.

"I . . . I'm sorry to cause all that, uh, commotion, sir."

"That's all right. You weren't hurt, were you?"

"Uh, no . . . I don't think so. Just embarrassed."

Leoh said nothing. They rode the slideway in silence through the busy station and out to the enclosed berths where the planetary shuttles were docked. They boarded one of the ships and found a pair of seats.

"Just how long have you been with the Star Watch, lieutenant?"

"Six weeks, sir. Three weeks aboard a starship bringing me out to Perseus Alpha VI, a week at the planetary base there, and two weeks aboard the cruiser SW4-J188. That is, it's been six weeks since I received my commission. I've been at the Academy . . . the Star Watch Academy on Mars . . . for four years."

"You got through the Academy in four years?"

"That's the regulation time, sir."

"Yes, I know."

The ship eased out of its berth. There was a moment of freefall, then the drive engine came on and the gravfield equilibrated.

"Tell me, lieutenant, how did you get picked for this assignment?"

"I wish I knew, sir," Hector said, his lean face twisting into a puzzled frown. "I was working out a program for the navigation officer . . . aboard the cruiser. I'm pretty good at that . . . I can work out computer programs in my head, mostly. Mathematics was my best subject at the Academy . . ."

"Interesting."

"Yes, well, anyway, I was working out this program when the captain himself came on deck and started shaking my hand and telling me that I was being sent on special duty on Acquatainia by direct orders of the Commander-in-Chief. He seemed very happy . . . the captain, that is.''

"He was no doubt pleased to see you get such an unusual assignment," Leoh said tactfully.

"I'm not so sure," Hector said truthfully. "I think he regarded me as some sort of a problem, sir. He had me on a different duty-berth practically every day I was on board the ship."

"Well now," Leoh changed the subject, "what do you know about psychonics?"

"About what, sir?"

"Eh . . . electroencephalography?"

Hector looked blank.

"Psychology, perhaps?" Leoh suggested, hopefully. "Physiology? Computer molectronics?"

"I'm pretty good at mathematics!"

"Yes, I know. Did you, by any chance, receive any training in diplomatic affairs?"

"At the Star Watch Academy? No, sir."

Leoh ran a hand through his thinning hair. "Then why did the Star Watch select you for this job? I must confess, lieutenant, that I can't understand the workings of a military organization."

Hector shook his head ruefully, "Neither do I, sir."

VII

The next week was an enervatingly slow one for Leoh, evenly divided between tedious checking of each component of the dueling machine, and shameless ruses to keep Hector as far away from the machine as possible.

The Star Watchman certainly wanted to help, and he actually *was* little short of brilliant in doing intricate mathematics completely in his head. But he was, Leoh found, a clumsy, chattering, whistling, scatterbrained, inexperienced bundle of noise and nerves. It was impossible to do constructive work with him nearby.

Perhaps you're judging him too harshly, Leoh warned himself. *You just might be letting your frustrations with the dueling machine get the better of your sense of balance.*

The professor was sitting in the office that the Acquatainians had given him in one end of the former lecture hall that held the dueling machine. Leoh could see its impassive metal hulk through the open office door.

The room he was sitting in had been one of a suite of offices used by the permanent staff of the machine. But they had moved out of the building completely, in deference to Leoh, and the Acquatainian government had turned the other cubbyhole offices into sleeping rooms for the professor and the Star Watchman, and an auto-kitchen. A combination cook-valet-handyman appeared twice each day—morning and evening—to handle any special chores that the cleaning machines and auto-kitchen might miss.

Leoh slouched back in his desk chair and cast a weary eye on the stack of papers that recorded the latest performances of the machine. Earlier that day he had taken the electroencephalographic records of clinical cases of catatonia and run them through the machine's input unit. The machine immediately rejected them, refused to process them through the amplification units and association circuits.

In other words, the machine had recognized the EEG traces as something harmful to a human being.

Then how did it happen to Dulaq? Leoh asked himself for the thousandth time. It couldn't have been the machine's fault; it must have been something in Odal's mind that simply overpowered Dulaq's.

"Overpowered?" That's a terribly unscientific term, Leoh argued against himself.

Before he could carry the debate any further, he heard the main door of the big chamber slide open and then bang shut, and Hector's off-key whistle shrilled and echoed through the high-vaulted room.

Leoh sighed and put his self-contained argument off to the back of his mind. Trying to think logically near Hector was a hopeless prospect.

"Are you in, doctor?" Hector's voice rang out.

"In here."

Hector ducked in through the doorway and plopped his rangy frame on the office's couch.

"Everything going well, sir?"

Leoh shrugged. "Not very well, I'm afraid. I can't find anything wrong with the dueling machine. I can't even *force* it to malfunction."

"Well, that's good, isn't it?" Hector chirped happily.

"In a sense," Leoh admitted, feeling slightly nettled at the youth's boundless, pointless optimism. "But, you see, it means that Kanus's people can do things with the machine that I can't."

Hector frowned, considering the problem. "Hm-m-m . . . yes, I guess that's right, too, isn't it?"

"Did you see the girl back to her ship safely?" Leoh asked.

"Yes, sir," Hector replied, bobbing his head vigorously. "She's on her way back to the communications booth at the space station. She said to tell you she enjoyed her visit very much."

"Good. It was, eh, very good of you to escort her about the campus. It kept her out of my hair . . . what's left of it, that is."

Hector grinned. "Oh, I liked showing her around, and all that— And, well, it sort of kept *me* out of your hair, too, didn't it?"

Leoh's eyebrows shot up in surprise.

Hector laughed. "Doctor, I may be clumsy, and I'm certainly no scientist . . . but I'm not completely brainless."

"I'm sorry if I gave you that impression . . ."

"Oh no . . . don't be sorry. I didn't mean that to sound so . . . well, the way it sounded . . . that is, I know I'm just in your way . . ." He started to get up.

Leoh waved him back to the couch. "Relax, my boy, relax. You know, I've been sitting here all afternoon wondering what to do next. Somehow, just now, I came to a conclusion."

"Yes?"

"I'm going to leave the Acquataine Cluster and return to Carinae."

"What? But you can't! I mean . . ."

"Why not? I'm not accomplishing anything here. Whatever it is that this Odal and Kanus have been doing, it's basically a political problem, and not a scientific one. The professional staff of the machine here will catch up to their tricks sooner or later."

"But, sir, if you can't find the answer, how can they?"

"Frankly, I don't know. But, as I said, this is a political problem more than a scientific one. I'm tired and frustrated and I'm feeling my years. I want to return to Carinae and spend the next few months considering beautifully abstract problems about instantaneous transportation devices. Let Massan and the Star Watch worry about Kanus."

"Oh! That's what I came to tell you. Massan has been challenged to a duel by Odal!"

"What?"

"This afternoon, Odal went to the Council building. Picked an argument with Massan right in the main corridor and challenged him."

"Massan accepted?" Leoh asked.

Hector nodded.

Leoh leaned across his desk and reached for the phone unit. It took a few minutes and a few levels of secretaries and assistants, but finally Massan's dark, bearded face appeared on the screen above the desk.

"You have accepted Odal's challenge?" Leoh asked, without preliminaries.

"We meet next week," Massan replied gravely.

"You should have refused."

"On what pretext?"

"No pretext. A flat refusal, based on the certainty that Odal or someone else from Kerak is tampering with the dueling machine."

Massan shook his head sadly. "My dear learned sir, you still do not comprehend the political situation. The government of the Acquataine Cluster is much closer to dissolution than I dare to admit openly. The coalition of star groups that Dulaq had constructed to keep the Kerak Worlds neutralized has broken apart completely. This morning, Kanus announced that he would annex Szarno. This afternoon, Odal challenges me."

"I think I see . . ."

"Of course. The Acquatainian government is paralyzed now, until the outcome of the duel is known. We cannot effectively intervene in the Szarno crisis until we know who will be heading the government next week. And, frankly, more than a few members of our Council are now openly favoring Kanus and urging that we establish friendly relations with him before it is too late."

"But, that's all the more reason for refusing the duel," Leoh insisted.

"And be accused of cowardice in my own Council meetings?" Massan smiled grimly. "In politics, my dear sir, the *appearance* of a man means much more than his substance. As a coward, I would soon be out of office. But, perhaps, as the winner of a duel against the invincible Odal . . . or even as a martyr . . . I may accomplish something useful."

Leoh said nothing.

Massan continued, "I put off the duel for a week, hoping that in that time you might discover Odal's secret. I dare not postpone the duel any longer; as it is, the political situation may collapse about our heads at any moment."

"I'll take this machine apart and rebuild it again, molecule by molecule," Leoh promised.

As Massan's image faded from the screen, Leoh turned to Hector. "We have one week to save his life."

"And avert a war, maybe," Hector added.

"Yes." Leoh leaned back in his chair and stared off into infinity.

Hector shuffled his feet, rubbed his nose, whistled a few bars of off-key tunes, and finally blurted, "How can you take apart the dueling machine?"

"Hm-m-m?" Leoh snapped out of his reverie.

"How can you take apart the dueling machine?" Hector repeated. "Looks like a big job to do in a week."

"Yes, it is. But, my boy, perhaps we . . . the two of us . . . can do it."

Hector scratched his head. "Well, uh, sir . . . I'm not very . . . that is, my mechanical aptitude scores at the Academy . . ."

Leoh smiled at him. "No need for mechanical aptitude, my boy. You were trained to fight, weren't you? We can do the job mentally."

VIII

It was the strangest week of their lives.

Leoh's plan was straightforward: to test the dueling machine, push it to the limits of its performance, by actually operating it—by fighting duels.

They started off easily enough, tentatively probing and flexing their mental muscles. Leoh had used the dueling machine himself many times in the past, but only in tests of the machine's routine performance. Never in actual combat against another human being. To Hector, of course, the machine was a totally new and different experience.

The Acquatainian staff plunged into the project without question, providing Leoh with invaluable help in monitoring and analyzing the duels.

At first, Leoh and Hector did nothing more than play hide-and-seek, with one of them picking an environment and the other trying to find his opponent in it. They wandered through jungles and cities, over glaciers and interplanetary voids, seeking each other—without ever leaving the booths of the dueling machine.

Then, when Leoh was satisfied that the machine could reproduce and amplify thought patterns with strict fidelity, they began to fight light duels. They fenced with blunted foils—Hector won, of course, because of his much faster reflexes. Then they tried other weapons—pistols, sonic beams, grenades—but always with the precaution of imagining themselves to be wearing protective equipment. Strangely, even though Hector was trained in the use of these weapons, Leoh won almost all the bouts. He was neither faster nor more accurate, when they were target-shooting. But when the two of them faced each other, somehow Leoh almost always won.

The machine projects more than thoughts, Leoh told himself. *It projects personality.*

They worked in the dueling machine day and night now, enclosed in the booths for twelve or more hours a day, driving themselves and the machine's regular staff to near-exhaustion. When they gulped their meals, between duels, they were physically ragged and sharp-tempered. They usually fell asleep in Leoh's office, while discussing the results of the day's work.

The duels grew slowly more serious. Leoh was pushing the machine to its limits now, carefully extending the rigors of each bout. And yet, even though he knew exactly what and how much he intended to do in each fight, it often took a conscious effort of will to remind himself that the battles he was fighting were actually imaginary.

As the duels became more dangerous, and the artificially amplified hallucinations began to end in blood and death, Leoh found himself winning more and more frequently. With one part of his mind he was driving to analyze the cause of his consistent success. But another part of him was beginning to really enjoy his prowess.

The strain was telling on Hector. The physical exertion

of constant work and practically no relief was considerable in itself. But the emotional effects of being "hurt" and "killed" repeatedly were infinitely worse.

"Perhaps we should stop for a while," Leoh suggested after the fourth day of tests.

"No. I'm all right."

Leoh looked at him. Hector's face was haggard, his eyes bleary.

"You've had enough," Leoh said quietly.

"Please don't make me stop," Hector begged. "I . . . I can't stop now. Please give me a chance to do better. I'm improving . . . I lasted twice as long in this afternoon's two duels as I did in the ones this morning. Please, don't end it now . . . not while I'm completely lost—"

Leoh stared at him. "You want to go on?"

"Yes, sir."

"And if I say no?"

Hector hesitated. Leoh sensed he was struggling with himself. "If you say no," he answered dully, "then it will be no. I can't argue against you any more."

Leoh was silent for a long moment. Finally he opened a desk drawer and took a small bottle from it. "Here, take a sleep capsule. When you wake up we'll try again."

It was dawn when they began again. Leoh entered the dueling machine determined to allow Hector to win. He gave the youthful Star Watchman his choice of weapon and environment. Hector picked one-man scoutships, in planetary orbits. Their weapons were conventional force beams.

But despite his own conscious desire, Leoh found himself winning! The ships spiraled about an unnamed planet, their paths intersecting at least once in every orbit. The problem was to estimate your opponent's orbital position, and then program your own ship so that you arrived at that position either behind or to one side of him. Then you could train your guns on him before he could turn on you.

The problem should have been an easy one for Hector, with his knack for intuitive mental calculation. But Leoh scored the first hit—Hector had piloted his ship into an excellent firing position, but his shot went wide; Leoh maneuvered around clumsily, but managed to register an inconsequential hit on the side of Hector's ship.

In the next three passes, Leoh scored two more hits. Hector's ship was badly damaged now. In return, the Star Watchman had landed one glancing shot on Leoh's ship.

They came around again, and once more Leoh had outguessed his younger opponent. He trained his guns on Hector's ship, then hesitated while his hand poised above the firing button.

Don't kill him again, he warned himself. *His mind can't accept another defeat.*

But Leoh's hand, almost of its own will, reached the button and touched it lightly. Another gram of pressure and the guns would fire.

In that instant's hesitation, Hector pulled his crippled ship around and aimed at Leoh. The Watchman fired a searing blast that jarred Leoh's ship from end to end. Leoh's hand slammed down on the firing button, whether he intended to do it or not, he did not know.

Leoh's shot raked Hector's ship but did not stop it. The two vehicles were hurtling directly at each other. Leoh tried desperately to avert a collision, but Hector bored in grimly, matching Leoh's maneuvers with his own.

The two ships smashed together and exploded.

Abruptly, Leoh found himself in the cramped booth of the dueling machine, his body cold and damp with perspiration, his hands trembling.

He squeezed out of the booth and took a deep breath. Warm sunlight was streaming into the high-vaulted room. The white walls glared brilliantly. Through the tall windows he could see trees and people and clouds in the sky.

Hector walked up to him. For the first time in several

days, the Watchman was smiling. Not much, but smiling.
"Well, we broke even on that one."

Leoh smiled back, somewhat shakily. "Yes. It was . . .
quite an experience. I've never died before."

Hector fidgeted. "It's, uh, not so bad, I guess . . . It
does sort of, well, shatter you, you know."

"Yes. I can see that now."

"Another duel?" Hector asked, nodding his head toward
the machine.

"Let's get out of this place for a few hours. Are you
hungry?"

"Starved."

They fought seven more duels over the next day and a
half. Hector won three of them. It was late afternoon when
Leoh called a halt to the tests.

"We can still get in another one or two," the Watchman pointed out.

"No need," Leoh said. "I have all the data I require.
Tomorrow Massan meets Odal, unless we can put a stop to
it. We have much to do before tomorrow morning."

Hector sagged into the couch. "Just as well. I think I've
aged seven years in the past seven days."

"No, my boy," Leoh said gently. "You haven't aged.
You've matured."

IX

It was deep twilight when the groundcar slid to a halt on
its cushion of compressed air before the Kerak Embassy.

"I still think it's a mistake to go in there," Hector said.
"I mean, you could've called him on the tri-di just as
well, couldn't you?"

Leoh shook his head. "Never give an agency of any
government the opportunity to say 'hold the line a moment' and then huddle together to consider what to do with
you. Nineteen times out of twenty, they'll end by passing

your request up to the next higher echelon, and you'll be left waiting for weeks.''

"Still," Hector insisted, "you're simply stepping into enemy territory. It's a chance you shouldn't take.''

"They wouldn't dare touch us.''

Hector did not reply, but he looked unconvinced.

"Look," Leoh said, "there are only two men alive who can shed light on this matter. One of them is Dulaq, and his mind is closed to us for an indefinite time. Odal is the only other one who knows what happened.''

Hector shook his head, skeptically. Leoh shrugged, and opened the door of the groundcar. Hector had no choice but to get out and follow him as he walked up the pathway to the main entrance of the Embassy. The building stood gaunt and gray in the dusk, surrounded by a precisely clipped hedge. The entrance was flanked by a pair of tall evergreen trees.

Leoh and Hector were met just inside the entrance by a female receptionist. She looked just a trifle disheveled—as though she had been rushed to the desk at a moment's notice. They asked for Odal, were ushered into a sitting room, and within a few minutes—to Hector's surprise—were informed by the girl that Major Odal would be with them shortly.

"You see," Leoh pointed out jovially, "when you come in person they haven't as much of a chance to consider how to get rid of you.''

Hector glanced around the windowless room and contemplated the thick, solidly closed door. "There's a lot of scurrying going on on the other side of that door, I'll bet. I mean . . . they may be considering how to, uh, get rid of us . . . permanently.''

Leoh shook his head, smiling wryly. "Undoubtedly the approach closest to their hearts—but highly improbable in the present situation. They have been making most efficient and effective use of the dueling machine to gain their ends.''

Odal picked this moment to open the door.

"Dr. Leoh . . . Lt. Hector . . . you asked to see me?"

"Thank you, Major Odal; I hope you will be able to help me," said Leoh. "You are the only man living who may be able to give us some clues to the failure of the dueling machine."

Odal's answering smile reminded Leoh of the best efforts of the robot-puppet designers to make a machine that smiled like a man. "I am afraid I can be of no assistance, Dr. Leoh. My experiences in the machine are . . . private."

"Perhaps you don't fully understand the situation," Leoh said. "In the past week, we have tested the dueling machine here on Acquatainia, exhaustively. We have learned that its performance can be greatly influenced by a man's personality, and by training. You have fought many duels in the machines. Your background of experience, both as a professional soldier and in the machines, gives you a decided advantage over your opponents.

"However, even with all this considered, I am convinced that you cannot kill a man in the machine—under normal circumstances. We have demonstrated that fact in our tests. An unsabotaged machine cannot cause actual physical harm.

"Yet you have already killed one man and incapacitated another. Where will it stop?"

Odal's face remained calm, except for the faintest glitter of fire deep in his eyes. His voice was quiet, but had the edge of a well-honed blade to it: "I cannot be blamed for my background and experience. And I have not tampered with your machines."

The door to the room opened, and a short, thick-set, bullet-headed man entered. He was dressed in a dark street suit, so that it was impossible to guess his station at the Embassy.

"Would the gentlemen care for refreshments?" he asked in a low-pitched voice.

"No, thank you," Leoh said.

"Some Kerak wine, perhaps?"

"Well—"

"I don't, uh, think we'd better, sir," Hector said. "Thanks all the same."

The man shrugged and sat at a chair next to the door.

Odal turned back to Leoh. "Sir, I have my duty. Massan and I duel tomorrow. There is no possibility of postponing it."

"Very well," Leoh said. "Will you at least allow us to place some special instrumentation into the booth with you, so that we can monitor the duel more fully? We can do the same with Massan. I know that duels are normally private and you would be within your legal rights to refuse the request. But, morally—"

The smile returned to Odal's face. "You wish to monitor my thoughts. To record them and see how I perform during the duel. Interesting. Very interesting—"

The man at the door rose and said, "If you have no desire for refreshments, gentlemen—"

Odal turned to him. "Thank you for your attention."

Their eyes met and locked for an instant. The man gave a barely perceptible shake of his head, then left.

Odal returned his attention to Leoh. "I am sorry, professor, but I cannot allow you to monitor my thoughts during the duel."

"But—"

"I regret having to refuse you. But, as you yourself pointed out, there is no legal requirement for such a course of action. I must refuse. I hope you understand."

Leoh rose from the couch, and Hector popped up beside him. "I'm afraid I do understand. And I, too, regret your decision."

Odal escorted them out to their car. They drove away, and the Kerak major walked slowly back into the Embassy building. He was met in the hallway by the dark-suited man who had sat in on the conversation.

"I could have let them monitor my thoughts and still crush Massan," Odal said. "It would have been a good joke on them."

The man grunted. "I have just spoken to the chancellor on the tri-di, and obtained permission to make a slight adjustment in our plans."

"An adjustment, Minister Kor?"

"After your duel tomorrow, your next opponent will be the eminent Dr. Leoh," Kor said.

X

The mists swirled deep and impenetrable about Fernd Massan. He stared blindly through the useless viewplate in his helmet, then reached up slowly and carefully to place the infrared detector before his eyes.

I never realized an hallucination could seem so real, Massan thought.

Since the challenge by Odal, he realized, the actual world had seemed quite unreal. For a week, he had gone through the motions of life, but felt as though he were standing aside, a spectator mind watching its own body from a distance. The gathering of his friends and associates last night, the night before the duel—that silent, funereal group of people—it had all seemed completely unreal to him.

But now, in this manufactured dream, he seemed vibrantly alive. Every sensation was solid, stimulating. He could feel his pulse throbbing through him. Somewhere out in those mists, he knew, was Odal. And the thought of coming to grips with the assassin filled him with a strange satisfaction.

Massan had spent a good many years serving his government on the rich, but inhospitable, high-gravity planets of the Acquataine Cluster. This was the environment he had chosen: crushing gravity; killing pressures; atmosphere of ammonia and hydrogen, laced with free radicals of sulphur and other valuable but deadly chemicals; oceans of liquid methane and ammonia; "solid ground" consisting of quickly crumbling, eroding ice; howling, superpowerful winds that could pick up a mountain of ice and hurl it halfway around the planet; darkness; danger; death.

He was encased in a one-man protective outfit that was half armored suit, half vehicle. There was an internal grav field to keep him comfortable in 3.7 gees, but still the suit was cumbersome, and a man could move only very slowly in it, even with the aid of servomotors.

The weapon he had chosen was simplicity itself—a hand-sized capsule of oxygen. But in a hydrogen/ammonia atmosphere, oxygen could be a deadly explosive. Massan carried several of these "bombs"; so did Odal. *But the trick,* Massan thought to himself, *is to know how to throw them under these conditions; the proper range, the proper trajectory. Not an easy thing to learn, without years of experience.*

The terms of the duel were simple: Massan and Odal were situated on a rough-topped iceberg that was being swirled along one of the methane/ammonia ocean's vicious currents. The ice was rapidly crumbling; the duel would end when the iceberg was completely broken up.

Massan edged along the ragged terrain. His suit's grippers and rollers automatically adjusted to the roughness of the topography. He concentrated his attention on the infrared detector that hung before his viewplate.

A chunk of ice the size of a man's head sailed through the murky atmosphere in a steep glide peculiar to heavy gravity and banged into the shoulder of Massan's suit. The force was enough to rock him slightly off-balance before the servos readjusted. Massan withdrew his arm from the sleeve and felt the inside of the shoulder seam. *Dented, but not penetrated.* A leak would have been disastrous, possibly fatal. Then he remembered: *Of course—I cannot*

*be killed except by direct action of my antagonist. That is
one of the rules of the game.*

Still, he carefully fingered the dented shoulder to make
certain it was not leaking. The dueling machine and its
rules seemed so very remote and unsubstantial, compared
to this freezing, howling inferno.

He diligently set about combing the iceberg, determined
to find Odal and kill him before their floating island
disintegrated. He thoroughly explored every projection,
every crevice, every slope, working his way slowly from
one end of the berg toward the other. Back and forth, cross
and recross, with the infrared sensors scanning three-
hundred-sixty degrees around him.

It was time-consuming. Even with the suit's servomotors and propulsion units, motion across the ice, against
the buffeting wind, was a cumbersome business. But Massan
continued to work his way across the iceberg, fighting
down a gnawing, growing fear that Odal was not there at
all.

And then he caught just the barest flicker of a shadow
on his detector. Something, or someone, had darted behind
a jutting rise of the ice, off by the edge of the iceberg.

Slowly and carefully, Massan made his way toward the
base of the rise. He picked one of the oxy-bombs from his
belt and held it in his right-hand claw.

Massan edged around the base of the ice cliff, and stood
on a narrow ledge between the cliff and the churning sea.
He saw no one. He extended the detector's range to maximum, and worked the scanners up the sheer face of the
cliff toward the top.

There he was! The shadowy outline of a man etched
itself on the detector screen. And at the same time, Massan
heard a muffled roar, then a rumbling, crashing noise,
growing quickly louder and more menacing.

He looked up the face of the ice cliff and saw a small
avalanche of ice tumbling, sliding, growling toward him.
That devil set off a bomb at the top of the cliff!

Massan tried to back out of the way, but it was too late. The first chunk of ice bounced harmlessly off his helmet, but the others knocked him off-balance so repeatedly that the servos had no chance to recover. He staggered blindly for a few moments, as more and more ice cascaded down on him, and then toppled off the ledge into the boiling sea.

Relax! he ordered himself. *Do not panic! The suit will float you. The servos will keep you right-side-up. You cannot be killed accidentally; Odal must perform the* coup-de-grace *himself.*

Then he remembered the emergency rocket units in the back of the suit. If he could orient himself properly, a touch of a control stud on his belt would set them off, and he would be boosted back onto the iceberg. He turned slightly inside the suit and tried to judge the iceberg's distance through the infrared detector. It was difficult, especially since he was bobbing madly in the churning currents.

Finally he decided to fire the rocket and make final adjustments of distance and landing site after he was safely out of the sea.

But he could not move his hand.

He tried, but his entire right arm was locked fast. He could not budge it an inch. And the same for the left. Something, or someone, was clamping his arms tight. He could not even pull them out of their sleeves.

Massan thrashed about, trying to shake off whatever it was. No use.

Then his detector screen was lifted slowly from the viewplate. He felt something vibrating on his helmet. The oxygen tubes! They were being disconnected.

He screamed and tried to fight free. No use. With a hiss, the oxygen tubes pulled free of his helmet. Massan could feel the blood pounding through his veins as he fought desperately to free himself.

Now he was being pushed down into the sea. He screamed again and tried to wrench his body away. The frothing sea filled his viewplate. He was under. He was being held under. And now . . . now the viewplate itself was being loosened.

No! Don't! The scalding, cold methane-ammonia sea seeped in through the opening viewplate.

"It's only a dream!" Massan shouted to himself. "Only a dream. A dream. A—"

XI

Dr. Leoh stared at the dinner table without really seeing it. Coming to this restaurant had been Hector's idea. Three hours earlier, Massan had been removed from the dueling machine—dead.

Leoh sat stolidly, hands in lap, his mind racing in many different directions at once. Hector was off at the phone, getting the latest information from the meditechs. Odal had expressed his regrets perfunctorily, and then left for the Kerak Embassy, under a heavy escort of his own plain-clothes guards. The government of the Acquataine Cluster was quite literally falling apart, with no man willing to assume responsibility . . . and thereby expose himself. One hour after the duel, Kanus's troops had landed on all the major planets of the Szarno Confederacy; the annexation was a *fait accompli.*

And what have I done since I arrived on Acquatainia? Leoh demanded of himself. *Nothing. Absolutely nothing. I have sat back like a doddering old professor and played academic games with the machine, while younger, more vigorous men have USED the machine to suit their purposes.*

Used the machine. There was a fragment of an idea in that phrase. Something nebulous, that must be approached carefully or it will fade away. Used the machine . . . used it . . . Leoh toyed with the phrase for a few moments, then gave it up with a sigh of resignation. *Lord, I'm too tired even to think.*

Leoh focused his attention on his surroundings and scanned the busy dining room. It was a beautiful place, really; decorated with crystal and genuine woods and fabric draperies. Not a synthetic in sight. The waiters and cooks and busboys were humans, not the autocookers and servers that most restaurants employed. Leoh suddenly felt touched at Hector's attempt to restore his spirits—even if it *was* being done at Star Watch expense.

He saw the young Watchman approaching the table, coming back from the phone. Hector bumped two waiters and stumbled over a chair before reaching the relative safety of his own seat.

"What's the verdict?" Leoh asked.

Hector's lean face was bleak. "Couldn't revive him. Cerebral hemorrhage, the meditechs said—induced by shock."

"Shock?"

"That's what they said. Something must've, uh, overloaded his nervous system . . . I guess."

Leoh shook his head. "I just don't understand any of this. I might as well admit it. I'm no closer to an answer now than I was when I arrived here. Perhaps I should have retired years ago, before the dueling machine was invented."

"Nonsense."

"No, I mean it," Leoh said. "This is the first real intellectual puzzle I've had to contend with in years. Tinkering with machinery . . . that's easy. You know what you want, all you need is to make the machinery perform properly. But this . . . I'm afraid I'm too old to handle a real problem like this."

Hector scratched his nose thoughtfully, then answered. "If you can't handle the problem, sir, then we're going to have a war on our hands in a matter of weeks. I mean, Kanus won't be satisfied with swallowing the Szarno group . . . the Acquataine Cluster is next . . . and he'll have to fight to get it."

"Then the Star Watch can step in," Leoh said, resignedly.

"Maybe . . . but it'll take time to mobilize the Star Watch. . . . Kanus can move a lot faster than we can. Sure, we could throw in a task force . . . a token group, that is. But Kanus's gang will chew them up pretty quick. I . . . I'm no politician, sir, but I think I can see what will happen. Kerak will gobble up the Acquataine Cluster . . . a Star Watch task force will be wiped out in the battle . . . and we'll end up with Kerak at war with the Terran Commonwealth. And it'll be a real war . . . a big one."

Leoh began to answer, then stopped. His eyes were fixed on the far entrance of the dining room. Suddenly every murmur in the busy room stopped dead. Waiters stood still between tables. Eating, drinking, conversation hung suspended.

Hector turned in his chair and saw at the far entrance the slim, stiff, blue-uniformed figure of Odal.

The moment of silence passed. Everyone turned to his own business and avoided looking at the Kerak major. Odal, with a faint smile on his thin face, made his way slowly to the table where Hector and Leoh were sitting.

They rose to greet him and exchanged perfunctory salutations. Odal pulled up a chair and sat with them.

"I assume that you've been looking for me," Leoh said. "What do you wish to say?"

Before Odal could answer, the waiter assigned to the table walked up, took a position where his back would be to the Kerak major, and asked firmly, "Your dinner is ready gentlemen. Shall I serve it now?"

Leoh hesitated a moment, then asked Odal, "Will you join us?"

"I'm afraid not."

"Serve it now," Hector said. "The major will be leaving shortly."

Again the tight grin broke across Odal's face. The waiter bowed and left.

"I have been thinking about our conversation of last night," Odal said to Leoh.

"Yes?"

"You accused me of cheating in my duels."

Leoh's eyebrows arched. "I said someone was cheating, yes—"

"An accusation is an accusation."

Leoh said nothing.

"Do you withdraw your words, or do you still accuse me of deliberate murder? I am willing to allow you to apologize and leave Acquatainia in peace."

Hector cleared his throat noisily. "This is no place to have an argument . . . besides, here comes our dinner."

Odal ignored the Watchman. "You heard me, professor. Will you leave? Or do you accuse me of murdering Massan this afternoon?"

"I—"

Hector banged his fist on the table and jerked up out of his chair—just as the waiter arrived with a large tray of food. There was a loud crash. A tureen of soup, two bowls of salad, glasses, assorted rolls, vegetables, cheeses and other delicacies cascaded over Odal.

The Kerak major leaped to his feet, swearing violently in his native tongue. He sputtered back into basic Terran: "You clumsy, stupid oaf! You maggot-brained misbegotten peasantfaced—"

Hector calmly picked a salad leaf from the sleeve of his tunic. Odal abruptly stopped his tirade.

"I am clumsy," Hector said, grinning. "As for being stupid, and the rest of it, I resent that. I am highly insulted."

A flash of recognition lighted Odal's eyes. "I see. Of course. My quarrel here is not with you. I apologize." He turned back to Leoh, who was also standing now.

"Not good enough," Hector said. "I don't, uh, like the . . . tone of your apology."

Leoh raised a hand, as if to silence the younger man.

"I apologized; that is sufficient," Odal warned.

Hector took a step toward Odal. "I guess I could insult your glorious leader, or something like that . . . but this seems more direct.'' He took the water pitcher from the table and poured it calmly and carefully over Odal's head.

A wave of laughter swept the room. Odal went white. ''You are determined to die.'' He wiped the dripping water from his eyes. ''I will meet you before the week is out. And you have saved no one.'' He turned on his heel and stalked out.

''Do you realize what you've done?'' Leoh asked, aghast.

Hector shrugged. ''He was going to challenge you—''

''He will still challenge me, after you're dead.''

''Um-m-m, yes, well, maybe so. I guess you're right— Well, anyway, we've gained a little more time.''

''Four days,'' Leoh shook his head. ''Four days to the end of the week. All right, come on, we have work to do.''

Hector was grinning broadly as they left the restaurant. He began to whistle.

''What are you so happy about?'' Leoh grumbled.

''About you, sir. When we came in here, you were, uh, well . . . almost beaten. Now you're right back in the game again.''

Leoh glanced at the Star Watchman. ''In your own odd way, Hector, you're quite a boy . . . I think.''

XII

Their groundcar glided from the parking building to the restaurant's entrance ramp, at the radio call of the doorman. Within minutes, Hector and Leoh were cruising through the city, in the deepening shadows of night.

''There's only one man,'' Leoh said, ''who has faced Odal and lived through it.''

''Dulaq,'' Hector agreed. ''But . . . for all the information the medical people have been able to get from him, he might as well be, uh, dead.''

''He's still completely withdrawn?''

Hector nodded. "The medicos think that . . . well,
maybe in a few months, with drugs and psychotherapy and
all that . . . they might be able to bring him back."

"It won't be soon enough. We've only got four days."

"I know."

Leoh was silent for several minutes. Then: "Who is
Dulaq's closest living relative? Does he have a wife?"

"I think his wife is, uh, dead. Has a daughter though.
Pretty girl. Bumped into her in the hospital once or twice—"

Leoh smiled in the darkness. Hector's term, "bumped
into," was probably completely literal.

"Why are you asking about Dulaq's next-of-kin?"

"Because," Leoh replied, "I think there might be a
way to make Dulaq tell us what happened during his duel.
But it is a very dangerous way. Perhaps a fatal way."

"Oh."

They lapsed into silence again. Finally he blurted, "Come
on, my boy, let's find the daughter and talk to her."

"Tonight?"

"Now."

She certainly is a pretty girl, Leoh thought as he explained very carefully to Geri Dulaq what he proposed to
do. She sat quietly and politely in the spacious living room
of the Dulaq residence. The glittering chandelier cast touches
of fire on her chestnut hair. Her slim body was slightly
rigid with tension, her hands were clasped in her lap. Her
face—which looked as though it could be very expressive—
was completely serious now.

"And that is the sum of it." Leoh concluded. "I believe
that it will be possible to use the dueling machine itself to
examine your father's thoughts and determine exactly what
took place during his duel against Major Odal!"

She asked softly, "But you are afraid that the shock
might be repeated, and this could be fatal to my father?"

Leoh nodded wordlessly.

"Then I am very sorry, sir, but I must say no." Firmly.

"I understand your feelings," Leoh replied, "but I hope you realize that unless we can stop Odal and Kanus immediately, we may very well be faced with war."

She nodded. "I know. But you must remember that we are speaking of my father, of his very life. Kanus will have his war in any event, no matter what I do."

"Perhaps," Leoh admitted. "Perhaps."

Hector and Leoh drove back to the university campus and their quarters in the dueling machine chamber. Neither of them slept well that night.

The next morning, after an unenthusiastic breakfast, they found themselves standing in the antiseptic-white chamber, before the looming, impersonal intricacy of the machine.

"Would you like to practice with it?" Leoh asked.

Hector shook his head. "Maybe later."

The phone chimed in Leoh's office. They both went in. Geri Dulaq's faced showed on the tri-di screen.

"I have just heard the news. I did not know that Lieutenant Hector had challenged Odal." Her face was a mixture of concern and reluctance.

"He challenged Odal," Leoh answered, "to prevent the assassin from challenging me."

"Oh . . . You are a very brave man, lieutenant."

Hector's face went through various contortions and slowly turned a definite red, but no words issued from his mouth.

"Have you reconsidered your decision?" Leoh asked.

The girl closed her eyes briefly, then said flatly, "I am afraid I cannot change my decision. My father's safety is my first responsibility. I am sorry."

They exchanged a few meaningless trivialities—with Hector still thoroughly tongue-tied and ended the conversation on a polite, but strained, note.

Leoh rubbed his thumb across the phone switch for a moment, then turned to Hector. "My boy, I think it would be a good idea for you to go straight to the hospital and check on Dulaq's condition."

"But . . . why . . ."

"Don't argue, son. This could be vitally important."

Hector shrugged and left the office. Leoh sat down at his desk and drummed his fingers on the top of it. Then he burst out of the office and began pacing the big chamber. Finally, even that was too confining. He left the building and started stalking through the campus. He walked past a dozen buildings, turned and strode as far as the decorative fence that marked the end of the main campus, ignoring students and faculty alike.

Campuses are all alike, he muttered to himself, *on every human planet, for all the centuries there have been universities. There must be some fundamental reason for it.*

Leoh was halfway back to the dueling machine facility when he spotted Hector walking dazedly toward the same building. For once, the Watchman was not whistling. Leoh cut across some lawn and pulled up beside the youth.

"Well?" he asked.

Hector shook his head, as if to clear away an inner fog. "How did you know she'd be at the hospital?"

"The wisdom of age. What happened?"

"She kissed me. Right there in the hallway of the—"

"Spare me the geography," Leoh cut in. "What did she say?"

"I bumped into her in the hallway. We, uh, started talking . . . sort of. She seemed, well . . . worried about me. She got upset. Emotional. You know? I guess I looked pretty forlorn and frightened. I am . . . I guess. When you get right down to it, I mean."

"You aroused her maternal instinct."

"I . . . I don't think it was that . . . exactly. Well, anyway, she said that if I was willing to risk my life to save yours, she couldn't protect her father any more. Said she was doing it out of selfishness, really, since he's her only living relative. I don't believe she meant that, but she said it anyway."

They had reached the building by now. Leoh grabbed

Hector's arm and steered him clear of a collision with the half-open door.

"She's agreed to let us put Dulaq in the dueling machine?"

"Sort of."

"Eh?"

"The medical staff doesn't want him to be moved from the hospital . . . especially not back to here. She agrees with them."

Leoh snorted. "All right. In fact, so much the better. I'd rather not have the Kerak people see us bring Dulaq to the dueling machine. So instead, we shall smuggle the dueling machine to Dulaq!"

XIII

They plunged to work immediately. Leoh preferred not to inform the regular staff of the dueling machine about their plan, so he and Hector had to work through the night and most of the next morning. Hector barely understood what he was doing, but with Leoh's supervision, he managed to dismantle part of the dueling machine's central network, insert a few additional black boxes that the professor had conjured up from the spare parts bins in the basement, and then reconstruct the machine so that it looked exactly the same as before they had started.

In between his frequent trips to oversee Hector's work, Leoh had jury-rigged a rather bulky headset and a hand-sized override control circuit.

The late morning sun was streaming through the tall windows when Leoh finally explained it all to Hector.

"A simple matter of technological improvisation," he told the bewildered Watchman. "You have installed a short-range transceiver into the machine, and this headset is a portable transceiver for Dulaq. Now he can sit in his hospital bed and still be 'in' the dueling machine."

Only the three most trusted members of the hospital staff were taken into Leoh's confidence, and they were hardly enthusiastic about Leoh's plan.

"It is a waste of time," said the chief psychophysician, shaking his white-maned head vigorously. "You cannot expect a patient who has shown no positive response to drugs and therapy to respond to your machine."

Leoh argued, Geri Dulaq coaxed. Finally the doctors agreed. With only two days remaining before Hector's duel with Odal, they began to probe Dulaq's mind. Geri remained by her father's bedside while the three doctors fitted the cumbersome transceiver to Dulaq's head and attached the electrodes for the automatic hospital equipment that monitored his physical condition. Hector and Leoh remained at the dueling machine, communicating with the hospital by phone.

Leoh made a final check of the controls and circuitry, then put in the last call to the tense little group in Dulaq's room. All was ready.

He walked out to the machine, with Hector beside him. Their footsteps echoed hollowly in the sepulchral chamber. Leoh stopped at the nearer booth.

"Now remember," he said, carefully, "I will be holding the emergency control unit in my hand. It will stop the duel the instant I set it off. However, if something should go wrong, you must be prepared to act quickly. Keep a close watch on my physical condition; I've shown you which instruments to check on the control board—"

"Yes, sir."

Leoh nodded and took a deep breath. "Very well then."

He stepped into the booth and sat down. The emergency control unit rested on a shelf at his side; he took it in his hands. He leaned back and waited for the semihypnotic effect to take hold. Dulaq's choice of this very city and the stat-wand were known. But beyond that, everything was locked and sealed in Dulaq's subconscious mind. Could the machine reach into that subconscious, probe past the lock and seal of catatonia, and stimulate Dulaq's mind into repeating the duel?

Slowly, lullingly, the dueling machine's imaginary, yet very real, mists enveloped Leoh. When the mists cleared, he was standing on the upper pedestrian level of the main commercial street of the city. For a long moment, everything was still.

Have I made contact? Whose eyes am I seeing with, my own or Dulaq's?

And then he sensed it—an amused, somewhat astonished marveling at the reality of the illusion. Dulaq's thoughts!

Make your mind a blank, Leoh told himself. *Watch. Listen. Be passive.*

He became a spectator, seeing and hearing the world through Dulaq's eyes and ears as the Acquatainian Prime Minister advanced through his nightmarish ordeal. He felt the confusion, frustration, apprehension, and growing terror as, time and again, Odal appeared in the crowd—only to melt into someone else and escape.

The first part of the duel ended, and Leoh was suddenly buffeted by a jumble of thoughts and impressions. Then the thoughts slowly cleared and steadied.

Leoh saw an immense and totally barren plain. Not a tree, not a blade of grass; nothing but bare, rocky ground stretching in all directions to the horizon and a disturbingly harsh yellow sky. At his feet was the weapon Odal had chosen. A primitive club.

He shared Dulaq's sense of dread as he picked up the club and hefted it. Off on the horizon he could see a tall, lithe figure holding a similar club walking toward him.

Despite himself, Leoh could feel his own excitement. He had broken through the shock-created armor that Dulaq's mind had erected! Dulaq was reliving the part of the duel that had caused the shock.

Reluctantly, he advanced to meet Odal. But as they drew closer together, the one figure of his opponent seemed to split apart. Now there were two, four, six of them. Six Odals, six mirror images, all armed with massive, evil clubs, advancing steadily on him.

Six tall, lean, blond assassins, with six cold smiles on their intent faces.

Horrified, completely panicked, he scrambled away, trying to evade the six opponents with the half-dozen clubs raised and poised to strike.

Their young legs and lungs easily outdistanced him. A smash on his back sent him sprawling. One of them kicked his weapon away.

They stood over him for a malevolent, gloating second. Then six strong arms flashed down, again and again, mercilessly. Pain and blood, screaming agony, punctuated by the awful thudding of solid clubs hitting fragile flesh and bone, over and over again, endlessly.

Everything went blank.

Leoh opened his eyes and saw Hector bending over him.

"Are you all right, sir?"

"I . . . I think so."

"The controls all hit the danger mark at once. You were . . . well, sir, you were screaming."

"I don't doubt it," Leoh said.

They walked, with Leoh leaning on Hector's arm, from the dueling machine booth to the office.

"That was . . . an experience," Leoh said, easing himself onto the couch.

"What happened? What did Odal do? What made Dulaq go into shock? How does—"

The old man silenced Hector with a wave of his hand. "One question at a time, please."

Leoh leaned back on the deep couch and told Hector every detail of both parts of the duel.

"Six Odals," Hector muttered soberly, leaning back against the doorframe, "six against one."

"That's what he did. It's easy to see how a man expecting a polite, formal duel can be completely shattered by the viciousness of such an attack. And the machine amplifies every impulse, every sensation.''

"But how does he do it?" Hector asked, his voice suddenly loud and demanding.

"I've been asking myself the same question. We've checked over the dueling machine time and again. There is no possible way for Odal to put in five helpers . . . unless—''

"Unless?"

Leoh hesitated, seemingly debating with himself. Finally he nodded his head sharply, and answered, "Unless Odal is a telepath.''

"Telepath? But—''

"I know it sounds far-fetched. But there have been well-documented cases of telepathy for centuries throughout the Commonwealth.''

Hector frowned. "Sure, everybody's heard about it . . . natural telepaths . . . but they're so unpredictable . . . I don't see how . . .''

Leoh leaned forward on the couch and clasped his hands in front of his chin. "The Terran races have never developed telepathy, or any of the extrasensory talents. They never had to, not with tri-di communications and superlight starships. But perhaps, the Kerak people are different—''

Hector shook his head. "If they had, uh, telepathic abilities, they would be using them everywhere. Don't you think?''

"Probably so. But only Odal has shown such an ability, and only . . . *of course!*''

"What?"

"Odal has shown telepathic ability only in the dueling machine.''

"As far as we know.''

"Certainly. But look, suppose he's a natural telepath . . . the same as a Terran. He has an erratic, difficult-to-control talent. Then he gets into a dueling machine. The machine amplifies his thoughts. And it also amplifies his talent!''

"Ohhh."

"You see . . . outside the machine, he's no better than any wandering fortuneteller. But the dueling machine gives his natural abilities the amplification and reproducibility that they could never have unaided.''

Hector nodded.

"So it's a fairly straightforward matter for him to have five associates in the Kerak Embassy sit in on the duel, so to speak. Possibly they are natural telepaths also, but they needn't be.''

"They just, uh, pool their minds with his, hm-m-m? Six men show up in the duel . . . pretty nasty.'' Hector dropped into the desk chair.

"So what do we do now?''

"Now?'' Leoh blinked at his young friend. "Why . . . I suppose the first thing we should do is call the hospital and see how Dulaq came through.''

Leoh put the call through. Geri Dulaq's face appeared on the screen.

"How's your father?'' Hector blurted.

"The duel was too much for him,'' she said blankly. "He is dead.''

"No,'' Leoh groaned.

"I . . . I'm sorry,'' Hector said. "I'll be right down there. Stay where you are.''

The young Star Watchman dashed out of the office as Geri broke the phone connection. Leoh stared at the blank screen for a few moments, then leaned far back in the couch and closed his eyes. He was suddenly exhausted, physically and emotionally. He fell asleep, and dreamed of men dead and dying.

Hector's nerve-shattering whistling woke him up. It was full night outside.

"What are you so happy about?'' Leoh groused as Hector popped into the office.

"Happy? Me?"

"You were whistling."

Hector shrugged. "I always whistle, sir. Doesn't mean I'm happy."

"All right," Leoh said, rubbing his eyes. "How did the girl take her father's death?"

"Pretty hard. Cried a lot."

Leoh looked at the younger man. "Does she blame . . . me?"

"You? Why, no, sir. Why should she? Odal . . . Kanus . . . the Kerak Worlds. But not you."

The old professor sighed, relieved. "Very well. Now then, we have much work to do, and little more than a day in which to finish it."

"What do you want me to do?" Hector asked.

"Phone the Star Watch commander—"

"My commanding officer, all the way back at Alpha Perseus VI? That's a hundred light-years from here."

"No, no, no." Leoh shook his head. "The Commander-in-Chief, Sir Harold Spencer. At Star Watch Central Headquarters. That's several hundred parsecs from here. But get through to him as quickly as possible."

With a low whistle of astonishment, Hector began punching buttons on the phone switch.

XIV

The morning of the duel arrived, and precisely at the agreed-upon hour, Odal and a small retinue of Kerak representatives stepped through the double doors of the dueling machine chamber.

Hector and Leoh were already there, waiting. With them stood another man, dressed in the black-and-silver of the Star Watch. He was a blocky, broad-faced veteran with iron-gray hair and hard, unsmiling eyes.

The two little groups of men knotted together in the

center of the room, before the machine's control board.
The white-uniformed staff meditechs emerged from a far
doorway and stood off to one side.

Odal went through the formality of shaking hands with
Hector. The Kerak major nodded toward the other Watchman. "Your replacement?" he asked mischievously.

The chief meditech stepped between them. "Since you
are the challenged party, Major Odal, you have the first
choice of weapon and environment. Are there any instructions or comments necessary before the duel begins?"

"I think not," Odal replied. "The situation will be
self-explanatory. I assume, of course, that Star Watchmen
are trained to be warriors and not merely technicians. The
situation I have chosen is one in which many warriors have
won glory.".

Hector said nothing.

"I intend," Leoh said firmly, "to assist the staff in
monitoring this duel. Your aides may, of course, sit at the
control board with me."

Odal nodded.

"If you are ready to begin, gentlemen," the chief
meditech said.

Hector and Odal went to their booths, Leoh sat at the
control console, and one of the Kerak men sat down next
to him.

Hector felt every nerve and muscle tense as he sat in
the booth, despite his efforts to relax. Slowly the tension
eased, and he began to feel slightly drowsy. The booth
seemed to melt away . . .

He was standing on a grassy meadow. Off in the distance were wooded hills. A cool breeze was hustling puffy
white clouds across a calm blue sky.

Hector heard a snuffling noise behind him, and wheeled
around. He blinked, then stared.

It had four legs, and was evidently a beast of burden. At
least, it carried a saddle on its back. Piled atop the saddle
was a conglomeration of what looked to Hector—at first

glance—like a pile of junk. He went over to the animal and examined it carefully. The "junk" turned out to be a long spear, various pieces of armor, a helmet, sword, shield, battle-ax and dagger.

The situation I have chosen is one in which many warriors have won glory. Hector puzzled over the assortment of weapons. They came straight out of Kerak's Dark Ages. No doubt Odal had been practicing with them for months, even years. He might not need five helpers.

Warily, Hector put on the armor. The breastplate seemed too big, and he was somehow unable to tighten the greaves on his shins properly. The helmet fit over his head like an ancient oil can, flattening his ears and nose and forcing him to squint to see through the narrow eye-slit.

Finally, he buckled on the sword and found attachments on the saddle for the other weapons. The shield was almost too heavy to lift, and he barely struggled into the saddle with all the weight he was carrying.

And then he just sat. He began to feel a little ridiculous. *Suppose it rains?* he wondered. But of course it wouldn't.

After an interminable wait, Odal appeared, on a powerful trotting charger. His armor was black as space, and so was his animal. *Naturally,* Hector thought.

Odal saluted gravely with his great spear from across the meadow. Hector returned the salute, nearly dropping his spear in the process.

Then, Odal lowered his spear and aimed it—so it seemed to Hector—directly at the Watchman's ribs. He pricked his mount into a canter. Hector did the same, and his steed jogged into a bumping, jolting gallop. The two warriors hurtled toward each other from opposite ends of the meadow.

And suddenly there were six black figures roaring down on Hector!

The Watchmen's stomach wrenched within him. Automatically he tried to turn his mount aside. But the beast had no intention of going anywhere except straight ahead.

The Kerak warriors bore in, six abreast, with six spears aimed menacingly.

Abruptly, Hector heard the pounding of other hoof beats right beside him. Through a corner of his helmet-slit he glimpsed at least two other warriors charging with him into Odal's crew.

Leoh's gamble had worked. The transceiver that had allowed Dulaq to make contact with the dueling machine from his hospital bed was now allowing five Star Watch officers to join Hector, even though they were physically sitting in a starship orbiting high above the planet.

The odds were even now. The five additional Watchmen were the roughest, hardiest, most aggressive man-to-man fighters that the Star Watch could provide on a one-day notice.

Twelve powerful chargers met head on, and twelve strong men smashed together with an ear-splitting *clang!* Shattered spears showered splinters everywhere. Men and animals went down.

Hector was rocked back in his saddle, but somehow managed to avoid falling off.

On the other hand, he could not really regain his balance, either. Dust and weapons filled the air. A sword hissed near his head and rattled off his shield.

With a supreme effort, Hector pulled out his own sword and thrashed at the nearest rider. It turned out to be a fellow Watchman, but the stroke bounced harmlessly off his helmet.

It was so confusing. The wheeling, snorting animals. Clouds of dust. Screaming, raging men. A black-armored rider charged into Hector, waving a battle-ax over his head. He chopped savagely, and the Watchman's shield split apart. Another frightening swing—Hector tried to duck and slid completely out of the saddle, thumping painfully on the ground, while the ax cleaved the air where his head had been a split-second earlier.

Somehow his helmet had been turned around. Hector

tried to decide whether to thrash blindly or lay down his sword and straighten out the helmet. The problem was solved for him by the *crang!* of a sword against the back of his helmet. The blow flipped him into a somersault, but also knocked the helmet completely off his head.

Hector climbed painfully to his feet, his head spinning. It took him several moments to realize that the battle had stopped. The dust drifted away, and he saw that all the Kerak fighters were down—except one. The black-armored warrior took off his helmet and tossed it aside. It was Odal. Or was it? They all looked alike. *What difference does it make?* Hector wondered. *Odal's mind is the dominant one.*

Odal stood, legs braced apart, sword in hand, and looked uncertainly at the other Star Watchmen. Three of them were afoot and two still mounted. The Kerak assassin seemed as confused as Hector felt. The shock of facing equal numbers had sapped much of his confidence.

Cautiously, he advanced toward Hector, holding his sword out before him. The other Watchmen stood aside while Hector slowly backpedaled, stumbling slightly on the uneven ground.

Odal feinted and cut at Hector's arm. The Watchman barely parried in time. Another feint, at the head, and a slash into the chest; Hector missed the parry but his armor saved him. Grimly, Odal kept advancing. Feint, feint, crack! and Hector's sword went flying from his hand.

For the barest instant everyone froze. Then Hector leaped desperately straight at Odal, caught him completely by surprise, and wrestled him to the ground. The Watchman pulled the sword from his opponent's hand and tossed it away. But with his free hand, Odal clouted Hector on the side of the head and knocked him on his back. Both men scrambled up and ran for the nearest weapons.

Odal picked up a wicked-looking double-bladed ax. One of the mounted Star Watchmen handed Hector a huge broadsword. He gripped it with both hands, but still staggered off-balance as he swung it up over his shoulder.

Holding the broadsword aloft, Hector charged toward Odal, who stood dogged, short-breathed, sweat-streaked, waiting for him. The broadsword was quite heavy, even for a two-handed grip. And Hector did not notice his own battered helmet lying on the ground between them.

Odal, for his part, had Hector's charge and swing timed perfectly in his own mind. He would duck under the swing and bury his ax in the Watchman's chest. Then he would face the others. Probably with their leader gone, the duel would automatically end. But, of course, Hector would not really be dead; the best Odal could hope for now was to win the duel.

Hector charged directly into Odal's plan, but the Watchman's timing was much poorer than anticipated. Just as he began the downswing of a mighty broadsword stroke, he stumbled on the helmet. Odal started to duck, then saw that the Watchman was diving face-first into the ground, legs flailing, and that heavy broadsword was cleaving through the air with a will of its own.

Odal pulled back in confusion, only to have the wild-swinging broadsword strike him just above the wrist. The ax dropped out of his hand, and Odal involuntarily grasped the wounded forearm with his left hand. Blood seeped through his fingers.

He shook his head in bitter resignation, turned his back on the prostrate Hector, and began walking away.

Slowly, the scene faded, and Hector found himself sitting in the booth of the dueling machine.

XV

The door opened and Leoh squeezed into the booth. "You're all right?"

Hector blinked and refocused his eyes on reality. "Think so—"

"Everything went well? The Watchmen got through to you?"

"Good thing they did. I was nearly killed anyway."

"But you survived."

"So far."

Across the room, Odal stood massaging his forehead while Kor demanded: "How could they possibly have discovered the secret? Where was the leak?"

"That is not important now," Odal said quietly. "The primary fact is that they have not only discovered our secret, but they have found a way of duplicating it."

"The sanctimonious hypocrites," Kor snarled, "accusing us of cheating, and then they do the same thing."

"Regardless of the moral values of our mutual behavior," Odal said dryly, "it is evident that there is no longer any use in calling on telepathically-guided assistants. I shall face the Watchman alone during the second half of the duel."

"Can you trust them to do the same?"

"Yes. They easily defeated my aides a few minutes ago, then stood aside and allowed the two of us to fight by ourselves."

"And you failed to defeat him?"

Odal frowned. "I was wounded by a fluke. He is a very . . . unusual opponent. I cannot decide whether he is actually as clumsy as he appears to be, or whether he is shamming and trying to make me overconfident. Either way, it is impossible to predict his behavior. Perhaps he is also telepathic."

Kor's gray eyes became flat and emotionless. "You know, of course, how the chancellor will react if you fail to kill this Watchman. Not merely defeat him. He must be killed. The aura of invincibility must be maintained."

"I will do my best," Odal said.

"He must be killed."

The chime that marked the end of the rest period sounded. Odal and Hector returned to their booths. Now it was Hector's choice of environment and weapons.

Odal found himself enveloped in darkness. Only gradually did his eyes adjust. He saw that he was in a spacesuit. For several minutes he stood motionless, peering into the darkness, every sense alert, every muscle coiled for immediate action.

Dimly he could see the outlines of jagged rock against a background of innumerable stars. Experimentally, he lifted one foot. It stuck, tackily, to the surface. *Magnetized boots*, Odal was right. It was a small planetoid, perhaps a mile or so in diameter. Almost zero gravity. Airless.

Odal swiveled his head inside the fishbowl helmet of his spacesuit and saw, over his right shoulder, the figure of Hector—lank and ungainly even with the bulky suit. For a moment, Odal puzzled over the weapon to be used. Then Hector bent down, picked up a loose stone, straightened, and tossed it softly past Odal's head. The Kerak major watched it sail by and off into the darkness of space, never to return to the tiny planetoid.

A warning shot, Odal thought to himself. He wondered how much damage one could do with a nearly weightless stone, then remembered that inertial mass was unaffected by gravitational fields, or lack of them. A fifty-pound rock might be easier to lift, but it would be just as hard to throw—and it would do just as much damage when it hit, regardless of its gravitational "weight."

Odal crouched down and selected a stone the size of his fist. He rose carefully, sighted Hector standing a hundred yards or so away, and threw as hard as he could.

The effort of his throw sent him tumbling off-balance, and the stone was far off-target. He fell to his hands and knees, bounced lightly and skidded to a stop. Immediately he drew his feet up under his body and planted the magnetized soles of his boots firmly on the iron-rich surface.

But before he could stand again, a small stone *pinged*

lightly off his oxygen tank. The Star Watchman had his range already!

Odal scrambled to the nearest upjutting rocks and crouched behind them. *Lucky I didn't rip open the spacesuit,* he told himself. Three stones, evidently hurled in salvo, ticked off the top of the rocks he was hunched behind. One of the stones bounced into his fishbowl helmet.

Odal scooped up a handful of pebbles and tossed them in Hector's general direction. That should make him duck. Perhaps he'll stumble and crack his helmet open.

Then he grinned to himself. That's it. Kor wants him dead, and that is the way to do it. Pin him under a big rock, then bury him alive under more rocks. A few at a time, stretched out nicely. While his oxygen supply gives out. That should put enough stress on his nervous system to hospitalize him, at least. Then he can be assassinated by more conventional means. Perhaps he will even be as obliging as Massan, and have a fatal stroke.

A large rock. One that is light enough to lift and throw, yet also big enough to pin him for a few moments. Once he is down, it will be easy enough to bury him under more rocks.

The Kerak major spotted a boulder of the proper size, a few yards away. He backed toward it, throwing small stones in Hector's direction to keep the Watchman busy. In return, a barrage of stones began striking all around him. Several hit him, one hard enough to knock him slightly off-balance.

Slowly, patiently, Odal reached his chosen weapon—an oblong boulder, about the size of a small chair. He crouched behind it and tugged at it experimentally. It moved slightly. Another stone *zinged* off his arm, hard enough to hurt. Odal could see Hector clearly now, standing atop a small rise, calmly firing pellets at him. He smiled as he coiled, catlike, and tensed himself. He gripped the boulder with his arms and hands.

Then in one vicious, uncoiling motion he snatched it up,

whirled around, and hurled it at Hector. The violence of his action sent him tottering awkwardly as he released the boulder. He fell to the ground, but kept his eyes fixed on the boulder as it tumbled end-over-end, directly at the Watchman.

For an eternally long instant Hector stood motionless, seemingly entranced. Then he leaped sideways, floating dreamlike in the low gravity, as the stone hurtled inexorably past him.

Odal pounded his fist on the ground in fury. He started up, only to have a good-sized stone slam against his shoulder, and knock him flat again. He looked up in time to see Hector fire another. The stone puffed into the ground inches from Odal's helmet. The Kerak major flattened himself. Several more stones clattered on his helmet and oxygen tank. Then silence.

Odal looked up and saw Hector squatting down, reaching for more ammunition. The Kerak warrior stood up quickly, his own fists filled with throwing stones. He cocked his arm to throw—

But something made him turn to look behind him. The boulder loomed before his eyes, still tumbling slowly, as it had when he had thrown it. It was too close and too big to avoid. It smashed into Odal, picked him off his feet and slammed against the upjutting rocks a few yards away.

Even before he started to feel the pain in his midsection, Odal began trying to push the boulder off. But he could not get enough leverage. Then he saw the Star Watchman's form standing over him.

"I didn't really think you'd fall for it," Odal heard Hector's voice in his earphones. "I mean . . . didn't you realize that the boulder was too massive to escape completely after it had missed me? You could've calculated its orbit . . . you just threw it into a, uh, six-minute orbit around the planetoid. It *had* to come back to perigee . . . right where you were standing when you threw it, you know."

Odal said nothing, but strained every cell in his pain-wracked body to get free of the boulder. Hector reached over his shoulder and began fumbling with the valves that were pressed against the rocks.

"Sorry to do this . . . but I'm not, uh, killing you, at least . . . just defeating you. Let's see . . . one of these is the oxygen valve, and the other, I think, is the emergency rocket pack . . . now, which is which?" Odal felt the Watchman's hands searching for the proper valve. "I shouldn've dreamed up suits without the rocket pack . . . confuses things . . . there, that's it."

Hector's hand tightened on a valve and turned it sharply. The rocket roared to life and Odal was hurtled free of the boulder, shot uncontrolled completely off the planetoid. Hector was bowled over by the blast and rolled halfway around the tiny chink of rock and metal.

Odal tried to reach around to throttle down the rocket, but the pain in his body was too great. He was slipping into unconsciousness. He fought against it. He knew he must return to the planetoid and somehow kill the opponent. But gradually the pain overpowered him. His eyes were closing, closing—

And, quite abruptly, he found himself sitting in the booth of the dueling machine. It took a moment for him to realize that he was back in the real world. Then his thoughts cleared. He had failed to kill Hector.

And at the door of the booth stood Kor, his face a grim mask of anger.

XVI

The office was that of the new Prime Minister of the Acquataine Cluster. It had been loaned to Leoh for his conversation with Sir Harold Spencer. For the moment, it seemed like a great double room: half of it was dark, warm woods, rich draperies, floor-to-ceiling bookcases. The other half, from the tri-di screen onward, was the austere, metallic utility of a starship compartment.

Spencer was saying, "So this hired assassin, after killing four men and nearly wrecking a government, has returned to his native worlds."

Leoh nodded. "He returned under guard. I suppose he is in disgrace, or perhaps even under arrest."

"Servants of a dictator never know when they will be the ones who are served—on a platter." Spencer chuckled. "And the Watchman who assisted you, this Junior Lieutenant Hector, what of him?"

"He's not here just now. The Dulaq girl has him in tow, somewhere. Evidently it's the first time he's been a hero—"

Spencer shifted his weight in his chair. "I have long prided myself on the conviction that any Star Watch officer can handle almost any kind of emergency anywhere in the galaxy. From your description of the past few weeks, I was beginning to have my doubts. However, Junior Lieutenant Hector seems to have won the day . . . almost in spite of himself."

"Don't underestimate him," Leoh said, smiling. "He turned out to be an extremely valuable man. I think he will make a fine officer."

Spencer grunted an affirmative.

"Well," Leoh said, "that's the complete story, to date. I believe that Odal is finished. But the Kerak Worlds have made good their annexation of the Szarno Confederacy, and the Acquataine Cluster is still very wobbly, politically. We haven't heard the last of Kanus—not by a long shot."

Spencer lifted a shaggy eyebrow. "Neither," he rumbled, "has *he* heard the last from *us*."

The Future of Science:
Prometheus, Apollo, Athena

Every year, Science Fiction Writers of America—the professional organizations of SF writers, agents, and impedimenta—produces a Nebula Awards book, in which the stories honored with Nebula Awards are reprinted, together with solicited contributions from SFWA members. Several years ago Kate Wilhelm, who was editing that year's volume, asked me to write an essay on the future of scientific research. Although there have been many discoveries and developments in the time since I originally wrote this essay, its basic tenets still hold true.

Where is science heading? Is it taking us on a one-way ride to oblivion, or leading the human spirit upward to the stars? Science fiction writers have been predicting both, for centuries.

"I have but one lamp by which my feet are guided," Patrick Henry said, "and that is the lamp of experience.

I know of no way of judging of the future but by the past.''

Look at the past, at the way science and technology have affected the human race. Look far back. Picture all of humanity from the earliest *Homo erectus* of a half-million years ago as a single human being. Now picture science as a genie that will grant that person the traditional three wishes of every good fable.

We have already used up one of those wishes. We are working on the second one of them now. And the future of humankind, the difference between oblivion and infinity, lies in our choice of the third wish.

Our three wishes can be given classical names: Prometheus, Apollo, and Athena.

Prometheus

Long before there was science, perhaps even before there was speech, our primitive ancestors discovered technology. Modern man thinks of technology as the stepson of scientific research, but that is only a very recent reversal of a half-million-year-long situation. Technology—*tool-making*—came first. Science—*understanding*—came a long time later.

Look at the Prometheus legend. It speaks the truth as clearly as any modern science fiction story. It speaks of the first of our three wishes.

Prometheus brought the gift of fire. He saw from his Olympian height that man was a weak, cold, hungry, miserable creature, little better than the animals of the fields. At enormous cost to himself, Prometheus stole fire from the heavens and gave it to man. With fire, man became almost godlike in his domination of all the rest of the world.

Like most myths, the legend of the fire-bringer is fantastic in detail and absolutely correct in spirit. Anthropologists who have sifted through the fossil remains of early man have drawn a picture that is much less romantic, yet startlingly close to the essence of the Prometheus legend.

The first evidence of man's use of fire dates back some half-million years. The hero of the story is hardly godlike in appearance. He is *Homo erectus*, an ancestor of ours who lived in Africa, Asia, and possibly Europe during the warm millennia between the second and third glaciations of the Ice Age. *Homo erectus* was scarcely five feet tall. His skull was rather halfway between the shape of an ape's and our own. His brain case was only two-thirds of our size. But his body was fully human: he walked erect and had human, grasping hands.

And he was dying. The titanic climate shifts of the Ice Age caused drought even in tropical Africa, his most likely home territory. Forests dwindled. Anthropologists have found many *H. erectus* skulls scratched by leopard's teeth. Our ancestors were not well-equipped to protect themselves. Picture Moon Watcher and his tribe from Arthur C. Clarke's *2001*.

It was a gift from the skies that saved *Homo erectus* from oblivion. Not an extraterrestrial visitor, but a blast of lightning that set a bush afire. An especially curious and courageous member of the *erectus* clan overcame his very natural fear to reach out for the bright warm promise of the flames. No telling how many times our ancestors got nothing for their curiosity and courage except a set of burnt fingers and a yowl of pain. But eventually they learned to handle fire safely, and to use it.

With fire, humankind's technology was born.

Fire, the gift of Prometheus, satisfied our first wish, which was: feed me, warm me, protect me.

Fire not only frightened away the night-stalking beasts and gave our ancestors a source of warmth, it helped to change the very shape of their faces and their society.

Homo erectus was the world's first cook. He used fire to cook the food that had always been eaten raw previously.

Cooked food is softer and juicier than raw food. Cooking cuts down greatly on the amount of chewing that must be done. Our ancestors found that they could spend less time actually eating and have more time available for hunting or traveling or making better spear points.

More important, the apelike muzzle of *Homo erectus*, with its powerful jaw muscles, was no longer needed. Faces became more human. The brain case grew as the jaw shortened. No one can definitely say that these two face changes are related. But they happened at the same time. The apelike face of the early hominids changed into the present small-jawed, big-domed head of *Homo sapiens sapiens*.

Beyond that, fire was the first source of energy for any animal outside its own muscles. Fire liberated us from physical labor and unleashed forces that have made us masters of the world. Fire is the basis of all technology. Without fire we would have no metals, no steam, no electricity, no books, no cities, no agriculture, nothing that we would recognize as civilization.

The gift of Prometheus satisfied our first wish. It has fed us, kept us warm, protected us from our enemies. Too well. It has led to the development of a technology that is now itself a threat to our survival on this planet.

The price Prometheus paid for giving fire to us was to be chained eternally to a rock and suffer daily torture. Again, the myth is truer than it sounds. The technology that we have developed over the past half-million years is gutting the earth. Forests have been stripped away, mountains leveled, our air and water fouled with the wastes of modern industry.

For our first wish, the wish that Prometheus answered, was actually: feed me, warm me, protect me, *regardless of the consequences*. Our leopard-stalked ancestors gave no thought to the air pollution arising from their primitive fires. And our waist-coated entrepreneurs of the Industrial

Revolution did not care if their factories turned the mill-stream into an open sewer.

But today, when the air we breathe can kill us and the water is often unfit to drink, we care deeply about the consequences of technology.

The gift of Prometheus was a first-generation technology. It bought the survival of the human race at the price of eventual ecological danger. Now we seek a second-generation technology, one that can give us all the benefits of Prometheus's gift without the harmful by-products.

This is our second wish. We have already asked it, and if it is truly answered, it will be answered by Apollo. The sun god. The symbol of brilliance and clarity and music and poetry. The beautiful one.

Apollo

Although our first-generation technology predated actual science by some half-million years, the second-generation technology of Apollo cannot come about without the deep understandings that only science can bring us. To go beyond the ills of first-generation technology, we must turn to science, to the quality of mind that sees beyond the immediate and makes the desire to know, to understand, the central theme of human activity.

Science is something very new in human history. As new, actually, as the founding of America. In the year 1620, when the Puritans were stepping on Plymouth Rock, Francis Bacon published the book that signaled the opening of the scientific age: *Novum Organum*.

Men had pursued a quest for knowledge for ages before that date. Ancients had mapped the heavens, tribal shamans had started the study of medicine, mystics had developed some rudimentary understandings of the human mind, philosophers had argued about causes and origins. But it was not until the first few decades of the seventeenth century that the deliberate, organized method of thinking that we now call science was created.

It was in those decades, some 350 years ago, that Galileo began settling arguments about physical phenomena by setting up experiments and measuring the results. Kepler was deducing the laws that govern planetary motion. Bacon was writing about a new method of thinking and investigating the secrets of nature: the technique of inductive reasoning, a technique that requires a careful interplay of observation, measurement, and logic.

Bacon's landmark book, *Novum Organum,* was written and titled in reaction to Aristotle's *De Organum,* written some fifteen hundred years earlier as a summarization of all that was known about the physical universe. For fifteen hundred years, Aristotle's word was the last one on any subject dealing with "natural philosophy," or what we today call the physical sciences. For fifteen hundred years it was blindly accepted that a heavy body falls faster than a light one, that the Earth is the center of the universe, that the heart is the seat of human emotion. (And when have you seen a Valentine card bearing a picture of the brain or an adrenal gland?)

For fifteen hundred years, human knowledge and understanding advanced so little that the peasant of Aristotle's day and that of Bacon's would scarcely seem different to each other. This was not due to a Dark Age that blotted out ancient knowledge and prevented progress. For this fifteen-hundred-year stasis affected not only Europe, but the Middle East, Asia, Africa, and the Americas as well.

The lack of advancement during this long millennium and a half was due, more than anything else, to the limits of the ancient method of thought. Only incremental gains in technology could be made by people who accepted ancient authority as the answer to every question, who believed that the Earth was flat and placed at the exact center of the universe, who "knew" that empirical evidence was not to be trusted because it could be a trick played upon the senses by the forces of evil.

In the three hundred fifty years since the scientific method of thought has become established, human life has changed so enormously that a peasant of Bacon's time (or a nobleman, for that matter!) would be lost and bewildered in today's society. Today the poorest American controls more energy, at the touch of a button or the turn of an ignition key, than most of the high-born nobles of all time ever commanded. We can see and hear the world's history, current news, the finest artists, whenever we choose. We live longer, grow taller and stronger, and can blithely disregard diseases that scourged civilizations, generation after generation.

This is what science-based technology has done for us. Yet this is almost trivial, compared to what the scientific method of thinking has accomplished.

For the basic theme of scientific thought is that the universe is knowable. Man is not a helpless pawn of forces beyond his own ken. Order can be brought out of chaos.

Faced, then, with a first-generation technology that threatens to strangle us in its effluvia, we have already turned to science for the basis of a second-generation technology. We have turned to Apollo.

We recognize that it is Apollo's symbol—the dazzling sun—that will be the key to our second-generation technology. The touchstone of all our history has been our ability to command constantly richer sources of energy. *Homo erectus'* burning bush gave way to fires fueled by coal, oil, natural gas—the fossils of antediluvian creatures. Today we take energy from the fission of uranium atoms.

Tomorrow our energy will come from the sun. Either we will tap the sunlight steaming down on us and convert it into the forms of energy that we need, such as electricity or heat, or we will create miniature suns here on Earth and draw energy directly from them. This is thermonuclear fusion, the energy of the H-bomb. In thermonuclear fusion, the nuclei of light atoms such as hydrogen isotopes are forced together to create heavier nuclei and give off energy. This is the energy source of the sun itself, and the stars. It promises clean, inexpensive, inexhaustible energy for all the rest of human history.

The fuel for fusion is deuterium, the isotope of hydrogen that is in "heavy water." For every six thousand atoms of ordinary hydrogen in the world's oceans, there is one atom of deuterium. The fusion process is energetic enough so that the deuterium in one cubic meter of water (about two hundred twenty-five gallons) can yield 450,000 kilowatt-hours of energy. That means that a single cubic kilometer of sea water has the energy equivalent of all the known oil reserves on Earth. And that is using only one-six-thousandth of the hydrogen in the water.

Fusion power will be cheap and abundant enough to be the driving force of our second-generation technology. The gift of Apollo can provide all our energy needs for millions of years into the future.

There will eventually be no further need for fossil fuels or even fissionables. Which in turn means there will be no need to gut our world for coal, oil, gas, uranium. No oil wells. No black lung disease. No problems of disposing of highly radioactive wastes.

The waste products of the fusion process are clean, inert helium and highly energetic neutrons. The neutrons could be a radiation danger if they escape the fusion reactor, but they are far too valuable to let loose, for energetic neutrons are the philosopher's stone of the modern alchemists. They can transform the atoms of one element into atoms of another.

Instead of changing lead into gold, however, the neutrons will be used to transmute light metals such as lithium into the hydrogen isotopes that fuel the fusion reactors. They can also transmute the radioactive wastes of fission power plants into safely inert substances.

The energy from fusion can also be used to make the

ultimate recycling system. Fusion "torches" will be able to vaporize anything. An automobile, for example, could be flashed into a cloud of its component atoms—iron, carbon, chromium, oxygen, etc. Using apparatus that already exists today, it is possible to separate these elements and collect them, in ultra-pure form, for reuse. With effective and efficient recycling, the need for fresh raw materials will go down drastically. The mining and lumbering industries will dwindle; the scars on the face of the Earth will begin to heal.

Fusion energy will produce abundant electricity without significant pollution and with thousands of times less radiation hazard than modern power plants. With cheap and abundant energy there need be no such thing as a "have-not" nation. Sea water can be desalted and piped a thousand kilometers inland, if necessary. The energy to do it will be cheap enough. All forms of transportation—from automobiles to spacecraft—will either use fusion power directly or the electricity derived from fusion.

The gift of Apollo, then, can mark as great a turning point in human history as the gift of Prometheus. Like the taming of fire, the taming of fusion will so change our way of life that our descendants a scarce century from now will be hard put to imagine how we could have lived without this ultimate energy source.

Apollo is a significant name for humankind's second wish for another reason, too. Apollo was the title given to humanity's most ambitious exploration program. In the name of the sun god we reached the moon. Not very consistent nomenclature or mythology, perhaps, but extremely significant for the future of science and the human race.

For to truly fulfill our second wish, we must and will expand the habitat of the human race into space.

We live on a finite planet. We are already beginning to see the consequences of overpopulation and over-consumption of this planet's natural resources. Sooner or later, we must begin to draw our resources from other worlds.

We have already "imported" some minerals from the moon. The cost for a few hundred pounds of rocks was astronomically high: more than $20 billion. Clearly, more efficient modes of transportation must be found, and scientists and engineers are at work on them now.

It is interesting to realize that the actual cost of the energy it takes to send an average-size man to the moon and back—if you bought the energy from your local electric utility—is less than $200. There is much room for improvement in our space transportation systems.

Improvements are coming. Reusable space shuttles are replacing expendable rockets, delivering cargo and people into orbit with increasing efficiency and economy. Fusion energy itself will someday propel spacecraft. Scientists are working on very high-powered lasers that could boost spacecraft into orbit. And the eventual payoff of the esoteric investigations into subatomic physics might well be an insight into the basic forces of nature, an insight that may someday give us some control over gravity.

There is an entire solar system of natural resources waiting for us, once we have achieved economical means of operating in deep space. Many science fiction stories have speculated on the possibilities of "mining" the asteroids, that belt of stone and metal fragments in orbit between Mars and Jupiter.

There are thousands upon thousands of asteroids out there. A single ten-kilometer chunk of the nickel-iron variety (which is common) would contain approximately 20 million million tons of high-grade iron. That's 2×10^{13} tons. Considering that world steel production in 1973 was a bit less than a thousand million tons (10^9), this one asteroid could satisfy our need for steel for about ten thousand years!

The resources are there. And eventually much of our industrial operations will themselves move into space: into orbit around Earth initially, and then farther out, to the areas where the resources are.

There are excellent reasons for doing so. Industrial operations have traditionally been sited as close as possible to the source of raw material. This is why Pittsburgh is near the Pennsylvania coal fields and not far from the iron-ore deposits farther west. It is cheaper to transport finished manufactured products than haul bulky raw materials.

The very nature of space offers advantages for many industrial processes. The high vacuum, low gravity, and virtually free solar energy of the space environment will be irresistible attractions to designers of future industrial operations. Also, the problems of handling waste products and pollution emissions will be easier in space than on Earth.

The pressures of social history will push industry off-planet. We cannot afford to cover the Earth with factories. Yet the alternative is a cessation of economic growth—as long as industrial operations are limited to our finite planet.

Although studies such as the MIT/Club of Rome's "Limits of Growth" have urged a stabilized society, human nature usually wants to have its cake and eat it, too. It should be possible to maintain economic growth by expanding off-planet, and thereby avoid the catastrophic effects of polluting our world to death.

What about the ultimate pollution: overpopulation? Will our expansion into space simply allow the human race to continue its population explosion until civilization collapses under the sheer groaning weight of human flesh?

Many science fiction stories have depicted a rigidly stabilized future society, where vocation, recreation, and even procreation are strictly controlled by the state. Given modern techniques of behavior modification and genetic manipulation, this might someday be possible. Indeed, this is the world that the "Limits to Growth" inevitably leads to.

There is an alternative. In all of human history, the only sure technique for leveling off an expanding population has been to increase the people's standard of living. War, famine, pestilence inevitably lead to a higher birth rate. Modern science has reduced the death rate to the point where even a moderately rising birthrate is a threat to society.

If economic growth can be maintained or even accelerated by expanding the economy into space—and this growth is shared by all people everywhere on Earth—we may have the means for leveling off the population explosion without the repressions that most science fiction writers are haunted by.

Eventually, people will go into space to live. There will be no large-scale migrations—not for a century, at least. But within a few decades, we may see self-sufficient communities in orbit around the Earth, on the moon, and eventually farther out in space.

For the first time since the settling of the Americas, humankind will have an opportunity to develop new social codes. In the strange and harsh environments we will encounter in space, we will perforce evolve new ways of life. Old manners and customs will wither; new ones will arise.

Scientists such as astronomer Carl Sagan look forward to these "experimental communities." They point out that social evolution on Earth is stultified by the success of Western technological civilization. Nearly every human society on this planet lives in a Westernized culture. Variety among human cultures is being homogenized away. The new environment of space offers an opportunity to produce new types of societies, new ways of life that might teach those who remain on Earth how to live better, more fully, more humanly.

Which brings us to the last of humankind's three wishes, the most important one of all, the wish for the gift of Athena.

Athena

The gray-eyed goddess of civilization and wisdom. The warrior-goddess who was born with shield and spear in her hands, but who evolved from Homer's time to Pericles' into a goddess of counsel, of arts and industries, the protectress of cities, the patron deity of Athens.

It is to Athena that we must turn if we are to succeed in our long struggle against the darkness. For human history can be viewed as an attempt to countervene the inevitable chaos of entropy. We succeed as individuals, as a society, as a species, when we are able to bring order out of confusion, understanding out of mystery. Athena, whose symbol is the owl, represents the wisdom and self-knowledge that we so desperately need.

Knowledge we have. And we are acquiring more, so rapidly that people suffer "future shock" from their inability to digest the swift changes flowing across our lives. Wisdom is what we need; the gift of Athena. Self-understanding.

Human beings are understanding-seeking creatures. But when we seek understanding from authorities—in ivied towers of learning, or marbled halls of government, or dark caves of mysticism—we fall short of our goal. Proclamations from authorities are not understanding. When we as individuals give up our quest for understanding and allow others to think and decide for us, we allow the inevitable darkness to gather closer. The brilliant Aegean sunlight is what we seek, and we must turn to Athena's gift of wisdom to find it.

Science will be the crucial factor in finding Athena's gift. As a mode of thinking, a technique for learning and understanding, it is central to our search for self-knowledge.

Our first two wishes were largely focused outside ourselves. They were aimed at manipulating the world outside our skins. Our third and final wish concerns the universe within us: our bodies, our brains, our minds. Until now, scientific research has been mainly concerned with the physical world around us. Physics, chemistry, astronomy, engineering—all deal with the universe that we lay hands on. Even biology and sociology have dealt mainly with matters external to the individual human being. Medical research has been confined to chemistry, mysticism, and sharper surgical tools, until very recently.

But starting with psychology, the major thrust of scientific research has been slowly turning over the past century or so toward the universe inside our flesh.

Molecular biology is delving into the basic mechanics of what makes us what we are: the chemistry of genetic inheritance. Ethnology and psychology are probing the fundamentals of why we behave the way we do: the essence of learning and behavior. Neurophysiology is examining the basic structure and workings of the brain itself: the electrochemistry of memory and thought.

Many view this research with horror. From Mary Wollstonecraft Shelley's vision of Frankenstein, generations of writers and readers have feared scientists' attempts to tamper with the human mind and body. "There are some things that man was not meant to know," has become not only a cliché, but a rallying cry for the fearful and the ignorant.

Genetic manipulation could someday create an elite of geniuses who rule a race of zombies. Behavior modification techniques can turn every jailbird into a model prisoner, and make prisoners of us all. Psychosurgery is performed on the poor, the uninformed, the helpless.

Yet molecular biology may erase the scourge of cancer and genetic disease, bringing the human race to a pinnacle of physical perfection. Behavior modification techniques will someday unravel the tangled engrams of hopeless psychotics and restore them to the light of healthy adulthood. Brain research could bring quantum leaps in our abilities to understand and learn.

Human societies have developed in such a way that new ideas and new capabilities are acquired by the rulers long before the ruled ever hear of them. All societies are ruled by elites. But the eventual effect of our new knowledge is to destroy the elite, to spread the new capabilities among all the people. Far from fearing new knowledge, or shunning it, we must seek it out and embrace it wholeheartedly. For only out of the new knowledge that scientists are acquiring will we derive the understanding that we need to survive as individuals and as a species.

The gift of Athena is what we must have. And it must be shared by all of us, not merely an elite at the top of society. The gift of Prometheus gave us mastery of this world. The gift of Apollo is bringing us powers so vast that we can turn this planet into a paradise or a barren lifeless wasteland.

Only the wisdom of Athena can control the powers of modern science and technology. Only when all the people know what is possible will it be possible to know what to do. As long as an elite controls the power of science and technology, the masses will be manipulated. And such manipulation will inevitably lead to collapse and destruction.

We stand poised on the brink of godhood. The knowledge and wisdom that modern scientific research offers can help us to take the next evolutionary step, and transform ourselves into a race of intelligent beings who truly understand themselves and the universe around them. It is possible, by our own efforts, to climb as far above our present condition as we today are above primitive little *Homo erectus*.

The anthropologist Carleton Coon Painted the prospect twenty-five years ago, in his book, *The Story of Man:*

> A half-million years of experience in outwitting beasts on mountains and plains, in heat and cold, in light and darkness, gave our ancestors the equipment that we still desperately need if

we are to slay the dragon that roams the earth today, marry the princess of outer space, and live happily ever after in the deer-filled glades of a world in which everyone is young and beautiful forever.

We have the means within our grasp. The gift of Athena, like our first two gifts, actually comes from no one but ourselves.

POUL ANDERSON
Winner of 7 Hugos and 3 Nebulas

☐	53088-8	CONFLICT	$2.95
	53089-6		Canada $3.50
☐	48527-1	COLD VICTORY	$2.75
☐	48517-4	EXPLORATIONS.	$2.50
☐	48515-8	FANTASY	$2.50
☐	48550-6	THE GODS LAUGHED	$2.95
☐	48579-4	GUARDIANS OF TIME	$2.95
☐	53567-7	HOKA! (with Gordon R. Dickson)	$2.75
	53568-5		Canada $3.25
☐	48582-4	LONG NIGHT	$2.95
☐	53079-9	A MIDSUMMER TEMPEST	$2.95
	53080-2		Canada $3.50
☐	48553-0	NEW AMERICA	$2.95
☐	48596-4	PSYCHOTECHNIC LEAGUE	$2.95
☐	48533-6	STARSHIP	$2.75
☐	53073-X	TALES OF THE FLYING MOUNTAINS	$2.95
	53074-8		Canada $3.50
☐	53076-4	TIME PATROLMAN	$2.95
	53077-2		Canada $3.50
☐	48561-1	TWILIGHT WORLD	$2.75
☐	53085-3	THE UNICORN TRADE	$2.95
	53086-1		Canada $3.50
☐	53081-0	PAST TIMES	$2.95
	53082-9		Canada $3.50

Buy them at your local bookstore or use this handy coupon:
Clip and mail this page with your order

TOR BOOKS—Reader Service Dept.
P.O. Box 690, Rockville Centre, N.Y. 11571

Please send me the book(s) I have checked above. I am enclosing
$_____ (please add $1.00 to cover postage and handling).
Send check or money order only—no cash or C.O.D.'s.

Mr./Mrs./Miss _____

Address _____

City _____ State/Zip _____

Please allow six weeks for delivery. Prices subject to change without
notice.

GORDON R. DICKSON

☐	53567-7	Hoka! (with Poul Anderson)	$2.75
	53568-5		Canada $3.25
☐	48537-9	Sleepwalker's World	$2.50
☐	48580-8	The Outposter	$2.95
☐	48525-5	Planet Run *with Keith Laumer*	$2.75
☐	48556-5	The Pritcher Mass	$2.75
☐	48576-X	The Man From Earth	$2.95
☐	53562-6	The Last Master	$2.95
	53563-4		Canada $3.50

Buy them at your local bookstore or use this handy coupon:
Clip and mail this page with your order —————————————

TOR BOOKS—Reader Service Dept.
P.O. Box 690, Rockville Centre, N.Y. 11571

Please send me the book(s) I have checked above. I am enclosing
$————— (please add $1.00 to cover postage and handling).
Send check or money order only—no cash or C.O.D.'s.

Mr./Mrs./Miss ————————————————————————
Address ————————————————————————————
City ————————————— State/Zip ———————————
Please allow six weeks for delivery. Prices subject to change without
notice.

FRED SABERHAGEN

Buy them at your local bookstore or use this handy coupon:
Clip and mail this page with your order

TOR BOOKS—Reader Service Dept.
P.O. Box 690, Rockville Centre, N.Y. 11571

Please send me the book(s) I have checked above. I am enclosing
$_____ (please add $1.00 to cover postage and handling).
Send check or money order only—no cash or C.O.D.'s.

Mr./Mrs./Miss _____

Address _____

City _____ State/Zip _____

Please allow six weeks for delivery. Prices subject to change without
notice.

NEXT STOP:
SPACE STATION

". . . I am directing NASA to develop a permanently manned Space Station, and to do it within a decade." . . . President Ronald Reagan, State of the Union message, January 25, 1984.

Are you a person of vision? Are you excited about this next new stepping stone in mankind's future? Did you know that there is a magazine that covers these developments better than any other? Did you know that there is a non-profit public interest organization, founded by famed space pioneer Dr. Wernher von Braun, that actively supports all aspects of a strong U.S. space program? That organization is the NATIONAL SPACE INSTITUTE. If you're a member, here's what you'll get:

- 12 big issues of Space World magazine. Tops in the field. Follow the political, social and technological aspects of all Space Station developments—and all other space exploration and development too!
- VIP package tours to Kennedy Space Center to watch a Space Shuttle launch—the thrill of a lifetime!
- Regional meetings and workshops—get to meet an astronaut!
- Exclusive Space Hotline and Dial-A-Shuttle services.
- Discounts on valuable space merchandise and books.
- and much, much more!

So if you are that person of vision, your eyes upon the future, excited about the adventure of space exploration, let us send you more information on how to join the NSI. Just fill in your name and address and our packet will be on its way. AND, we'll send you a FREE Space Shuttle Launch Schedule which is yours to keep whatever you decide to do!

Name _____

Address _____

City, State, & Zip_____

NATIONAL SPACE INSTITUTE
West Wing Suite 203
600 Maryland Avenue, S.W.
Washington, D.C. 20024
(202) 484-1111